BERRY GROVE BED AND BREAKFAST

SARAH HOPE

Boldwood

First published in 2019. This edition first published in Great Britain in 2024 by Boldwood Books Ltd.

Cover Design by Head Design Ltd

Cover Illustration: Shutterstock

A CIP catalogue record for this book is available from the British Library.

Paperback ISBN 978-1-80549-131-6

Large Print ISBN 978-1-80549-130-9

Hardback ISBN 978-1-80549-129-3

Ebook ISBN 978-1-80549-132-3

Kindle ISBN 978-1-80549-133-0

Audio CD ISBN 978-1-80549-124-8

MP3 CD ISBN 978-1-80549-125-5

Digital audio download ISBN 978-1-80549-127-9

Boldwood Books Ltd
23 Bowerdean Street
London SW6 3TN
www.boldwoodbooks.com

For my children,
Let's change our stars
xXx

1

Skimming her eyes across her notes, Kim Reynolds nodded in agreement. By the end of the meeting, they'd have the contract signed and she'd be well on her way to achieving her target. After securing the company three million pounds' worth of client campaigns this tax year there would be nothing to stop her from being promoted to partner.

Smiling confidently, she looked around her, Mr Hitches was engaged and hanging on to every word the advertising team were telling him. In the ten years she'd worked at Pinnel's Incorporated she'd learnt to spot the signs of a sure deal and Mr Hitches was displaying the classic signs of a man itching to sign.

Tapping her pen against her notepad, Kim pushed her chair back and stood up. 'Thank you, John. So, as you can see if you choose Pinnel's Incorporated to run this campaign, we will deliver outstanding results. Not to mention the fact that you will be our number one priority.' Walking to the front of the room, Kim clicked onto a fresh set of PowerPoint slides. 'I'll now take you through our forecasts for the upcoming season.'

Out of the corner of her eye, she could see Tara, her PA, peering through the window, frantically waving and trying to catch her attention. Smiling, she looked around at the group of clients and her team. 'Patrick, could you discuss this next slide? Thank you. Excuse me for one moment.'

Closing the door quietly behind her, Kim took hold of Tara's elbow and led her further down the corridor away from the conference room. 'I thought I told you not to disturb me? You do know who I've got in there and what's at stake, don't you?'

'Yes, yes. I'm ever so sorry Ms Reynolds but I have an urgent call for you.' Nodding her head, Tara's blonde curls bounced around her face much like a doll Kim remembered from childhood.

'It had better be good.' Pursing her lips, Kim reminded herself that she must keep her cool, the last thing she needed was to let Tara and her drama get in the way of this deal.

'It's a teacher from Mia's school. I tried to take a message, but she was very insistent that she spoke to you.'

Rolling her eyes, Kim took the phone. 'Hello, Ms Reynolds speaking.'

'Afternoon, Ms Reynolds, I'm Mrs Oakbury, Mia's tutor from school. I'm afraid she has left the campus without permission.'

'What do you mean, "left the campus"?'

'She's not here.'

'Yes, she is. She messaged me this morning to say she'd got to school safely.'

'I'm sorry, I'm not making myself very clear. She was here this morning, that's right, but she's not turned up to her history lesson.'

'Well, she's probably just gone to the toilet or something. Maybe she's talking to the teacher from her previous lesson.'

'She was seen running out of the school gates after her English lesson before break.'

'Why didn't you say that?' She'd never much liked Mrs Oakbury, she always spoke in riddles. 'Well, find her then.'

'With all due respect, we don't have the staff to chase truanting teens across town. We can, of course, inform the police if you are unable to look for her yourself.'

'Look for her?' Surely it was the job of the school to keep its pupils safe? To stop them from running off? 'I'm in the middle of a meeting, a very important meeting. I cannot just up and leave.'

'Shall I ask the police to send officers out to find her then?'

Kim narrowed her eyes and glanced back at the conference room. It should be her in there; she needed to close this deal. Her future career hung on this meeting. 'No, I'll find her and return her to school.' Punching the End Call button, Kim threw the phone at Tara, who expertly caught it. 'I'll be back soon.'

'But, Ms Reynolds, you're in the middle of a meeting.'

Ignoring Tara's whining, Kim pushed open the door and jogged to the lift. The sooner she could find Mia and drop her back off at school, the higher the chance that she wouldn't lose the company Mr Hitches' custom.

* * *

Throwing the door to her bright blue two-seater sleek car open, Kim pulled out her phone and connected it to the hands-free system.

'Pick up, pick up.' Pulling out of the car park, she cursed as the familiar voicemail message filled the interior. 'Mia, I know that you're ignoring me, but as soon as you get this message ring me and let me know where you are.'

Pulling onto the motorway, she tapped her fingers against the steering wheel and rolled her eyes as the car in front failed to seize the opportunity to pull out in front of a lorry, forcing Kim to brake and match his snail's pace. At this rate, she wouldn't even get back to Hulberry before the meeting came to a close, let alone find Mia, return her to school and make the journey back to the office.

Flashing her indicators, Kim slipped in the lane to the right, praying that the car coming up would have the foresight to realise her plan. Breathing a sigh of relief, she put her hand up to thank them.

* * *

As she turned into Hulberry, she tried Mia's phone again.

'Mia, this is getting beyond a joke. I've just come into town, ring me back now and tell me where you are or, even better, get yourself back to school.' What was she playing at? She was normally such a good girl. Kim pulled the visor down against the sun. Mia knew not to truant.

Turning into the town centre, Kim slowed the car down, searching the pavement. If she'd come into town, she certainly wouldn't be getting dinner money tomorrow, or for the rest of her school life for that matter. She would have to take a packed lunch. There were no excuses; there was a perfectly good canteen at school. Kim drummed her fingers against the steering wheel. Fine, not a perfectly good canteen, Mia was always complaining that they ran out of the half decent food before she managed to get there, but that wasn't the point, Mia knew it was wrong to walk out of school, for whatever reason.

'You've got to be kidding me!' Slamming her brakes on and waving her hands in the air, she swerved to miss the taxi pulling out in front of her. 'You know the funny little stick by your steering wheel? It's called an indicator. Use it!'

Rounding the corner, she peered down the pedestrianised

cobbles leading to the precinct. There was no sign of Mia. No teenagers at all in fact, just the custom handful of parents pushing buggies or chasing after screaming toddlers, amongst the waves of pensioners on their daily excursion to the shops. Where was she? Where else would she have gone? Didn't all truants go downtown? The handful of times Kim had skipped secondary school it was town that she and her friends had swarmed to. Town and the park. Of course! The park.

Switching her hazard warning lights on, she quickly completed a three-point-turn, narrowly missing the 'No Entry' sign to the pedestrianised area before holding her hand up in thanks to the impatient driver flashing his lights.

Clenching her teeth as she crept along in the queue leading back up to the roundabout, Kim checked her phone again. Nothing. If Mia had run out of school to go drinking on a park bench, or worse to meet a boy, she'd be grounded until she was twenty-five. At least.

* * *

Slamming the car door behind her, Kim jogged the short distance to the iron gates of the People's Park. Shielding her eyes from the low Spring sun, she scanned the open space. The small swing park to her right stood eerily empty. Checking her watch, she cursed. She really did need to get back.

Taking a deep breath, Kim pulled her thin suit jacket around her and hurried around the perimeter of the park, looking down the alleyways leading back into town and behind the toilet blocks.

Halfway around she paused, leaned her hand against the trunk of a tree to steady herself and slipped her shoe off. Rubbing the heel of her foot, she watched as a dog walker jogged past her and again muttered curse words under her breath. Surely one of the teachers from Mia's school should be doing this, not her. She paid good money in her taxes, a good chunk which she was sure went into the education system and yet here she was chasing after her daughter who she had entrusted into the care of the local comprehensive. It was ridiculous. Slipping her high-heeled shoe back on, she picked up her pace and marched the distance back to her car.

Releasing the hand brake, she reversed out of the car park and joined the road towards home. She was out of ideas. Maybe Mia had written something in that blue notebook she had hidden in her sock drawer. There was a small chance she'd written her plans in there or at least scribbled down a friend's address or something. Anything to give Kim a clue as to her whereabouts.

Thirty-two minutes she'd been out of the office now. Thirty-two minutes of Mr Hitches being spoken at by Patrick. She pinched the bridge of her nose, Patrick was good at his job and she could trust him to schmooze mid-grade clients, but whether he had the talent to reel Mr Hitches in, she wasn't so sure. The advertising team would be showcasing their marketing proposals before they broke for a break and then she was up again for the closing pitch. That, she definitely needed to be there for.

* * *

Rounding the corner into their close, Kim took the corner a little too fast, the tyres screeching on the warm tarmac. There she was, her small figure hunched on the front doorstep, her blue coat hood pulled up despite the sunny weather.

Pulling onto the driveway, Kim came to a standstill and switched off the engine. Throwing the car door open, she sprinted the few steps towards Mia. 'Mia, are you okay? Why on earth aren't you at school?'

Shrugging her shoulders, Mia remained seated on the step, her body facing towards the front door.

'Mia, I'm talking to you. Look at me, please.' Crossing her arms, Kim checked her watch. She needed to get back to the office, if she didn't head back soon, she'd get stuck in the lunchtime rush and she could wave goodbye to the promotion.

Dipping her head lower, Mia's face was completely covered by her hood.

'Mia, please? You know how important today is for me. I've been working towards this meeting for months, you know that. A lot rides on me bringing this account in for the firm. They'll give me a partnership. Think of the holidays we could go on and the things we could buy!' This was getting ridiculous; whatever Mia was upset about didn't warrant her running out of school. And why would she choose to play up today when she knew about the meeting? It was pure selfishness.

'Right, if you're not going to tell me what this nonsense is about then hurry up and get in the car. I should have just about enough time to drop you back off at school.'

'Mum, no.' Turning her head towards Kim, Mia's lips trembled.

'You're very pale. Are you feeling okay?' Holding the back of her hand against Mia's forehead, she shook her head. 'You don't feel hot. Come on, it's only another three hours until home-time anyway and then we'll discuss this properly.'

'Mum, I can't go back there. At least let me have today off. Please?' Staring up at her, Kim noticed that Mia's dark green eyes were red-rimmed as though she'd been crying.

'Have you been crying?'

'No. Maybe a little. I can't go back today. Please, Mum, not today. Just let me have today off, please?'

'You've got to go back today. I've had your form tutor on the phone. They know you're truanting. Now, get in the car before I miss the end of the meeting too.' Spinning on her heels, she retreated to the car and waited until Mia had joined her and clicked her seatbelt on before reversing.

'Mum, I really really don't want to go back to school.' Wrapping her arms around herself, she peered out of the side window.

'Is there something wrong? Is something upsetting you at school?' Glancing at the clock, Kim calculated that she would have just about enough time to drop Mia outside the school gates and make it onto the motorway before eleven fifty. The offices were only a couple of junctions away, so she'd be back in the meeting before twenty past.

'It doesn't matter.'

Straining to hear Mia's mumbling, Kim rolled her eyes. If there was nothing wrong, then why did she have to choose today to play truant? Why not yesterday? Or tomorrow? Any other day would have been better than today. And Mia knew that. 'You'll be fine going back to school then.'

* * *

Watching Mia slope into school, Kim narrowed her eyes at Mrs Oakbury. She was sure she'd just been taken for a mug. Mrs Oakbury had probably been sat having a cup of tea without a care in the world while Kim had been running around looking for Mia, who the school had allowed to run out of their care in the first place.

Pulling the visor down, she checked her hair and make-up in the mirror. Smoothing her dark hair back into a high bun, she then re-applied her lipstick, smacking her lips together to even out the shade.

Checking her mobile, she tutted. She'd had four missed calls from the office. Placing the mobile back into its holder, she restarted the engine. She didn't have the time to call them back and, besides, she'd be there in twenty-five minutes if she hurried.

2

Crawling along, Kim indicated to turn right off the roundabout and drummed her fingers against the steering wheel. The traffic was hardly moving. She'd hoped it was just the congestion on the roundabout but by the looks of it, it was a hold up on the motorway.

Drat. She couldn't miss the end of the meeting. She had to be there to conclude everything her team had showcased. It already looked unprofessional that she had walked out halfway through, although hopefully Tara had used her initiative and spun a story about her being called away to an emergency to do with a different client. At least that way there was the slim possibility that Mr Hitches would think that if he were to entrust Pinnel's, existing clients would always take precedence over new. That, or he'd think she was putting other clients ahead of his own interests already and he wouldn't entrust his company into their hands at all.

As the cars inched along, she could feel her heart pounding in her chest. The increase in its rhythm couldn't be good, she knew that. She was sure she'd already taken her high blood pressure statins; she always took them with her 6am coffee before she woke Mia up and left for work. Trying to shake off the advice of Dr Thomas to slow down, she focused on the car in front. She'd be able to take things easier once this account was in the bag. Once she was promoted to partner, she'd no longer need to prove herself. She chose not to think about Lawrence who had been on long-term sick leave due to stress whose position she was desperately trying to fill. It would be different for her; it would be a different sort of stress than what she was feeling now. Plus, with every year that passed and Mia grew older the less Kim had to feel guilty for working such long hours.

As the traffic crept around the slight curve to the left, Kim could see the telltale blue flashing lights half a mile ahead. Breathing a sigh of relief, she smiled; she'd get there in time. She'd be past the accident scene in less than ten minutes and then could push her way into the fast lane. All was not lost.

Staring ahead as the bumper sticker on the Nissan in front flaunted the idea that 'Adoption was the best option' flagged by two bright red paw prints, she rolled her eyes. What was the point? What was the point of any of these bumper stickers? The only time anyone would get close enough to read the small print emblazoned across the car in front was in a traffic jam. Surely most people would be in a hurry, thinking about where they were going or where they should be, not taking divine advice from a piece of plastic film?

As the traffic slowed even further, Kim followed the lead of the Nissan and crossed over into the outside lane to avoid the cones placed to indicate the closure of the other two.

Up ahead she could see two ambulances, a fire engine and three police cars flanking the accident scene. It must have been a bad crash to warrant that many emergency vehicles. A lorry stood at an angle, covering the farthest lane and it looked like a car, no two cars, were also involved. A red Land Rover lay on its side slightly in front of the lorry and a dark blue hatchback stood a few metres away down the motorway. The side and rear of the car had been crumpled, making it impossible to tell the make or model. Kim shivered, the roof had been cut off, presumably to release someone trapped inside.

Trying to keep her eyes on the Nissan's bumper sticker, Kim murmured a small prayer begging for the crash victim's safety. Slamming her brakes on, Kim gripped the steering wheel as the Nissan came to an abrupt stop in front of her. A horn sounded as the car behind her narrowly missed bumping into her and veered perilously close to the crash barrier.

Ducking her head below the rear-view mirror, she refused to lock into eye contact with the irate driver behind her. He could shout all the obscenities in the world at her, it hadn't been her fault he hadn't been paying attention. She peered ahead to try to work out why the line of traffic passing the accident had stopped. She was well aware of the phenomenon that people slowed down to gawp at traffic accidents, but it was the traffic beyond the accident scene that had stopped. It was her and the people immediately ahead and behind her who were now adjacent to the scene.

Looking down, she fiddled with the top of the gear stick, smoothing the leather encasing it. She would not look. She would not look. Ever since being involved in a crash in her late teens and being the subject of strangers' pitying glances, Kim avoided at all costs to be drawn in to watch other people's worst nightmares unfold. She touched the photograph of Mia stuck in the visor. Unbeknown to her she'd been pregnant with her at the time. It had been during the check-up at the hospital afterwards that she had been told she was carrying her. She shook her head. She didn't need to think about that now.

Replacing her hands on the steering wheel, she began going through the closing speech for Mr Hitches that she'd rewritten the previous evening. Mia had been acting strangely yesterday too, complaining that Kim hadn't been taking any notice of her. In truth, Kim had lost her temper and ended up sending Mia to her room. She hadn't been able to cope with the incessant whining and pleading. She remembered now, Mia hadn't wanted to go to school today. She'd said something, given a reason, Kim was sure, but she hadn't been listening properly. Had Mia just wanted to completely jeopardise today for her? She'd tried to stop her being able to concentrate on the speech last night and now with this silly running away from school business, it all added up, didn't it? Mia had been trying to stop her sealing the deal. Why, though? Kim only wanted to better things for them. She only wanted to give Mia the best life she could.

Having Mia so early on in life had been tough, and she'd had a lot to prove. Her own parents hadn't believed in her, had told her that a baby would ruin her future. Well, she'd shown them. She'd finished college, gone to university and, after landing a great job in the City she'd worked her butt off to climb the corporate ladder. She hadn't let Mia's birth stop her doing anything. In fact, it was Mia and Kim's need to provide for her that had fuelled her ambitions.

Getting this final promotion and being accepted as a partner would show beyond doubt to everyone that she could handle this single mum thing.

Screaming from outside jolted Kim out of her thoughts. Glancing across, she watched paralysed, as a woman ran towards a huddle of paramedics kneeling around a figure on the tarmac. Her hands reaching out, the woman, donned in bloodstained jeans and a thin blood splattered jumper, pushed her way into the huddle. Flittingly two of the paramedics nearest Kim's car sank back on their haunches allowing the woman into the middle. In that moment, Kim watched as the two paramedics on the farthest side fought to resuscitate a crash victim. She watched as arms pulsed up and down on the limp body and oxygen was forced into their lungs.

With her fingers gripping the steering wheel, Kim forced herself to breathe. She hadn't seen anyone this close to death, not since that night on the side of the road all those years ago. A picture of her best friend's limp body lying there as the paramedics futilely tried to revive her flashed through her mind. She remembered holding Miriam's head in her arms as the paramedics, beaten by fate, extracted tubes and pads from her lifeless body.

At the time, Kim had felt so alone, her and Miriam's body being on an island of strange calmness as the world sped around them, but it had been the eyes of the strangers, slowing down and staring out of their car windows, gawping and revelling in her pain that had haunted her nightmares for years to come.

A fresh wave of despair, louder this time, escaped the woman's lungs and drew Kim's eyes to the figure on the ground. Lying on the black tarmac was the pale face of a teenage girl, her eyes closed, her chest still. She could only have been a year or so older than Mia.

Having accepted the poor woman into the huddle, the paramedics surrounded the young girl again, their backs forming a barrier against the ogling drivers.

Setting her eyes forward again, Kim tried to block out the desperate wailings of the mother.

'Come on. Please, come on.' Muttering to the Nissan in front of her, Kim tapped her foot against the accelerator, willing to use it again.

Suddenly, as if answering her prayers, the Nissan crawled forward, inching faster and faster.

Looking in the rear-view mirror, Kim breathed a sigh of relief as she watched the teenager being lifted onto a stretcher, a paramedic holding a bag of fluid above her. They'd won. This time the paramedics had won and brought the girl back from the dead.

Turning off at the next junction instead of continuing towards the offices, Kim pulled in at the service station and drove to the back of the car park.

With the engine still running, she unclipped her seat belt and stepped out into the warm spring air. Leaning her back against the door, she took a deep shuddering breath. That girl could have died. It could have been them. It could have been Mia. She watched as people busied about their daily lives, the businessmen and women jumping out of their small sports cars to grab a coffee or a sandwich on their way to important meetings, parents trying to cajole their offspring to get in the car again for the next leg of their journey, even a couple of police officers walking towards their car, cardboard cups in hand, laughing and joking as if oblivious to what had occurred only a couple of miles down the road.

Life continued as normal. It had been the same after Miriam had died, their classmates went back to college the next day, studying for a future Miriam no longer had, her desk space swallowed up the following fortnight by a new student. Even her boyfriend of the time had started seeing someone else barely three months later. Kim was sure he went on to marry her. The worst thing had been reading in the local newspaper that the drunk driver who had caused the crash had got away without being charged due to some technical fault or loophole or something. Kim hadn't understood it at the time and since then had purposely not looked into it knowing that if she did it would consume her until she believed justice had been done.

Her phone rang, vibrating across the dashboard where she had thrown it when she'd stopped.

'Hello?'

'Ms Reynolds? It's Tara. Will you be back in the office soon? Only Patrick has been looking for you. They're taking a break before closing the meeting.'

'Meeting?' Kim shook her head. This was why she didn't allow herself to think about her personal life during the working day; it obscured her vision and muddied her goals. 'Meeting. Right. Yes, I'll be there.'

'Ms Reynolds?'

'Yes?'

'Are you okay? I hope you don't mind me asking, but you sound different, a little... umm...'

'I'm fine.' Stabbing the End Call button, Kim slid back into the driver's seat. As she pulled the visor down to check her make-up Mia's photograph fluttered out, coming to land on her knee. Picking it up, Kim looked at it, a five-year-old Mia grinning into the camera lens stared back at her. Where had that happy little girl gone? Today's Mia was sullen, moody and quiet. Too quiet. She was sure she hadn't been that quiet when she had been Mia's age. Kim thought back over the past week. She had hardly even seen Mia, let alone heard about her days at school or spent any quality time with her.

What had Mia done over the weekend? Kim rubbed her temples, trying to extract memories she knew hadn't been there to begin with. She didn't have a clue what Mia had done to keep herself occupied over the weekend or after school any day for the past few weeks, for that matter. Kim had been shut away in the study at home or been putting in extra hours at the office consumed with preparing for this deal. Fair enough. It was a big deal. A massive deal that would hopefully allow her to provide more for Mia.

Before that then, last month, last year even, how had Mia spent her free time? She didn't know. Kim didn't have a clue what Mia liked to do, what her interests were, who her friends were. Anything.

Turning her head towards the sun, Kim closed her eyes. There was always some deal, some reason why Kim had to spend this one last day/week/month chasing a client rather than spending time with the only person who really meant anything to her, her daughter.

And today? What had she been thinking forcing Mia to go straight back into school? She hadn't even given her own daughter five minutes of her precious time to tell her what was worrying her, to tell her why she had run out of school. Even if it had been a stupid reason, it had been big enough, scary enough to make her Mia, the child whose teachers always complained she was too shy, too quiet, to run out of school and run home. She didn't usually put a foot wrong at school or at home. Something must have happened, and Kim had shut her down, hadn't listened to her. She'd only been thinking about the damn deal. She'd put work above her daughter time and time again.

The shrill ringtone of her mobile interrupted her thoughts.

'Yes?'

'Ms Reynolds? Are you here now? Are you in the office? Mr Hitches is ready to go back into the meeting.' Tara's voice, one that Kim would normally have described as being whiney suddenly sounded terrified.

'I'm sorry, Tara, I'm not coming in.'

'What? I mean, sorry, I mean, what do you mean you're not coming in?'

'I mean just that. I'm not going to be able to make it back into the office today. My daughter needs me.'

'But what about Mr Hitches? There's a lot riding on you bringing Mr Hitches' custom into the business. You always say...'

'I know what I always say, but Patrick will be fine. I need to go now. Bye, Tara.'

Shutting the car door, Kim drove back to the school.

3

Kim wandered around the school campus until she found a sign for the reception. Inside, she tapped on the glass partition.

'May I help you?' A young woman with a sharp cut dark bob slid open the partition, the smell of coffee wafting through the small gap.

'Yes. I'm here for my daughter.'

'Can I see the appointment card please?'

'Appointment card? No, she doesn't have an appointment. I'm just here to pick her up. She ran out of school earlier and I've just dropped her off, but need to speak to her.'

'So, she's not ill or being sent home?'

'No, I just need to speak to her.'

'With all due respect, we cannot just let every pupil whose parent wants a chat come and go. It would become very disruptive during lessons.'

Was she trying to be condescending or did it just come naturally to her? Taking a deep breath, she tried again. 'I realise that, but it is of great importance I speak to her now.'

'Lunchtime will be in...' Ignoring the oversized watch on her wrist, the woman peered at a clock behind her. 'Forty-five minutes, I could see if I can arrange for her to call you?'

'No, as I said, there have already been some issues this morning and I would like to speak to her now. Her form tutor is Mrs Oakbury, she is aware of what has happened today if you need to seek confirmation and my daughter's name is Mia Reynolds. If it is not possible to speak to her I am happy to contact Ofsted and discuss my concerns about the school's inadequacy to keep its pupils safe and in school for the entirety of the six compulsory hours.'

'I'm sure that won't be necessary. Mia Reynolds, you say? I shall see if I can locate her. Please take a seat.'

'Thank you.' Perching on the indicated blue plastic chair, Kim crossed her legs and smiled as the receptionist scurried about looking in folders, presumably at timetables, to locate Mia's whereabouts.

Fifteen minutes later, she was ushered through the door into the foyer. 'If you could follow me, Mrs Oakbury is in her office and would like a little chat.'

'Thank you.' Stepping into a small sparse office, she was greeted by Mrs Oakbury.

'I will have Mia sent for in a moment, but first I wanted a quiet word with you.'

'Okay.' She slipped into the chair opposite Mrs Oakbury and placed her handbag at her feet.

'Now, as you are aware, Mia has always been a very quiet but diligent student. Someone who we, as her teachers, can rely on to set a good example both in the work she produces and in her behaviour. I am aware there are ongoing issues with her friendship circle that Mia is working through, but as that situation has been going on a fair while now and it is only now that Mia has begun to display this troubling behaviour, I wanted a quick chat with you to see how life is at home.'

'Life at home?'

'Yes. Have there been any changes or anything you can think of which may explain this sudden change in behaviour?'

'No, not at all. Everything at home is...' Looking at the wall to the side of Mrs Oakbury, Kim watched as the shadow from a large willow tree outside the window danced against the stark white wall. Things weren't 'fine' at home. She was realising that. '...the same. Things at home are the same as they have always been.'

'Right, okay. Well, that's good to hear. Sometimes when there are changes in a student's home life, they exhibit changes in behaviour at school. Now, as you are probably aware from the recent parents' evening, Mia's grades have been consistently dipping since... let me check.' Flicking open a folder, Mrs Oakbury scanned the printed document in front of her. 'Since October time.'

'I didn't come.'

'Sorry?'

'I said, I was unable to make the last parents' evening.' Uncrossing her legs, she gripped her hands together in her lap. When was the last time she had been able to make one of Mia's parents' evenings? She had been to one since she had joined secondary school two years ago, hadn't she? She must have.

'Oh, I see. Well, has Mia spoken to you about her grades or why she's been struggling in class?'

'No.' Kim cleared her throat. 'No, she hasn't mentioned it.'

'This may come as a bit of a shock to you then.' Mrs Oakbury slid the document towards Kim. 'As you can see, all of last year Mia's grades were in the top five per cent of second-year students and, indeed, back in September she was still producing work worthy of being placed in the top ten per cent. So, as you can see, since the beginning of this academic year her grades have dropped slightly but nothing really notable. Teacher expectations increase year on year and so slipping into the top ten per cent instead of the five per cent was probably written off due to a shift in expectations, but it's here,' Leaning across the table, Mrs Oakbury prodded her finger against the sheet. 'Since the beginning of October, when we see the sudden decline in grades.'

'It's a big drop in grades. Why? What happened in October?'

'That's what we need to work out. I've had reports of Mia not completing or handing homework in and not finishing the work set during lesson time. In fact, a big project was due in last Friday in History and she still has not handed anything in. It could be that she is simply not trying her best, but I'm afraid, if something doesn't change then she could well find herself unable to catch up with her peers.'

Kim shook her head. None of this made any sense. She'd never had to worry about Mia's schoolwork before. She'd always been such a bright girl, had always found anything academic quite easy. 'You mentioned a friendship issue?'

'Yes, I'm sure Mia has spoken to you about it before. It seems the issues may be continuing. Oh hello, Mia. Come on in.'

Peering behind her, Kim spotted Mia standing in the doorway. Pushing her chair back, she stood up. 'Mia.'

'Mum, why are you here?' A warm blush crept up Mia's pale face, joining the red around her eyes.

'I've come to take you home.' Kim tried to catch her eye but instead Mia looked down, twisting a crumpled tissue in her hand. What had happened to turn her happy little girl into this? When had it happened? Kim shook her head. How was she ever going to make it up to her?

'Home? I got the message that you wanted to speak to her.'

'Yes, well, I forgot to mention she has a dental appointment so

I need her to come with me.' Walking the short distance towards her daughter, Kim held her by the elbow and guided her back towards the door.

'Right, in future, Ms Reynolds, we do have a protocol we rely on parents to follow when requesting time off for appointments.'

'I'll try to remember. Thank you for your time.'

* * *

Stepping through the reception doors, the warm air enveloped them as Kim led them to the car.

They drove in silence, Mia looking out of the window and Kim concentrating on the road ahead. Surprisingly, there wasn't much traffic and they were home within a few minutes.

Pulling onto the driveway, Kim yanked the hand brake before twisting around to face Mia.

'Mia, what's been happening at school?' She reached out to her, laying her hand on Mia's forearm before being shrugged off.

'Nothing.' She continued to stare out of the side window, apparently transfixed on the rose bush in the front garden which was beginning to bloom.

'There is something going on. I know there is. Mrs Oakbury mentioned an issue with a friend.'

Mia snorted before glancing at Kim and back towards the rose bush.

'What's that for? Is there a problem with your friends?'

'It doesn't matter.' Shaking her head, Mia played with the tissue still in her hands.

'It does matter. If there's something wrong, I'd like to know.'

'Why?'

'What do you mean "why"? I'm your mum, that's why.'

'You've never cared before.'

Leaning forward, Kim strained to hear Mia's whisper. She nodded, she probably deserved that. More than deserved it. 'I've always cared.'

'No, you haven't. You never ask me how I am or how my day was or what I'm doing at school.' Mia let out a small sob. 'Or anything.'

'Oh, Mia. I'm sorry. I've been...'

'Busy with work, I know. That's what you always say.' Mia's voice became quieter still. 'But, sometimes, just sometimes, it would be nice for you to think about me, to give me a bit of the attention you give work.'

Squeezing her eyes shut, Kim drew a deep breath in. 'I'm sorry. I've only been doing what I thought was right. I only work to provide for us, to give you a nice life.'

'Look,' Mia waved her hand, taking in the detached house with a double garage. 'I don't need this. I don't need the latest electronics or the promise of fantastic holidays which we never get to go on anyway because you're always too busy. I need you, Mum. Not things.'

Leaning forward, Kim used the pads of her fingers to wipe away the tears streaming down Mia's cheeks. 'I've got it all wrong, haven't I?'

Shaking her head, Mia pushed the passenger door open. 'I'm going to have a shower.'

'Okay, I'll get us some lunch and then you can tell me what's been happening at school.' Watching Mia walk into the house, her head low and her shoulders slumped, Kim lowered her forehead to the steering wheel. She had got this all wrong. Completely wrong. And it was Mia, the one person she did all of this for, who had suffered.

* * *

'Do you want me to blow dry your hair for you?' Standing up from the sofa, Kim walked towards Mia, taking her towel from her and patting her hair dry.

'No, the heat makes my curls all fuzzy. I normally leave it to dry naturally.'

'Okay. Here, come and sit down, I've got you a cheese and ham toastie.'

'Thanks.' Mumbling, Mia sat down, pulling her legs up underneath her and resting her plate on her knees.

'Are you ready to tell me about what's been happening between you and your friends now?'

'It doesn't matter.'

'Mia, please don't shut me out. I know I've been pretty preoccupied recently but, please, talk to me.'

'I haven't got any friends.'

'Yes, you have. How about that girl, Anna, was it? Who was always round here last year?'

'Amelia? No, I'm not friends with her any more.'

'Fair enough. Is that what's wrong? You've had a falling out with Amelia?'

'Yes, no. Look, it doesn't matter. There's nothing you or anyone else can do anyway. Just drop it.' Looking down, Mia poked at her toastie.

'It does matter and there are a lot of things that we can do to make it better. Maybe we can invite her round again? That way you can both spend some time together and sort it out? It's normal to fall out with your friends at our age. You wait, you'll be best mates again in a few days.'

'No, we won't and no, that won't help.'

'Well, I can talk to the school then. Mrs Oakbury seems nice. I bet she could help.'

'She knows. At least, she knows some of it.'

'But if I have a word, there might be something else she can try, something she's not thought of.'

'Just leave it, Mum. Please? Me and Amelia will never be friends again.'

'Okay, well, how about all the other girls in your class then? Are they nice?'

'I really don't want to talk about it.' Ripping the crusts off the bread, Mia pushed them to the side of her plate.

'I'm sorry, Mia, but we are going to talk about it.' Pulling her legs up onto the sofa, Kim twisted around to look at her. 'I know I've let you down, really let you down, but things are going to change. I'm going to start coming home from the office earlier.'

'You won't. You've promised me that before and you ended up spending more time there.' Mia looked up from her plate, her eyes tearing up again.

'Did I? When was that?'

'On my tenth birthday. You got home really late and told me you'd buy the best birthday present ever but I asked for you to spend more time with me instead.'

'This time I promise.'

'You promised last time, too.' Mia pulled a string of cheese from the toastie, wiping it across the crusts at the edge of the plate.

'Did I? I'm sorry.' Leaning forward, Kim put her hand on Mia's leg. 'Please? Tell me what's been happening with your friends?'

'I've already told you, I don't have any friends. And I mean any. Any. Any. Any. No friends. Amelia's turned everyone in my tutor group against me. No one talks to me any more. And I hate it. I hate school. And I hate myself. I hate all of it. Okay?' Jumping up, Mia threw her plate onto the coffee table in front of her, causing the picked apart ham and cheese toastie to fly across the smooth table finally coming to land on the floor on the other side.

'Mia, why didn't you tell me?' Standing up, Kim strode the few steps towards Mia.

'Don't. Just don't.' Holding her hands up in front of her, Mia took a shuddering breath before turning and running upstairs.

Letting her arms collapse against her sides, Kim watched as Mia disappeared, the slam of her bedroom door echoing through the house.

The shrill ringtone of her mobile broke the silence that followed.

'Yes?'

'Ms Reynolds?'

'Tara, I can't deal with this right now.' Placing her finger and thumb against her temples she closed her eyes.

'Mr Pinnel wishes to meet with you.'

Perching on the edge of the sofa, Kim dug her nails into the cushion. 'I'm sorry, Tara. I won't be back in right now.'

'Shall I schedule it for later this afternoon then? I believe it's quite urgent.'

'No, not today. I won't be back in today. I really must go. Goodbye, Tara.' Sliding her mobile across the table, Kim bent her head. Mr Hitches must have declined their offer. There would be no promotion. The best-case scenario for her now would be to get a telling off from Mr Pinnel or even be taken off some of the more lucrative clients' accounts. The worst-case scenario and she'd be picking up her P45. Yanking out her hairband, she let her dark hair fall from the bun she had created this morning and flow down her back. Although only a few short hours had passed, it felt like a lifetime ago.

Pushing herself to standing, she slipped her high heels off and padded upstairs.

'Mia, can I come in?' Pushing the door to Mia's bedroom open,

Kim paused, allowing her eyes to adjust to the darkness. Mia must have closed her curtains. 'Mia, sweetheart.'

Picking her way through the clothes and books scattering the carpet, she made her way towards Mia's bed and lowered herself onto the starry red and white duvet cover. 'Budge up.' Swinging her legs up, Kim edged next to Mia and enveloped her in her arms, breathing a sigh of relief when she wasn't pushed away. 'We need to have that chat now, sweetheart. I know I've been distracted with work for a very long time, but I want to try to make it up to you now. Are you ready to tell me what's been going on?'

Mia nodded and pulled the duvet up to her chin. 'If I have to.'

'Yes, you do. That's the only way we can work out how to proceed and make things better.'

'Okay. It all started just before half term in October. Me and Amelia had been to the roller disco at the weekend, and at school Lucy was talking to us and asked us what we had done at the weekend.' Mia took a shuddering breath. 'And I answered her. I told her that me and Amelia had gone to the roller disco.'

'Okay. And then what?'

'Amelia pulled me aside, and we went on a walk around the playground because it was lunchtime, and she told me never to answer for her again. I told her that I hadn't answered for her because Lucy had asked both of us. So I hadn't, had I? But she told me Lucy had been speaking to her and that Lucy wouldn't even bother speaking to me at all if I wasn't friends with her.'

'That's not nice. What did you say to her?'

'I told her that she would be, that I had been friends with Lucy in primary school, so of course, I was friends with her too. Lucy had been in my class since I was seven, hadn't she? Do you remember?'

Kim nodded. She vaguely remembered something about a Lucy from primary school.

'She then trod on my foot on purpose so it really hurt and told me that I was stupid and no one would be friends with me if I didn't hang around with her.'

'Oh, Mia. Why didn't you tell me?'

'I was going to but then you had to work late, again, and by the time you got home I was asleep.'

Kim ran her fingers through Mia's dark curls and kissed her head. It had started in October. October. Five months ago. She had been dealing with this alone for five months. She had felt she couldn't speak to her own mother about it for five months.

'It was the next day it all started.' Whispering, Mia spoke into her duvet.

'When what started?'

'She turned everyone against me. It started with Lucy, Rachel and Macey, and then she just kept on going. Now, no one speaks to me. Not in my tutor group or any of the lessons.'

'No one?'

'No one. Apart from a couple of girls in my art class who don't like Amelia anyway and even they're probably only talking to me to try to annoy her.' A sob wracked through her small body, vibrating against Kim's side.

'Mrs Oakbury told me you'd spoken to her about it. What did she suggest?'

'At first she spoke to Amelia and her parents and made Amelia apologise.'

'Okay. And did that help?'

'No, it got worse. Everyone just called me a snitch and a telltale and said that they would never talk to me ever again because I would only tell of them too. It's horrible, Mum. When I walk down the corridor everyone just turns their backs on me.'

'Oh, darling, you should have told me. You should have made me listen.' Kim shook her head. 'I shouldn't have said that. You shouldn't have had to make me listen. I should have realised something wasn't right.'

'I was going to tell you and then things just got worse and worse and I didn't know how to. Plus, if I said it out loud then it would make it more real.'

'Come here.' Pulling her closer, Kim wiped the tears from Mia's cheeks with a tissue. 'We will make this okay. Tomorrow we'll go into school and speak to your head teacher, okay?'

'I don't want to. It'll only make things worse like it did before.'

'It won't. The head teacher will have dealt with so many horrible little bullies in her time, she'll know how to sort it out properly.'

'Can't I just have tomorrow off? Just tomorrow, please? I don't think I can face going back yet.'

'No, I'm afraid not. We need to face this thing head on and show them we mean business this time.'

'I can't. I just can't, Mum. Please don't make me go back in. Not tomorrow, please?' Twisting her head, Mia buried her face in Kim's suit jacket.

'Hey, okay, we'll take tomorrow off.'

'We? You'll stay off too?' Lifting her chin, Mia looked at Kim, her eyes glistening with tears and her cheeks flushed.

'Yes, tomorrow we'll have a home day.'

'Thank you.'

4

Jolting awake on the sofa, Kim opened her eyes, blinking to try to adapt to the dim glow coming from the TV. She'd been back there, at the crash scene, only it hadn't been a stranger running to the lifeless figure on the floor, it had been her. In the dream she had been calling Miriam's name, knowing it would be her who the paramedics would be working on. Screaming Miriam's name over and over, she'd knelt down beside her and pushed the paramedics away to get to her. Holding her head in her arms, she'd whispered into her ear. She'd thanked her for being the closest friend anyone could ever ask for. She'd promised her that she'd always remember her. It had been then that Miriam's head had turned towards her in her arms. Only all along it hadn't been Miriam. It had been Mia. It had been Mia who the paramedics had been trying to save, Mia who had been dying on the cold tarmac.

Pinching her eyes shut, that was all she could see, Mia's dark eyes staring back at her; lifeless and yet somehow still pleading.

Swinging her legs around, she stood up, still wobbly from sleep. Padding into the kitchen she checked the time on the cooker, 1:25. Switching on the kettle, she spooned a heaped teaspoon of coffee granules into her mug. There was no point even trying to get back to sleep. She'd only wake again in another twenty minutes and she didn't want to be taken back there again, not to a place where dreams muddled with reality and played on the mind.

Taking her mug back through to the living room, she perched on the edge of the sofa and took a sip, letting the scalding, bitter liquid hit the roof of her mouth. A loud whoop of delight escaped the TV and pierced through the dark silence. Looking up, she allowed herself to empty her mind and focus on the couple on the programme. It looked as though they were looking around houses. A man in a flat cap walked into the spacious light room the couple were wandering around in.

'Follow me.'

Diligently, the couple followed Mr Flat Cap down the hallway and through a doorway.

'Here, is the icing on the cake. As you can see, not only is this a wonderful house, but there is a workshop attached and beyond this a small shop floor. You will not only be able to kit out this space so you can create your pottery, but you will be able to sell it quite literally on your doorstep too.'

Five minutes of umming and ahhing and it seemed that they had decided to put an offer in. As it is with such TV programmes before the credits rolled a photograph of the couple, complete with a newly acquired Labrador, filled the screen with text telling the world how much they were loving their new life in the countryside.

Hefting her weight, Kim pulled her legs up underneath her and settled her head against the back cushions. She sipped her coffee as the next programme in the series introduced another couple (why were these programmes all about couples?) who had decided to escape the London Rat Race and flee into the countryside, chasing the idyllic dream of becoming landlords.

Maybe that's what she should do, quit her job, take Mia away from the bullies and start a new life in the countryside, far away from all that was getting them down here. Laughing at herself, she reminded herself it wasn't as easy as that. There was her impending promotion, although she had likely screwed that up, and Mia's education, she'd moved them here because the secondary school had been the best one for miles around. Plus, of course, there were the practical things like the mortgage. She'd be daft to sell now, in another five years she would have paid it all off. No, real life wasn't as simple as they made it out to be on TV.

Pulling her pyjama sleeves down to her fingers, Kim wrapped her arms around herself. It was no good, she was still cold. Placing her coffee down, she stood up and padded upstairs.

Standing on her tiptoes, she gently pulled a pale pink jumper from the top shelf of her wardrobe and pulled it over her head. That was better. Perching on the edge of her bed, she rubbed her eyes; she'd need a few more cups of coffee if she was going to evade the nightmares for a bit longer.

As she walked past Mia's room, the sound of sobbing stopped her. 'Mia, are you awake?'

The sobbing abruptly stopped. Kim stepped in and slid onto the bed next to Mia, who was curled up under the duvet. Rubbing her hand across Mia's back, she consoled her. 'It's okay. We'll sort it, sweetheart. School won't be like this forever.'

'I don't think I can go back. I just don't think I can do it.' Pulling the duvet down to her chin, Mia's red, swollen eyes shone in the semi-darkness. 'Please, please, don't make me go back. Ever. I can't do it. I can't.'

'Let's just take one day at a time, shall we?' Wrapping her arms around her, she wiped Mia's tear-soaked hair from her cheeks and kissed her on the top of the head.

'I really, really can't.' Sobs wrecked through her, shaking her body.

'Shush, it's okay. Try to get some sleep now.' Stroking her cheek as she had done when she was a baby, Kim blinked back her own tears. How could she have been so blind as to what had been going on in her own daughter's life? She was her mother. Her job was to protect her, and she had failed.

She waited until Mia's shoulders had finally stopped shaking before leaning over and checking she had fallen to sleep. Slipping out from under the duvet, Kim went back downstairs. How was she ever going to get her to step foot inside that school again? Yes, she could demand to see the head teacher, but what good would that really do? If things had got worse after Mrs Oakbury had spoken to this Amelia, what would happen once the head teacher had intervened? It was a gamble, a huge gamble, but what other choice did she have? She had to protect Mia and get these bullies to stop. She couldn't sit back and do nothing; she had done that for far too long already. Kim pinched the top of her nose and reminded herself that she hadn't done anything because Mia hadn't told her what was happening, but the truth was, that was only because Kim hadn't been present, not emotionally or physically, most of the time.

Things had to change. Swirling the remaining cold coffee around her mug, she watched as the brown liquid coated the ceramic momentarily before slipping back down to the bottom. Maybe the only real option here was to remove Mia from the school altogether? But to where? Her present school was the best secondary for miles around. Unless she was to get the coach, but even then she was sure the next half decent one would take at least an hour each way.

Sliding the laptop out from the side of the sofa, Kim flipped the lid and fired it up. Waiting for it to load, her eyes were drawn to the collection of school photographs on the mantelpiece. From left to right they showed a snapshot of Mia's schooling. In each one her hair was a little longer and her smile a little smaller, until the most recent one taken just before last Christmas in which Mia's grin had been the largest. When Mia had shown her the photo, Kim had told her how happy she had looked and that she was proud of her for becoming so independent and making the most of secondary school.

Setting the laptop on the cushion next to her, Kim stood up and strode across the room. Picking up the photograph, she looked down at it. Mia's smile may have been the biggest out of all the photographs, but it was only now that Kim noticed the smile didn't reach her eyes. At all. Her eyes were glazed as though she had been hiding something, and she had, she had been hiding how sad she had been feeling. Kim could see that now. The slight turn of her lips at the ends of her smile, the tiny crease in her forehead and her dull, listless eyes were obvious now.

Taking the photograph back to the sofa, Kim placed it on the coffee table in front of her, Mia's eyes locking into hers. Her little girl had changed. Her little girl's happy-go-lucky outlook had been squashed. She was being robbed of her very personality. Every day she went to that school, every time someone ignored her or was unkind to her told her she was unworthy. Amelia had planted a seed in her little girl, a seed that was making her doubt her very self, and each day the bullies watered it. Soon it would become her and Mia would be changed, altered for life.

Squeezing her hands into fists, Kim willed herself to be distracted from the pain, the knowledge of what was happening, but she couldn't be. She had been too easily distracted with work, promotion, money, the hunger to make Mia's life better, and she'd got it all wrong. Mia was right. She didn't need a bigger house, the promise of exclusive holidays that they would never take. Mia needed her, and at this moment she also needed to be taken away from the reality Amelia had turned her life into.

Curling her legs up underneath her, Kim balanced the laptop on her knees. They needed to get away. Not a holiday though, that would just prolong the inevitable. No, they needed to get away properly. Maybe, just maybe, these people on the series playing out in the background were right; maybe starting over again wasn't taking a step back. Maybe it was actually taking a step forward, being strong enough to jump into change.

She had enough holiday rolled over from years of working non-stop to be able to quit work and not have to work out the notice period. The house, well, yes she had almost paid off the mortgage but maybe she just needed to view that as a positive, instead of thinking she was so close to owning it outright she needed to think that she'd built up a good deposit to put down on another place.

Downing the last cold dregs of coffee, she clicked through to the search engine. There was no point looking at the popular house buying and selling websites yet, she didn't have a clue where they would even move to. She hadn't spoken to her parents since Mia was born and they didn't have any other family to speak off. The odd aunt and uncle scattered around the country and a few cousins Norfolk way, but no one she really communicated with on a regular basis, apart from polite correspondence at Christmas and birthdays anyway. She shrugged; she'd been too busy building her career, proving herself she guessed, to have spent any real time putting the effort into keeping in touch. As for friends, she had her work colleagues but didn't have anyone she'd particularly call a 'friend'. Again, partly because she had dedicated her life to the office but also, if she was completely honest, subconsciously she had promised herself she would never get close enough to another friend to care about them the way she had Miriam.

She typed 'places to escape and live in UK' into the search bar and began scrolling past the numerous websites offering the low-down on the Top Ten Places to Live in the UK. Maybe she should have worded the search differently. Just as she was about to clear the search, her eyes focused on a website offering 'the best rural places to buy and live in the countryside'. Clicking through, the screen was soon filled with photographs of idyllic stone cottages and windy country walkways. In big, bold font she was asked if she was 'dreaming of a better country life?' Yes, that she was. Nope, she did not want to move to the Orkney Islands, however picturesque they might be. Devon, though? Maybe. She remembered going on camping trips there when she had been a child. It could be an option.

Looking up at the TV, she let herself be drawn into the programme again, this time the family were moving to Scotland to open up a dog training school. At least she didn't need to worry about getting another job. With her CV and the reference she'd be able to coax out of Mr Pinnel she should be able to walk into another job with ease. She might even go part-time, at least until Mia had settled into her new school. She knew one thing for certain though; she would not be sucked into corporate life again at the expense of Mia's welfare.

Looking back down at the laptop, a pop-up advert shot across the screen. Instead of clicking the cross to shut it down instantly as she normally did, Kim focused in on the text. It was for some property selling site. Now she had a vague idea of where they could move, or at least a vague idea of one of their options, it wouldn't hurt to do a bit of window shopping. Clicking through to the site, she entered 'Devon' into the search bar at the top of the page and waited for it to load. Wow, property was certainly a lot cheaper than where they were now and there were some beautiful homes up for sale too. Scrolling through page after page, she studied dozens of photos and floorplans. The majority of them were lovely, but there was nothing that was jumping out at her. With their current home, as soon as she'd seen the pictures in the estate agents' window she'd known it was where she had wanted to continue to raise Mia. There hadn't been anything particularly striking or different about their home but it had just been, Kim shook her head, she'd just known it was the one.

Clicking through to the final page in her search, her eyes were drawn to a whitewashed stone house, a large house much bigger than what she and Mia needed, but there was something special about it. Blossom trees framed the door and shielded the windows, the sun glinting in the old-fashioned lead panelled windows. She clicked through to the details and that's when she realised that it was, in fact, a Bed and Breakfast. That made more sense.

Clicking back through to the main site, she stared at the slogan to the right underneath the title of the website, 'Your life does not get better by chance. It gets better by change'. According to the caption underneath, the author of the quote was a Jim Rohn. He knew what he was talking about, she'd give him that. It made sense. If she were to make more time for Mia and make life better for them both then things would have to change and the only person who could make decisions that big was herself.

Moving house was only half of the solution. Even if she took a few weeks out before looking for another job, she would eventually have to go back out to work and the corporate world was all she knew, all she was trained to do, and with a corporate job came corporate hours. No, the only way she was going to be able to secure Mia's future happiness was to make real, lasting changes.

And, ultimately, that meant giving up her goal of working towards a partnership in a firm, giving up her corporate lifestyle.

She pushed the laptop onto the sofa and made her way into the kitchen, pausing at the bottom of the stairs to listen for Mia. Silence. Hopefully she was still asleep and wouldn't be woken by fears about facing her bullies again. Holding on to the bottom of the banister, her eyes fell on Mia's school bag thrown on top of her black patent school shoes. Bringing the dark purple cloth bag to the bottom of the stairs, she unzipped it and pulled out the pile of school books, English, maths, history exercise books and her homework planner, and sat on the bottom step. Flicking through Mia's English book, she noticed that the amount of writing had decreased dramatically from the first few pages through to the current ones. In fact, for the past three weeks or so, Mia had barely scribbled the date and first sentence. What had she been doing in the remaining lesson time?

She shook her head, no wonder her grades had fallen, she had hardly been doing any of the work set. Standing back up, she shuffled the books into a neat pile, placing them back into Mia's school bag. Turning back towards the kitchen, she bent to pick up a couple of stray pieces of paper that must have fallen from Mia's books. Just as she was about to slip them back in the bag, she glanced down at them. Gripping the banister and lowering herself to the bottom step, Kim forced herself to read Mia's scrawly black handwriting. In the middle of the first page, in large bold bubble writing, Mia had written 'Hate Life', around the word, spidery lines led to numerous circles each containing a reason for Mia's hate. The statements included, 'I'm rubbish – worthless', 'no one wants to be my friend', 'ugly', 'everyone hates me'. Pinching the top of her nose, Kim closed her eyes. How could Mia think like this? What had those girls been saying to her?

Opening her eyes, she focused in on the remaining statement.

As hard as it was to read, she needed to know how Mia was feeling. The final statement had been written in the smallest and neatest handwriting and the circle of black ink around it was so dark it looked as though Mia had circled around it time and time again. Peering at the paper closely, Kim read the words, letting them sink into her and pierce her heart. 'Even my own mother doesn't want to spend time with me – I AM too much of a horrible human being'.

Standing up, Kim ran to the back door. Pulling it wide open, she let the cool night air embrace her. Looking up at the stars, she tried to search out Orion's Belt. Having located the three stars, evenly spaced in a line, she focused on the middle one before letting her vision pan out until she could see Orion. Danny had taught her that trick. One night during the weeks before taking her final exams, she had panicked that she wouldn't be able to revise everything she needed to know for her Business Studies GCSE. She had believed that even if she did, she'd forget it as soon as she got into the stuffy PE hall. Holding her hand, he had led her outside into the darkness. Quietening her panic, he had shown her Orion's Belt, had made her focus on each of the three stars in turn before allowing her eyes to take in all of Orion. He had told her that her Business Studies exam was much like one of these stars; it was important but it wasn't the whole picture. Taking her in his arms, he had reminded her that she had her whole life to accomplish what she wanted to and one little exam wouldn't be the end of her journey. She had a lifetime to explore. A whole lifetime to succeed in what she chose to.

Looking up at those stars now, Kim remembered his words, as clear as though he had muttered them in her ear moments ago, 'life is made up of lots of little events, little stars, don't focus too much on one thing or you will never see the whole picture'. And that's what she had been doing; she had been focusing too much on work, on her goal of becoming a partner, that she hadn't seen what had been right in front of her. She hadn't noticed Mia's pain. It was in that moment that she knew what she had to do. She had to do what she should have done when she'd become a mum less than three years after Danny had calmed her exam nerves; she had to put her daughter first.

Striding back inside and into the living room, she took her position back on the sofa and lifted the laptop onto her knees. Pressing the back arrow, she scanned the website until she found the advert for the Bed and Breakfast again. Taking a deep breath, she clicked the 'Contact Seller' button and emailed a short message querying the general state of the business being offered. Opening another browser she logged into her work emails. Ignoring the dozens of new messages, she wrote a curt email to Mr Pinnel thanking him for the opportunities his business had given her before handing her resignation in and detailing how the holiday she had accrued over the years would more than cover her notice period. Without hesitating, she pressed 'send'.

Quickly pushing the laptop onto the coffee table, Kim stood up, strode into the kitchen and flicked the kettle on. It was done now. She had made her decision and there was no going back. She'd move Mia far away from the grips of the bullying and learn to be the mother Mia deserved. It would be an adventure, and the challenge of owning her own business would feed her need for success. How hard could it be to run a small Bed and Breakfast? After all of her experience in the business world, it should be a breeze.

* * *

Sipping her coffee, she focused on the TV shopping programme which had taken over from the previous show and let the calm, soothing tones of the woman and man duo wash over her. Whenever Mia had been poorly, or she hadn't been able to sleep for whatever reason, Kim had turned to the late-night shopping channel takeover, letting the repetitive nature of the show lull Mia to sleep while Kim zoned out hugging a small Mia on her lap before dragging herself into work the next day.

Just as she watched the peroxide blonde demonstrate the cleaning abilities of a steam mop for the tenth time, she was jarred into consciousness by the ping of an email coming through.

It was a reply from the Bed and Breakfast. Sitting up straight, she opened the email and skimmed the contents. It sounded as though the accounts were in good order and the turnover had been quite profitable the previous tax year. They were eager to sell and would welcome her to view the property as soon as she wanted to. Apparently they were going away to visit friends at the weekend but were available the rest of the week.

Looking at the carriage clock on the mantelpiece, Kim noted it was almost a quarter to three in the morning. If she tried to get some sleep now, maybe they could go and view it tomorrow? There was no point waiting around. Plus, surely it would be better to view it sooner rather than thinking about it for a few days and either getting their hopes up or concocting reasons why it was just an impossible dream. Hugging her knees to her chest, she was the first to admit if she didn't commit to their new future soon she would be tempted to withdraw her resignation and opt to return to the corporate world where she was confident in her actions and decisions rather than take a chance on a new life.

Leaning forward over the laptop perching on the coffee table, Kim emailed the question back to the vendor, before standing up and padding to the rug chest under the bay window to retrieve a blanket.

Back on the sofa, she covered her legs, the soft warmth of the woollen blanket instantly making her feel sleepy and listened for the telltale ping of a reply. Sure enough, within two minutes, the vendor had replied to say that they were looking forward to her visit and to drop in at any time during the day tomorrow.

Closing the laptop, Kim settled onto the sofa and closed her eyes, letting the dull tones of the presenters finally lull her to sleep.

5

'Mia, it's time to wake up.' Leaning across the mound of duvet and blankets, Kim gently shook Mia's shoulders. 'Up you get now. I'm going to go and put some toast on for you, Get changed and come downstairs.'

Back downstairs in the kitchen, Kim opened the window, letting the cool, fresh spring air breeze into the room.

After barely three hours sleep, she had woken up at six o'clock tossing and turning unable to drift off again, and after checking the location of the Bed and Breakfast and realising it would take them just shy of four hours to get there, she had decided there was no reason to wait. If they left soon they should make good headway before the rush hour traffic began to clog up the motorways.

Putting two slices of bread into the toaster, she took her coffee over to the kitchen table and let the strong caffeine wake her while listening to the morning chorus of the blackbirds who nested in the garden.

Standing up once the toast had popped, Kim spread a thick coating of peanut butter across the toast.

'Mum, I can't have peanut butter while in my school uniform.'

Turning around, the plate in her hand, she watched as Mia walked into the kitchen wearing her navy uniform. The downward curve of her lips and the red rings around her eyes exposed the fact that she had been crying already.

'Here, sit down. No need to worry about that today. You're not going back there.'

'You mean I can really have today off? I thought you'd forgotten. I'll be good. I promise.'

'No. I don't mean you can have today off. I mean you're not going back to that school. Ever.'

'Really?'

Kim watched as Mia's eyes filled with fresh tears. Standing behind her, she wrapped her arms around Mia's shoulders, feeling the release of a deeply held fear being released as her body slumped back against her. 'Really. I told you things were going to change and they are. Starting from today.'

'Thank you. Thank you, Mum.'

'You don't need to thank me; I'm only doing what I should have done a long time ago.'

'I'll tidy up for you and I'll study online, I promise. And I have all my textbooks from school so I can read them if you need to go into the office. I promise I will.'

'I'm not going back to work, so you don't need to worry about that.'

'But what about your promotion? You've been working so hard to get your partnership? Have I messed it up for you? Have they fired you because I made you come out of your important meeting?' Looking up at her, Mia's bottom lip trembled.

'No, nothing of the sort. I emailed Mr Pinnel my resignation last night.' Slipping into the chair next to Mia, Kim picked her coffee mug up again. 'Listen, I've decided the best thing for us is to move away, to get a fresh start somewhere else. There's nothing keeping us here now. You're not going back to that school and I've quit work, so it's the perfect time for a new adventure. One where we can spend more time together.'

'Really? We're really moving?'

'Yes. I've been emailing the owner of a little Bed and Breakfast up in Devon and I've arranged for us to go and view it today, which is why I've got you up so early.'

'A Bed and Breakfast. Why? For us to stay at while we find somewhere to buy?'

'No, we're going to view the Bed and Breakfast, and if we like it, we can buy it. We can run it. Of course, we don't know what it's like yet and we'll make the decision together. This move is to make things better for you, so we'll decide together.'

'Wow. A Bed and Breakfast? Us running a Bed and Breakfast? What about you though? I thought you liked working in London?'

'I do. I did, but you're more important than all the partnerships in the world. Plus, it's time for me to try new things.' Smiling, Kim reminded herself that her leaving the corporate world could only be a good thing. Her work had shielded her eyes to what was important in her life for too long as it was.

'Are you sure? I don't want you regretting leaving the career you've worked so hard for.' Pulling the crusts off her toast, Mia looked up.

'When did you get so old and wise?' Smiling, Kim rubbed Mia's forearm. 'It's something I should have done a long time ago.'

'Okay. Awesome! When do we leave?'

'As soon as you've changed out of your uniform. I'll grab us some snacks for in the car, but we can always find a coffee shop at the services to stop at.'

'I'll go and change now then.' Taking the last piece of toast with her, Mia paused in the doorway and looked back at Kim. 'What's the name of the Bed and Breakfast?'

'Berry Grove B&B.'

'Ooh, I like that. Berry Grove B&B. It sounds really cute.'

* * *

Turning off the motorway at the junction, Kim turned the music down and listened to the satnav.

'How much further have we got?' Mia mumbled as she took a bite from the cupcake they had bought at the services a few miles back.

'It shouldn't be much further, about an hour if we're lucky with the traffic.' Kim glanced at the satnav. 'Can you pass me one of those mints, please?'

'How many rooms does it have? Is it really big? What's the garden like?'

Taking the mint, she let it dissolve in her mouth for a minute before crunching it. 'I'm not sure, to be honest. I saw it online and emailed them. It was very much a spur of the moment thing.'

'Weren't there any photos?'

'There was a photo of the front of it but I didn't scroll through the other photos.' Kim looked in her rear-view mirror as a motorbike sped up behind them, overtaking easily. Truth be told she had chosen not to look at the other photos. She knew they needed to get as far away from their old life as they could but she was still terrified she'd back out of moving so hadn't wanted to look at the photos in case she found an excuse not to jump. 'We'll be there soon enough anyway and it'll be nice for us both to see it in real-life for the first time. Most of the time those photos online don't do the places justice anyway.'

'I guess so. I'm just so excited! I can't believe we're actually moving and you're not going to make me go back to that school. I know you always say that we need to face our problems, but I just don't think I can.'

Out of the corner of her eye, Kim watched as Mia used her sleeve to wipe her cheeks. 'Sometimes the problems aren't worth facing and Amelia and her little gaggle of sheep are definitely not worth the aggro. Plus, we've got better things to be doing with our lives now.' Patting Mia's knee, she focused on the car in front. She would make this work. She had to.

Pausing at the crossroads in front, Kim steered left down a thin country lane. They sped past fields of cows, sheep, horses and numerous barns.

'Can I start going horse riding?'

'I don't see why not? If we decide to buy Berry Grove, then we can certainly look into it.'

'Oh, I hope we do buy it. If we do, when would we move in?'

'Probably not for a few months yet. We'd need to sell our house first. Hopefully by the summer though, ready for the tourist season.'

'What will I do about school? Will I have to go back in the meantime?' Mia's voice was barely audible above the engine noise.

'No, I'll teach you from home.'

'Really?'

'Yes, really. I meant what I said, things are changing. You are my priority.'

Nodding, Mia looked out of the window.

'We're almost there now.' Turning right, they drove into the small town and weaved their way up a steep hill along the High Street. Independent, quirky shops lined the cobbled street, people bustling in and out, the old-fashioned bells above the doors tinkling to announce their arrival or departure.

'Look up there, Mia.' At the top of the hill stood Aranel Castle, its sandy coloured towers standing to attention flanking the entrance.

'Wow. I didn't know there was a castle here!'

'Nor did I.' The small town was beautiful, and with the castle being here too, Kim was sure it must attract thousands of visitors a week during the height of summer, which could only be profitable for Berry Grove.

'Whereabouts is the B&B?' Peering out of the window, Mia watched as the car climbed the hill.

'From the looks of the satnav, it's just down at the end of the next lane.' Indicating, Kim turned left and squeezed down the narrow cobbled lane. Thin, tall shopfronts gave way to old cottages as the lane opened up towards the end.

'That's it! That's Berry Grove, isn't it, Mum?'

Following Mia's pointing finger, Kim took a deep breath in. At the end of the lane, a large whitewashed house stood, true to its photo online, pink blossom trees filled the front garden, camouflaging its stark difference to the small cottages on its approach. It certainly did look as charming as the photograph she had seen last night.

Pulling into the small car park to the right, Kim noted there were four other cars as she squeezed between a large four by four and a tiny mini. She nodded. It was good to see that even in early spring there was still business about.

'Right, let's go and have a look.' Checking her hair before she got out, Kim waited until Mia had joined her and they both walked around the side of the B&B to the front door. The front garden was laid to slabs, but tastefully so with huge old-fashioned weathered wooden pots planted with an abundance of colour. An array of bistro style metal tables and chairs were scattered across the yard, and to continue with the flowery theme on each stood a small pot perfectly planted with blooming perennials.

Above the wooden front door the words, 'Welcome to Berry Grove' had been carved into the stone many years previously. Taking the heavy lion metal knocker in her hand, Kim rapped it twice, a loud and satisfying dull thwack echoing around the yard.

Kim looked down at Mia as she edged closer to her.

'Good morning. You must be Kim Reynolds, is that right? I'm Jane Duncan and this is my husband, Bill.' Holding the door open a plump elderly couple ushered them in. 'We're so pleased you could come today.'

'Morning. Thank you for having us at such short notice. This is my daughter, Mia.'

'Welcome, Mia. Come in, come in. We don't stand on ceremony here.'

'Thank you.' Following the couple through the vast hallway, Kim took in the black and white polished ceramic tiles and the vintage décor.

'Now, would you like to have a sit down and go through the books or have a tour of the building first? Or, of course, you can have a rest after your long journey before we get down to business?' Turning to face them, Bill smiled, his bushy grey eyebrows raising a little as he asked the question.

'We're fine, thank you. We stopped off at the services not so long ago. Could you maybe show us around first?'

'Of course. As you can see, the hallway is both spacious and welcoming with plenty of room for pushchairs and wheelchairs to access the property. We have the front desk over there. Upon the insistence of our grandson, Harry, we have recently moved across to computerised booking forms and payments.'

Kim looked where he was pointing to a large, ornate dark wooden desk positioned to the right of the front door.

'Through here we have the guest sitting room. We allow our guests access to this room at all hours, and we've had many a review praising Berry Grove on offering family living rather than just the traditional bedrooms.'

Nodding, Kim made her way into the sitting room. It was a large room, decorated with pale cream wallpaper depicting a pattern of sprawling flowers and cream carpets covered with an array of dark maroon rugs of differing sizes. Two sofas were positioned along the outside walls in an L shape facing a large flat-screen television. Tall pot plants filled the bay window offering a fresh feel to the room at the same time as blocking some of the sunlight piercing through the glass. 'Very nice.'

'Thank you. We don't currently have an alcohol licence, although I'm sure it won't be a problem to obtain one if you wish. We've just never felt the need. We offer access to the kitchen day and night for guests to help themselves to drinks.' Jane smiled.

'What sort of clientele do you find comes here the most?'

'Mostly couples and families. The seaside is just a short drive or a twenty-minute walk down the road and, of course, the castle and grounds attract guests all year round. We also have a special deal with a national touring company who guarantee bookings, but we'll speak more about that when we go into the details.'

'That sounds promising.'

'It is. There are plenty of sightseeing attractions to entice guests. Two of Devon's most popular seaside towns are but a few miles away and we offer a slightly more upmarket country escape to the bustling seafront B&Bs.'

Kim nodded. Looking across at Mia, she smiled. Mia's face said it all. She was glowing with an excitement and happiness Kim hadn't seen for a very long time.

'In here, we have the kitchen. As you can see, we have space enough for these two big tables.'

The kitchen boasted the same black and white tiles as the hallway and the walls above the work surfaces were covered with multi-coloured splashback tiles, a feature wall was decorated in orange flowery wallpaper and the remaining walls painted yellow. Kim wasn't sure if the two colours complimented each other or clashed. The two large pine tables added to the farmhouse ambience.

'It's lovely.' After years of treating cooking as an inconvenience and a time sap, having the free time to experiment and cook properly would be a welcome change from the microwave ready meals they had grown accustomed to.

'I must admit I will really miss this room when we leave.' Jane looked around fondly. 'Of course, with the touring company bringing a lot of business our way and often groups of guests all staying here and having to get to their booked activities or tours at the same time, we have struggled to fit everyone in for breakfast at their required times. At the moment we rotate the guests, which can be quite frustrating, and so we have begun to build a conservatory, or an orangery if you like, on the back of the building.'

They followed Jane around the corner and through a small utility room which had been opened into an airy short corridor with a heavy-duty curtain hung at the end. Kim watched as Jane pulled the curtain aside to reveal the shell of a conservatory twice the size of the kitchen.

'There will be enough space for at least seven tables in here which will be plenty big enough to allow all the guests to eat together at breakfast time if they wish. It will also open up opportunities such as hosting conferences, small parties or wedding receptions or opening it up to the general public at lunchtimes, for example.'

'It sounds as though there's a lot of scope to increase the profit then?'

'Absolutely. We have a good team of local experienced builders who should complete the job within the next two months. So it will be ready in time for the summer holiday season, and that includes underfloor heating, the floor being laid, all electrics and also an extension to the patio area out the back. We haven't yet decided on the specifications for the flooring and other details so if you were to purchase you would have complete control on any of the final decisions.'

'Okay.' Looking around the shell of the room, Kim could see the huge potential. When it was finished it would look amazing and certainly add a substantial amount to the resale value of the property.

Letting the curtain fall back into place, Jane rubbed her hands together and smiled at them. 'Right, I'm going to leave you in Bill's capable hands to show you around the bedrooms while I cook us up a bit of lunch. We can eat while we discuss the finer details of the business.'

* * *

Back in the vast hallway, Kim and Mia followed Bill up the wide staircase. Sepia vintage photographs lined the walls showing off beautiful local sights and distracted the eye from the garishly patterned red and cream carpet.

'All of the seven bedrooms are of a similar standard, all with en suite, television, and tea and coffee making facilities.' Pausing outside the first door on the landing, Bill opened it, letting Kim and Mia step through first.

The flowery theme from the living room was continued with the pale cream wallpaper covered in pale pink climbing roses. The décor, although old-fashioned and not to Kim's taste, was pretty. Plus, if they did decide to buy Berry Grove, it wouldn't take much to modernise it.

By the time they had viewed all five bedrooms on the first

floor, the memory of each one had merged with the others and Kim wasn't sure if she would ever be able to differentiate between any of them, they were that alike.

'Up here, in the loft space, are the private quarters.' Leading them to another staircase, this one a little narrower than the main one, Bill looked back at Kim.

'I thought you said there were seven bedrooms?'

'Yes, there are. We have two bedrooms on the ground floor, which we normally reserve for guests with limited mobility. When we go back downstairs, remind me and I'll show you them.' Bill held a heavy fire door open for them as they reached the top of the narrow staircase.

The private quarters comprised of a small living room, a galley kitchen, a bathroom, one double bedroom and one single room. Kim nodded, it would take a lot of getting used to living in such a small space after being used to their large detached house, but she supposed, they would still have use of the communal kitchen and living room, which would be empty during the day so they would only be cooped up in the small flat in the evenings.

Back downstairs, Bill led them through to the kitchen where Jane had prepared a cream tea, complete with scones, jam, cream, a teapot and milk jug.

'So, what do you think? Do you like what you've seen so far?' Jane handed Kim and Mia each a plate and indicated to the dining chairs.

Taking the plate, Kim glanced at Mia who was still smiling and looking more relaxed than Kim could remember her being for a long time. 'Yes, definitely. I can imagine us being very happy living here. We just need to have a look through the accounts and see how viable it is.'

'Of course, dear.' Patting Kim on the forearm, Jane handed her the plate of scones to put on the table before sitting down at the chair opposite. 'There's plenty still to go through before you can make such a big decision. So, have you run a Bed and Breakfast before?'

'No, this would be the first time.'

'Do you come from a hospitality background then?'

'Umm, no. Until recently, I was working as a project coordinator for a firm in London.'

'Oh, I say. It certainly will be a change of career then, I imagine.'

Kim shifted in her seat and accepted the jam. 'Yes, it will.'

'What made you look into purchasing Berry Grove then, if you don't mind me asking?'

'Let's just say it's time for a change of direction and a better work-life balance. I need more time to spend with my daughter.' Resting her hand over Mia's, Kim smiled at her.

'If Aranel is anything, it's certainly a family orientated little town. There's plenty here for you to enjoy together, plenty of sights to see and adventures to be had. Our grandchildren love to visit here, don't they, Bill? They love exploring the nature reserve behind the castle grounds and spending time at the seaside. There are good schools too. The local secondary school is only a short coach ride or drive into the next town and has a very good Ofsted report. There's even a little youth club that one of the cafés down the High Street run.'

'That sounds nice, doesn't it, Mia?'

Mia nodded and took a gulp of her tea.

Staring at the red lights of the car in front, the pros and cons of buying Berry Grove whirred around in Kim's mind. The figures had certainly added up and the Bed and Breakfast was already making a tidy profit which had grown year on year over the past five years. Jane and Bill had been very open about the amount of money the business had been bringing in. When Kim had asked to see the accounts, Bill had piled the account books for the past seven years onto the table in front of her.

After buying the property, they lost money in the first two years and then had made a deal with a well-known touring and activity centre offering package holidays such as horse riding and Norman re-enactments which were held in the castle grounds. All Jane and Bill needed to do was to provide accommodation and although they had to give a small cut of the room fee to the company, it was guaranteed income during the quieter times of the year when otherwise they would have struggled to fill the rooms.

It seemed like a sound investment. The only thing that had initially concerned her was the half-built extension, but Bill and Jane had shown her the contract and plans drawn up by the architect detailing the price and timescale of the project. Anyway, if she did put an offer in by the time her house had sold and they were able to exchange, the building work would probably have been completed. If for whatever reason it wasn't, Jane had assured her that they would pay for the amount up until the point they left and then any remaining work would be completed and paid by the new owners, which seemed fair. Plus, the amount of potential extra income that would come from the extension would make the extra expense worth it, anyway.

* * *

Glancing across at Mia, who had fallen asleep, her head flopping forwards onto her chest, Kim gently pushed her head back against the headrest. She quite liked the idea of opening the orangery up as a café during lunchtimes. Berry Grove was close enough to the High Street to offer convenience, but being at the end of the little lane it offered the seclusion the more centralised coffee shops and cafés couldn't offer. She'd have to get word out about it though, as they would be too far out of the way to pick up foot traffic.

Slowing down, she pulled onto the slip road. Home was still two hours away, and she needed coffee.

It would be easy enough to market the lunchtime café though; she'd certainly had enough experience from working at Pinnel's. All it would need is a launch day and then word of mouth would more than likely do the rest.

Parking up at the garage, she ran in to grab a coffee from the machine. Standing in the queue, she listened as the young couple in front of her discussed their holiday plans for the year. It would be exciting to have the chance to make a difference to a total stranger's holiday. Exciting and terrifying at the same time.

Back in the car, Mia still soundly asleep, Kim took a long sip of her coffee, swilling the comforting bitterness around her mouth before swallowing. She had really enjoyed spending the day with her today, and she was sure Mia had too. She had certainly looked happy anyway. Closing her eyes, Kim literally couldn't remember the last time she had spent a whole day with Mia without work getting in the way. She wanted to say Christmas Day, but she knew that she would be lying. After Christmas Dinner she had holed herself up in her study to go through a new account and write some proposals.

They had been missing out on so much, both her and Mia. And with no other family around, she understood why Mia had been so lonely and felt so unwanted. Opening her eyes again, Kim looked across at her and studied her face, her cheeks rosy with the comfort of sleep. She could blame this Amelia girl for destroying Mia's confidence, but if she was completely truthful it had been her, Kim, who for as long as she could remember had prioritised work, a job, over her own daughter. That must have knocked Mia's confidence way more and much earlier than this Amelia and her gaggle of followers had.

'I promise, Mia, I'll make up for the times I have let you down.' Leaning over, she stroked Mia's cheek before placing her coffee mug in the holder and starting the engine.

6

Piling the last of their bags into the back of the car felt much like Tetris, only if she failed, she didn't lose points, she'd just lose her rag. Taking a deep breath, she tried again, taking the bags back out and reorganising them. When everything was balanced, she pulled the boot shut, quickly swiping her hand away at the last moment to prevent anything from falling.

'Did you manage to get everything in?'

'I sure did.' Turning around, she watched as Mia slipped into the passenger seat, two travel mugs in her hands. 'Don't you want to have a last look around?'

'No, I think I'll be okay. I'm just excited to get there now.'

'Okay. Just give me five minutes and we'll set off.' Shutting the passenger door for Mia, Kim walked back into the house. She couldn't help feeling that they were taking a step back by moving to Berry Grove. Yes, Berry Grove was huge compared to this place, but they would be squashed into the small two-bedroom flat while the grandeur of the place was left for the guests to enjoy.

Stepping into the large, airy family room at the back of the house, Kim ran her fingers along the breakfast bar. She'd had so many hopes and dreams pinned on this home. When she'd first viewed it she'd even let herself imagine that she might have met someone else to spend her life with, to have more children with, and to fill the house with the sound of happiness and laughter. Of course, that had been short-lived. The only time she'd ever felt half comfortable with another man besides Danny had been with Max, who ten months into the relationship she had discovered was still married.

Back out in the hallway, she climbed the stairs, her feet sinking into the plush cream carpet. She'd definitely miss the luxuries of this house.

It had been after her relationship with Max, or more specifically, the night his wife had turned up sobbing on her doorstep, that she had vowed never to let another man muddy her focus again. She had decided to work as hard as she could and get to the highest level of her career and she wouldn't let anyone stop her. His lies had awakened in her a need to be independent, to only trust and rely on herself. She had felt she had to show the world that she was in control. And she had been, for so many years now she had proved that despite her rocky start she could be independent, in control and a success. She could earn enough money for the big house and swanky cars.

Pushing Mia's bedroom door open, she let the lingering aroma of incense envelope her. She'd been wrong, she could see that now. The more successful in her career she had become, the more she had failed in real life. She had closed her heart off to any chance of romantic happiness, but more importantly, and the biggest regret she had, the more she had strived to be the 'good' mum who could provide a comfortable life for her child, the more she had pushed Mia away. Mia hadn't needed money, a big house or nice cars. She had needed a mum. She had needed love and time, and Kim hadn't given them to her. She had loved her, always, but she hadn't shown her that love, and she certainly hadn't given her time.

Running her hand down the banisters, she hurried back downstairs. It was time to go, time to leave her past mistakes and to build a new future. Closing the front door behind her, she checked her watch. The estate agent would be arriving soon to show some prospective buyers around for the second time. Hopefully, the new owners would be able to fill the house with the love it deserved.

* * *

'Right, are you ready to begin our new adventure?' Pulling off the handbrake, Kim let the car roll down the drive for the final time.

'More than ready, Mum.'

'Glad to hear it. This day may have come quicker than we had thought, but I think we're ready.'

'I think so, too.'

Kim smiled and silently said goodbye to their old life. Since they had viewed Berry Grove, everything had raced by. The following day she'd received a frantic phone call from Jane telling her that they were moving to go and look after her sister and her sister had taken a nasty tumble and so needed them more than ever. She'd then gone on to tell her they were sorry but would have to accept a past offer on the property even though it was lower than they had hoped to receive simply because the people were living in a rental property and were able to exchange quicker. At that point, Kim had looked over at Mia sat on the sofa with her iPad and asked that they could hold on until she had consulted with her financial advisor.

Two days later, Kim had organised a bridging mortgage based on the promise that when their old house sold, she would pay a large chunk of it off, and, three weeks later, here they were, travelling to their new life at Berry Grove. Glancing across at Mia, slouching back in her chair, her feet resting on the dashboard, she knew she'd made the right decision, however rushed it had felt.

* * *

Pulling onto the sweeping driveway, Berry Grove looked even more beautiful and idyllic than she had remembered.

'Home, sweet, home.'

'I can't believe we're actually here.'

'I know.' Getting out of the car, Kim paused to take in the large building. Could she really do this? Could she really run a Bed and Breakfast with no previous experience in the hospitality business? Shaking herself, it struck her that she'd find out tomorrow. Jane and Bill had made sure the bookings were cleared for today, but there were two bookings for tomorrow.

'What time is the lorry with all our stuff getting here?'

'Soon, hopefully.'

* * *

'Night, love you.' Kissing Mia on the forehead, Kim retreated out of her bedroom and went into the narrow galley kitchen. She'd scrubbed the work surfaces at least three times, but they still looked grubby. Switching the kettle on, she resisted the urge to grab the dishcloth again. She knew it was clean and it was just the dingy grey speckled colour that made them look dirty. She looked around, the cupboards were a veneered dark brown, scuff marks and loose handles included, and the floor was the cheapest of the cheap grey-green lino. It was fine, it was usable. It just wasn't her immaculate, new kitchen from their old place.

She poured the boiling water over the coffee granules. It didn't mean it couldn't be. If there was one thing the tired Bed and Breakfast didn't lack, it was potential. She had it all worked out, this year they'd focus on learning the trade and selling their old home, obviously. Next year, they could have a bit of fun and modernise. It was exciting. Daunting, but exciting all the same.

Carrying her mug through to the living room, Kim curled up on the sofa, clutching the hot mug to her. It was tomorrow she was worried about. Her people skills swung from being curt to colleagues on a lower pay scale than her being over-indulgent to the clients of Pinnel's. She wasn't sure she held the qualities to work with members of the public, much less welcome them into her new home. She took a long sip of coffee. She'd have to learn and learn quickly.

7

'Morning.' Taking the frying pan off of the hob, Kim turned around.

'Morning, Mum. Have we got guests already? I thought they weren't coming until later?' Yawning, Mia pulled her pink dressing gown tighter around herself and slipped into one of the dining chairs closest to the oven.

'We don't, but I thought I could do with the practice, so these are for us.' Gently moving the hash browns and bacon across to the other side of the plates, Kim slid the fried eggs into the space.

'Looks yummy. I don't think I've ever seen you make a cooked breakfast before.' Mia took the plate from Kim's hand.

'I have. Well, I used to. Admittedly, I probably haven't made one in about five years or so.'

'Looks good though.'

'I just hope I don't poison anyone.' Laughing, Kim grinned to hide the worry behind her eyes. What would happen if she did poison someone? Would they sue her? Cutting into her egg, she watched as the yolk ran towards the hash browns. She guessed that was why the insurance was so high. It'd be higher if they knew her cooking capabilities, or lack of, though.

'Nah, you won't. It's all going to be okay, you'll see.' Smiling confidently, Mia squirted tomato ketchup all over her plate.

'I'm sure it will be.'

'When will I have to start school?' Picking up her fork, Mia prodded a piece of bacon.

'We'll give it a couple of days for us to settle in and learn how to run this place, and then we'll go and have a look at the schools early next week.'

'Okay.'

'I've looked online and rung up the local authority, there's a couple with spaces within ten miles of here. So I figured we could go along and check them both out and then decide from there, what do you think?'

'All right, I guess. Does that mean I'll have to get a school bus though?'

'No, not to begin with anyway. I'll drive you in and if you find that some of your new friends take the bus then that'll be a decision you make. I'm happy to drive you there and back.' Squeezing Mia's hand, Kim smiled at her. 'This move is for us to spend more time together and, you never know, you might find someone nice who comes from here and whose parents want to lift share.'

'Okay, thanks, Mum.'

A shrill sound echoed around the kitchen making them both jump. It took Kim a few minutes to realise that it must be the doorbell. Jane and Bill must have had it wired up so that it sounded in the kitchen.

'I didn't think check-in time was until after two in the afternoon?'

'It isn't.' Frowning, Kim scraped back her chair. She hadn't even checked the guest rooms yet. Jane and Bill had assured her they would leave it ready to run, but she'd wanted to check them for herself before she welcomed anyone.

Striding down the hall towards the front door, Kim patted her hair down. She'd only quickly pulled it up into a bun before cooking breakfast and she hadn't even run a brush through it. Some first impression she would make on her first guests.

Smiling widely, she pulled open the front door. 'Good morning, I am the new owner here at Berry Grove and I wish to welcome you into our home. If you'd like to come through, I'll check you in at the desk.'

'Nice to meet you, boss. I'm Dave, one of the builders here to work on the extension.' He took Kim's hand, his handshake strong and his skin rough. 'Jane and Bill had said you were coming, so I thought I'd best come and introduce myself instead of going straight round the back to the extension as usual.'

'Of course, sorry.' Feeling a blush creep up her neck, she pulled on her neckline. Now she was looking properly and not panicking she took in the jeans and scruffy T-shirt and the bright orange hi-vis vest. 'Nice to meet you too. I'm Kim. Come through and I'll pop the kettle on for you.'

'No need, I always come prepared.' Dave held up a large thermos flask.

'Right, okay. Are you the only builder on site today?'

'No, Barry and John will be joining me in a bit, and then we have the Big Boss coming in to check on the progress in a couple of hours.' Picking up his rucksack, he squeezed past her. 'Like your top, by the way.'

Looking down, Kim laughed. She'd forgotten she was still in her pyjamas.

* * *

'I think we'd better go and get dressed, there's more of them coming in a bit.' Back in the kitchen, Kim placed the finished plates into the dishwasher. 'We'll then pop out and explore the town. We need to pick up some more sausages and eggs anyway and Jane left me a list of their suppliers. All local and down the High Street, I believe.'

'Okay. Maybe we can accidentally pop into that little bakery too on the way back?'

'Good idea.'

* * *

Pushing open the front door, Kim turned to Mia. 'Why don't you take these up to the flat and find a film for us to watch with those cakes while I pop this lot in the fridge down here?'

'Okay, what type of film do you fancy? Comedy or romance or something more action-packed?'

'You choose.' Watching Mia run up the stairs, the small white cardboard box of cakes in her hand, Kim smiled. She was already a different child. Or maybe she wasn't, she had spent so little time with her over the past years, she was well aware that she didn't really know her own daughter that well. But that was all changing now, and Mia looked a whole lot happier and more relaxed than she had been at their old home.

* * *

Squeezing the sausages into the already full fridge, Kim paused and listened as a loud bang filtered through the heavy curtain dividing the kitchen and the extension. She should probably go and offer them all a drink. Dave might have brought his own, but that didn't mean the other builders had.

Sweeping the curtain aside, she noticed that the other two builders, Barry and John, had arrived. There was also another man who was kneeling down sweeping his left hand across the floor and gripping a clipboard with the other. Presumably, he was the Big Boss Dave had been referring to.

Taking a step inside, Kim cleared her throat. 'Hi, can I get anyone a drink or a biscuit or anything?'

'Wow, I'd recognise that voice anywhere.' Slowly standing up, the Big Boss twisted around, tugging on his white shirt collar as he did so. 'Kim? It is you, isn't it, Kim?'

Standing still, she watched as the man walked towards her. Was it him? It didn't make any sense. Why would he even be here? They were hundreds of miles from where they'd grown up.

'Kim? I'm sorry, you probably don't even remember me.'

'I remember you, Danny.' Allowing herself to be pulled in for an awkward hug, she kept her arms loose by her sides as he embraced her.

'You look as gorgeous as ever.' Stepping back, he surveyed her. She noted he had kept his dimple, its cheekiness etched onto the right side of his face. 'Don't tell me you're the new owner of Berry Grove?'

Nodding, she kept her eyes fixed on his dimple.

'Congratulations then. I'm sure you and your husband will be very happy here. It's a lovely place and this extension is going to be an amazing addition when these chaps have finished.'

'Me.'

'Sorry?' Danny furrowed his eyebrows and took a step forward, trying to hear her.

Clasping her hands in front of her, she cleared her throat again. 'Me. I bought Berry Grove on my own.'

'Right, sorry, I didn't mean to be so presumptuous. Congratulations to you then.' Smiling, his dimple reappeared. 'I can't believe that after all this time we run into each other here, of all places. What a coincidence.'

'It definitely is.' Tearing her eyes away, she looked across at Barry and John who had stopped working, presumably to watch the show unfolding in front of them. 'Can I get you a drink?'

'That'd be grand, thanks. I'll have a coffee, no milk and two sugars please, and Barry here will have a classic builder's cuppa please?'

'Coming right up.' Turning on her heels, she battled with the curtain before falling into the solace of the kitchen. Slumping at one of the dining chairs, she put her elbows on the wooden surface and held her head in her hands. Danny, here? It wasn't possible. He couldn't be here. They were never supposed to see each other again.

'Hey, Kim. You okay?' Coming through to the kitchen, Danny placed his clipboard on the work surface and walked towards her.

'I'm fine. I just didn't expect to see you here.' Scraping the chair back, she stood up and stepped away from him.

'I know, it's weird, isn't it?' Laughing, he ran his hand through his thick black hair, pushing it to the side of his forehead.

'It certainly is.' He wore his hair in the same style as he had back then. The in-name had been 'curtains' all those years ago, although the hair stylists had probably renamed it with some modern term nowadays. 'How? Why are you here? The last I heard, you'd moved to Dubai.'

'Dubai? Wow, that was a lifetime ago. Yes, I landed a job out there after I'd finished travelling, but I only stayed a few years. I moved back to the UK, oh, um, at least eight years ago.'

'Eight years? Why didn't you look me up?'

Running his hand through his hair again, he leant back against the kitchen counter. 'Look you up?'

'I'm sorry. Why would you? Just ignore me. It's the shock of seeing you here.'

'No, you're right to ask. To be honest, I tried. Of course, you'd moved and your parents wouldn't tell me where you were.' He looked up at her, his dark green eyes holding her in his gaze. 'I don't blame them. They never had liked the idea of me swanning off and travelling instead of getting serious and going to uni.'

'So you did try then?'

'Yes, I did. And then I heard that Miriam had passed away and I guess I was a coward. I suddenly didn't want to find you and have to accept that she wasn't with us any more. We were only young, for goodness' sake. Plus, when your parents were so cagey about you moving away, I realised that you'd met someone else and started a new life. I had no right to interfere with that.' He held up his hands. 'That came out wrong, not that for one moment I'd have expected you to carry on from where we had been when I left.'

'That hadn't been the reason I moved away. I hadn't met anyone else.' She shook her head and gripped the counter behind her. He hadn't needed to know that. Why had she said it? 'It would have been nice, helpful, to have been able to speak to someone who had known Miriam as well as I had.'

'I'm sorry. What can I say? I was young and thought I was invincible. I didn't want to face up to the fact that someone my age had gotten ill and died.'

'She hadn't been ill.' Focusing on one of the garish orange flowers decorating the wallpaper on the opposite side of the room, she swallowed. 'There was a car accident. She died in my arms.'

'What?' Dropping onto a chair, he shook his head. 'I had no idea. I'm so sorry. If I'd known, if someone had told me, I would have come straight back. I would have cut my trip short. I would have been there for you. Were you hurt?'

Kim shook her head. 'Not physically.'

'I'm so sorry. Kim, that's awful.'

'You weren't to know.'

'I didn't. I didn't even know she had passed away until I got back to England. My parents must have known that I'd have come straight back if they'd me told me.' He furrowed his brow, his eyes darkening with concern. 'Why didn't you tell me? You knew I always wrote to you when I got to a place I was going to stay at for a while. You would have had my address.'

'I did. I wrote to you shortly after it had happened and told you to ring me, that I had something to tell you.' Clasping her hands in front of her, she looked down. 'You never did ring me.'

Looking down at his hands, he held them palms facing upwards on the table. 'I never got that letter. I wrote to you throughout my travelling though and never got any replies after the first two.'

'I moved out from my parents a month or so after it happened. I didn't have much contact after that so they wouldn't have forwarded anything.' Reaching across, she clicked the kettle on.

'You moved out? Why? What changed? I thought you always got on okay with them? I know they could be quite pushy, but they'd only wanted the best for you.'

'Yes, well, it doesn't matter. Did you want a drink?'

'Umm, yes, please?'

'Coffee, milk and one sugar still?'

'Yep, that hasn't changed.'

'Mum, are you coming up yet? I made you a coffee, but it'll be cold now.'

Twisting around, Kim watched as Mia strode into the kitchen before glancing at Danny and then back at Mia. 'Mia, I'll be up in a moment. Please go back up.'

'Oh, okay.' Pausing in the doorway, Mia's smile dropped for the first time since arriving at Berry Grove.

'Sorry, I didn't mean to snap. I was just...' Squeezing out a teabag, she mouthed 'sorry' again.

'Hi, Mia, I'm Danny, an old friend of your mums. We were just catching up on a few things. I'm afraid I've upset her by talking about an old friend of ours.' Standing up, Danny leant across the table and shook Mia's hand.

'Okay.' Mia smiled again. 'I'll see you up in a bit then, Mum.'

'Yes, sorry again, sweetheart.'

'No worries.' Grinning, she turned and walked away.

'Mia? You named her after Miriam?'

Kim nodded. Mia shouldn't have come down. They shouldn't have met. Not like this.

'A lovely girl you have there.'

'Here's your coffee. Shouldn't you be getting on with your work now?'

'Yes, of course. You don't pay me to sit around and talk, do you?' Standing up, he took the tray of mugs Kim held out to him and retreated back behind the curtain.

Dipping her head to the sink, she ran the water until it was freezing cold and splashed her face. Danny shouldn't be here. Mia shouldn't have come down. What had she been thinking talking to him like that, knowing that Mia was only just upstairs? That she could have come down at any moment? She was messing up again. They'd only just moved and already she had managed to mess everything up. Although this time, she knew it wouldn't be as easy to just up and leave and run from their problems.

8

Kim skimmed the computer screen on the front desk. 'We have a Mr and Mrs Towbridge coming to stay in Room 5 and a Mr Garret who is booked in to stay in Room 7. Why do you think Jane and Bill just didn't just fill up the rooms from Room 1 and up? It seems strange. They've just chosen random rooms.'

'I don't know. It does seem weird. Unless the people coming have been before and have asked for those rooms?' Mia leaned across the desk and tilted her head, trying to read what was on the screen. 'Danny seemed nice. Did he used to be your boyfriend?'

'What?' Jerking her head up, Kim looked at Mia. She'd promised herself she would never lie to her about her father, but she couldn't very well just blurt it out, could she?

She tapped a pen against the desk, the deep, dull thuds ringing through the silence of the hallway. Danny more than likely had a wife, had children. It wouldn't just be Danny's life she would turn upside down, it would have a knock-on effect with all his family too. And, of course, there was Mia, she was dealing with the aftershocks of being bullied and settling into a completely new way of life. She had so many obstacles to overcome before she could be truly settled here. She would have to face the reality of going back into the school system soon and that would be absolutely terrifying for her after what she'd been through at the hands of that Amelia. No, now was not a good time. At all.

'Mum? What's up?'

'Nothing. Sorry. I'm just feeling a bit nervous about welcoming our first guests, that's all.'

'Is that them?' A car pulled into the car park and Mia ran to the window. 'I think the car has gone into our car park. I think it's them!'

'Well, they're certainly punctual, aren't they?' Although check-in was from two o'clock, Jane had warned them that people would arrive from anything between two until ten at night. 'At least it will get our first ever check-in out of the way.'

'Yes, oh, look, they're coming.' Pressing her face against the glass, Mia turned to Kim and then back to the window. 'They're literally walking up the path now.'

'Come away from the window then. We don't want them thinking we're nosy. We need to pretend to be professional.' Shaking her arms and circling her shoulders, Kim tried to relax. 'Come behind the desk and give me some moral support.'

'You'll be fine, Mum. You're used to working with people and getting people to do what you want, like in all those meetings with all those big bosses and that. You can win over a couple of normal people.'

'You don't want me to act like I do, used to, at work, believe me.' Kim laughed.

'Here they are.' With her elbows resting on the desk, Mia smiled as a young couple came through the door and whispered, 'Should we have held it open for them?'

'I have no idea.' Turning to the couple as they approached the desk, Kim smiled. 'Good afternoon, you must be Mr and Mrs Towbridge?'

'Hi, yes we are. Are you the new owner? Jane mentioned that they were selling last time we came.' The blonde woman frowned slightly, shallow creases forming above her nose.

'Yes, we moved in yesterday actually. I'm Kim and this is my daughter, Mia.'

'You're our first ever guests!' Standing up straight, Mia grinned at them.

'In that case, it's our pleasure to be your first guests.' Mrs Towbridge smiled as the creases were replaced with impossibly smooth, flawless skin.

'Thank you. You're going to be staying in Room 5, if that's okay with you?'

'That'll be lovely, thank you. We came here three years ago on our honeymoon and ever since we've made it a tradition to return each year and Jane and Bill always promised us we could have the same room.'

'Happy anniversary then.' Smiling, Kim glanced at the computer screen. There was no note to say they were staying for a special occasion. If there had been she could have put a bottle of bubbly or organised to leave a fruit basket on the bed or something. Maybe Jane and Bill hadn't been planning to move when they had booked them in. They were staying for three nights so she'd organise something for tomorrow. It wouldn't be quite as special, but she didn't really have much choice, did she?

'Can I show them to their room and do the little tour thing you see on TV? Please, Mum?'

Frowning, Kim wanted to say yes, but it would hardly look professional, a teenage girl showing them around.

'That would be wonderful.' Mr Towbridge indicated for Mia to lead the way.

With Mia showing their guests to their room, Kim lowered her forehead onto the cool wood of the desk. Who knew running a Bed and Breakfast would be this difficult? She was so used to having to act professional in her previous role, but Mr and Mrs Towbridge had seemed to appreciate Mia's friendliness and eagerness more than Kim's stilted welcome. Maybe that was how she was supposed to act. Maybe people chose to stay at a Bed and Breakfast instead of one of those commercial inns because they liked being treated like old friends instead of customers. She shook her head, she couldn't even remember the last time she had stayed away from home. It had probably been the one occasion that she had taken Mia to the seaside down in Plymouth, but then they had stayed at one of those popular caravan parks. She literally had no experience of this life at all.

Hearing footsteps on the tiles, Kim lifted her head and smiled at Mia. 'How did it go?'

'Great, like really great. I showed them their room, but when I was telling them that there was a kettle to make a cup of tea and that, I realised I'd forgotten to show them the sitting room and the kitchen and the garden, but they said that they remembered it from last year anyway.'

'That's okay then. I'm sure you did a better job than I could have.' Holding out her arms, she waited until Mia had slipped back behind the counter and hugged her tightly, kissing the top of her head. 'Love you, Mia.'

'Love you too, Mum.' Pulling away, she looked at the computer screen. 'What do we do now? Just wait around for Mr Garret to turn up?'

'No, it's almost a quarter to three now so we'll just get on with our usual stuff. We'll hear when he comes anyway.'

'But shouldn't we wait for him?'

'No, it's fine. It could be he's coming after a work meeting or something, so he could be hours.' Shutting the key cupboard, Kim walked around the side of the desk.

'I guess so. I've just thought you won't be able to pick me up after school because guests might turn up while you're driving. Will that mean I'll have to get the school bus straight away?' Mia's eyes glistened and she looked down at the floor.

'I hadn't thought of that. It'll be fine though, I'll just make it clear when people book up a room that they won't be able to check-in between half two and half three. It'll be fine.' Hooking her index finger underneath Mia's chin, Kim lifted it gently until she looked at her. 'I've told you that you're my priority now, and I mean it, okay?'

'Okay.'

'Why don't we go and make some cookies or something that we can leave out for the guests?'

'Yes, okay. Are we going to make them up in the flat or down here? It's strange thinking we have two kitchens now, isn't it? Can we make them down here being as they're for the guests and the kitchen is bigger?'

'Yes, I guess it makes more sense.' As long as Danny didn't walk in, not that he should, he was here to do a job not to socialise. Anyway, hopefully he had left already; he had only been there to check up on things.

* * *

Mia set up the dining table with everything they needed while Kim made them both a hot chocolate.

'All set?'

'Yep. I can't find the sieve though.'

'I can't remember seeing it when we were packing either actually. Never mind, we'll just make do today and buy a new one another time. What type are we making?'

'Chocolate chip?'

'Yum, I was hoping you'd say that.' Turning on the small kitchen radio, Kim settled on a channel pumping out pop songs and joined Mia at the table.

'Hellooooo...'

'Danny? What are you doing in here?' She knew who it was even before she'd turned around; she'd remember his voice for as long as she lived. Wiping the flour from her hands down her jeans, she glanced at Mia who had stopped measuring out the sugar and was stood smiling at him.

'Sorry. I know when I'm getting in the way.' Holding his hands up in surrender, he backed away, grinning.

Biting down on her bottom lip, she momentarily closed her eyes. Why was he still here? 'Mia, I'm just going to go and see what he wants and I'll be back in a minute, okay? It's best you stay in here, the extension is still a building site.'

'Okay.'

Ducking through the curtain, Kim stood for a few minutes and watched as Danny scrutinised his clipboard, the muscles in his cheeks pulsing as he tried to work something out. She smiled; she'd properly fallen for him because of that look. During a French test, she had looked across at him and he'd been pulling that face, his head dipped, a pen behind his ear and his cheeks pulsing.

She cleared her throat, waiting as he turned around and grinned. 'Has everyone else clocked off for the day?'

'They sure have.'

'Sorry if I sounded rude back then. It still seems so surreal that you're here and that we've both ended up in the same place.'

'No worries. I shouldn't have startled you like that.' Placing his pen behind his ear, he strode towards her. 'Are you laughing at me?'

'Yes, I am. Sorry, it's just you used to do the same thing with your pen when we were younger.'

'You mean when you were madly in love with me?'

'Oi.' Patting him on the arm, she grinned. 'Something like that.'

'No need to be shy. I was madly in love with you too.' Crossing his arms across his chest, he stared at her. 'There was a time when I truly thought we'd spend the rest of our lives together.'

'Aw, but then you swanned off travelling. The promise of freedom and adventure enticing you away.'

'I was being serious. I used to dream about coming home early to find you waiting for me.'

'Really?' Scrunching her nose, she tilted her head and studied his face; he looked as though he was being sincere. She shook her head, he'd probably just learnt to lie like most other men.

'Yes, really.'

'Well, it was obviously a fleeting thought being as you ended up living in Dubai.'

'Yes, well, that hadn't quite been my first choice.' Dipping his head, he looked down at his clipboard, his dark hair falling in his eyes. 'When I couldn't get in contact with you I had to face the fact that you had moved on.'

Spluttering, she held her hand in front of her mouth. If only he had known the truth. 'It wasn't quite as clear cut as that.'

Shrugging, he looked back up at her. 'It was all a long time ago now. It obviously hadn't been the right path for us anyway.'

'Exactly. Everything happens for a reason and all that.' Grimacing, she wished she hadn't uttered those words. She didn't believe that sentiment for a second. Awful things didn't happen for a reason, Miriam hadn't died for a reason. Crossing her arms, she narrowed her eyes.

'Maybe.' Looking at her, his green eyes seemed to search her face for clues. 'Anyway, have you got a lucky boyfriend locked away somewhere?'

'Nope, it's me and Mia. She's all the family I need.'

'Fair enough. I'm assuming there once was a husband though?'

'And why would you assume that? Because I'm a lady of a certain age I must have fallen into the marriage trap at some point in my life?'

'No. Because you have Mia.' He smiled playfully.

'Right. No, I have never been married.' Fixing her eyes on a patch of drying plaster behind him, she continued. 'I used to work in the City. I didn't have time for anyone else in my life.'

'You weren't waiting for me then?' Smirking, he prodded her with the clipboard.

'No. Good job really or I'd still have been living at my parents pining for you.' Taking the clipboard from his hands, she looked down at it. 'What's this then?'

'Oh, just boring stuff about measurements and resources we need to order and that.'

'Nice. There's a lot more to do then?'

'Yep, I'm afraid so. We need to order the floor tiles by the end of next week if we're going to stick to schedule, so I'll bring over a couple of catalogues I have and some samples for you to choose from.'

'Brilliant, thanks. So how about you then?'

'Me? It's your choice really, isn't it?'

'Haha, very funny.' She passed him the clipboard. 'You've interrogated me on my past relationships. Now it's your turn to tell all.'

'I wouldn't say it was an interrogation, and to be fair you've been pretty sketchy about the whole subject.'

'Yes, well, it's a woman's prerogative as they say. So, go on then.'

'Your demanding ways haven't changed I see.' Hugging his clipboard to his chest, he nodded. 'Okay, here goes. I was married, yes. I met Penny out in Dubai when I'd given up on the hope of seeing you again, and things were good for a few years. Then, well, things got a bit more complicated and we decided to go our separate ways.'

'Is that why you stayed in Dubai?' She could feel her cheeks flushing with heat. That's why he hadn't come home then because he had met the love of his life.

'Yes, it is.' Clearing his throat, he looked at her. 'Don't look at me like that. If I had been able to keep in contact with you, you know that I would have come back. But you'd moved on and, so, I did too.'

'Hey, I'm not looking at you in "that" way or any other way.'

'All right, I'm only joking!'

'Sorry, it's been a bit of a strange day today. We booked in our first guests and to be honest it feels a bit weird to know there are strangers under our roof. We never even had people pop round to ours back home.'

'What? You didn't have your parents round or any of Mia's friends or anyone?' Frowning, Danny tilted his head, looking at her.

'I was always at work. Or if I wasn't, I was working from home which was why we decided to move here. We needed to get away from our old life. And, as I said before, I don't really have anything to do with my parents any more.'

'Why is that?'

'We ended up disagreeing on a few matters.' She couldn't really tell him that her parents had wanted her to get an abortion when she had found out she was pregnant with his child, and when she had refused, they had even got an advocate from the local adoption centre to visit her. They had been adamant that having Mia would be the end of her career goals. Well, she'd shown them. She'd more than proved herself, but at what cost? Shaking her head, she pushed all thoughts of her parents to the back of her mind again. 'I best get back to Mia anyway.'

'Yes, of course.' Stepping forward, Danny placed his hand on her forearm. 'I'm glad we've found each other after all these years.'

Smiling, she turned and walked away, leaving him standing in the middle of the extension, hugging his clipboard to his chest again.

9

Wiping the work surfaces in the communal kitchen, Kim hummed along to the quiet tunes on the radio. Mr Garret had arrived at a quarter to eight, a tall quiet man who had been polite but a little guarded when she had shown him to his room. Since Mia had gone to bed to read at about nine, Kim had been cleaning the kitchen and laying the tables ready for breakfast in the morning. It was a good job that she wasn't used to having a lie-in, guests could come down for breakfast anytime between seven and half-past eight which seemed a long time to be standing around in the kitchen waiting.

Opening the fridge, she double-checked there were enough sausages, eggs and bacon before switching the kettle on. Maybe a hot chocolate would calm her nerves and stop her thinking so much.

Waiting for the kettle to boil, she looked around the room. It still felt completely surreal that she'd gone from living in an immaculate house and working in the City to running Berry Grove. It was a beautiful place but, if she was honest, it was a little rough around the edges and the more she looked, the more she noticed little jobs that needed doing. One day, she'd get round to them. It really needed a complete makeover and modernisation, but maybe the tired look was part of the charm. It had worked for Jane and Bill, their profits had been good enough.

Slumping down in a chair, she rested her forehead on her hands. It would take some time to get used to it all. The pace was a lot calmer and slower than her career at Pinnel's. There was no fierce race to try to win a promotion to partner; she was her own boss now.

Looking down at her nails, she noticed how chipped they were, the fierce red manicure of her past life quickly wearing off. Soon they'd be naked, and there'd be no reason for her to have them redone. She fingered the small pendant that Mia had bought her for Christmas years ago and traced around the silver heart encasing the word 'Mum'. That's what all this was about; it was natural that it would take them both time to adjust, but when they did, they wouldn't look back. Hopefully.

Glancing across at the kettle, she stood ready to get her hot chocolate. The song on the radio faded into the next one and Kim sat back in her chair. She recognised it from just the first few beats, the unmistakable highs and lows, the lull before the song truly began. This had been their song, her and Danny's, when they had been dating. She listened to the rise and fall of the lyrics which had filled both of them with hope for their future.

The first time they had heard the song had been in a small café back home. He had pulled her to her feet in the middle of the café and they had danced, not caring for the onlookers, the young families whose children had clapped when they had finished or the elderly couple who had tutted all the way through. At the time, they had been oblivious to it all, locked away in their small world, just the two of them. When the song had ended, they had slipped back into their seats and continued eating their lunch and

Danny had promised her he would love her forever. Of course, she had believed him. He had probably believed himself too.

Closing her eyes, she tried to clear her mind of the memory. Instead, she tried to picture how she'd like to redecorate the kitchen, but the image of Danny standing there in his suit, clip-board in hand, the familiar grin on his face, kept flooding back into her mind's eye. Opening her eyes again, she pushed the chair back and switched the kettle back on. She was just nervous about cooking the breakfasts tomorrow.

Tapping the spoon against the edge of the work surface, she hummed along to the radio again, trying to push away any thoughts of having to tell Danny and Mia the truth. She knew she had to tell him though, and she would. Next time she saw him, she'd make herself. He deserved to know and so did Mia.

The shrill tone of the doorbell seared through the kitchen, drowning out the quiet tick of the kettle clicking off. Who on earth could that be at this time of the night? There wasn't anyone else booked in for today and she'd taken the 'Vacancies Available' sign down at eight o'clock as Jane and Bill had instructed her. Unless, of course, people just turned up on the off chance, which she supposed they might.

Keeping her foot jammed behind the front door, she inched it open. 'Danny?'

'Hi, sorry, I left something here earlier and was driving past so thought I'd pop by on the off chance you were still awake.' Grinning, he shifted on his feet, the light from the moon above him illuminating his chiselled jawline.

'Right, yes, of course.' This didn't count as the next time she saw him, did it? Surely it was still on the same day so didn't count? Opening the door, she let him slip through before following him to the kitchen.

'I'll just pop and get it then.'

'Okay.' She indicated towards the extension and slipped back into her seat. The hot chocolate would have to wait. Should she tell him? Now? There was nothing stopping her. Apart from the million questions and accusations that whirred around her head. How come he hadn't kept his promise? Why hadn't he come back for her? She knew he'd said he didn't know where she'd moved to, but he could have found her, if he'd wanted to. Had it been an easy decision for him to marry his ex? After blowing Kim a kiss from the terminal, had he ever thought of her again?

'You okay?'

Twisting around in her chair, she looked at him. Was he ready to become a father? 'Yes, I'm fine. Just tired that's all.'

'You're not fine. You look like you're worrying about something. You've got that look.'

'Oh, so now you remember *my* looks?'

'I do indeed. You used to get that same glazed look in your eyes before your exams.'

'Did I?' Kim rubbed her eyes with the pads of her thumbs. Were they both so similar to the teenagers they had been when they had last seen each other? It felt like a lifetime had passed. 'I wish it was that simple.'

'Your exams used to be your world back then.'

'I know. Still, it would be a lot easier if exams were the only things I had to worry about now.'

'Hey, I'll make us a hot choccie and you can tell me all about it.'

Nodding, she dipped her head and followed the natural grooves in the wooden table with her finger. She could do this. She could. She could do this for Mia.

'Here you go.' Smiling, Danny placed a mug on the table and sat down opposite her.

'Thank you.' Looking up, she smiled and wrapped her hands

around the hot mug, leaning over she breathed in the sweet aroma of cinnamon mixed with whipped cream. 'You remembered.'

'Of course, I remembered.' Taking a sip, he grinned at her, a smidge of cream smeared on his nose.

'You've got some... Here, come here.' Leaning forward, she wiped the cream from his nose.

'Thank you.' Reaching across, he took her hand. 'Now, what's worrying you?'

'There's something I need to talk to you about.'

'Okay, well, you can tell me anything. You don't need to worry about talking to me. Is there something wrong with the extension? If there is, I'm sure it can be easily fixed.'

'It's nothing to do with the extension.' Pulling her hand away, she rubbed it across her forehead. She was used to having difficult conversations; she was used to discussing problems and still winning her clients over. And they were millionaires, people with power. She knew Danny. He was right. She should be able to tell him anything. 'It's to do with something that happened when we were teenagers.'

'You're still angry with me.' Clasping his hands on the table in front of him, he shifted his gaze from Kim to his hands and back again.

'No, well, yes if I'm honest I am, but not why you think.'

'It's okay. I know.'

'You know?' She narrowed her eyes. 'How do you know? Why didn't you say anything before?'

'Because I assumed you knew that I was sorry.'

'Well, no, I didn't know you were sorry, but thanks for that.' He hadn't known, he didn't really have anything to feel sorry about, not really.

'I am. I knew something was wrong when my sister began avoiding all my questions about my friends back home, but I didn't do anything. I hadn't heard from you and assumed you had moved on, given up on waiting for me. I didn't blame you. It had been my decision to go travelling, and you had loved me, you had put your feelings aside and encouraged me because you knew that's what I wanted to do.'

Nodding, she took another sip of her hot chocolate.

'I should have pushed her for answers, for what was happening back home with you, with Miriam, with all my mates. But I promise you, at no point did it ever, ever occur to me that something as awful as Miriam passing away would have happened.' He clasped her hands in his. 'If I had known, I promise I would have been on the first plane home. I would have. I would not have let you deal with all that on your own whether you had moved on from me or not.'

'That's why you think I'm angry at you?'

'I don't blame you. You have every right to be angry at me.'

'That's not the reason I was angry.' Looking into his eyes, she took a deep breath. Out of the corner of her eye, she noticed a movement by the kitchen door. Pulling her hands away, she smiled broadly. 'Mr Garret, how may I help you?'

'I don't mean to disturb you, but I was just wondering if you had any local leaflets I could peruse. I'm hoping to make the most of my few days left in this part of the country and so would like to visit some local attractions.'

'Of course. Yes, there are some in the hallway. I'll show you where.' Pushing her chair back, she stood up, grateful for the distraction.

'I've had a look at those. They seem to be geared more towards families.'

'Oh, okay. Sorry.'

'Here sit down, mate. I've lived around here for five years now, I'm sure I can recommend some places. What kind of thing are you interested in?' Patting the chair beside him, Danny shook Mr Garret's hand.

'I'm interested in wildlife and history mainly.'

'This is the perfect location for you then. You must have seen the amazing castle at the top of the High Street?'

'Yes, I took a tour there this afternoon.'

'Brilliant. Well, if you turn left at the bottom of the High Street and follow the path around you will come to the nature reserve owned by the castle which is not only full of the Queen's swans but also has the only breeding population of the Blue Duck outside of its native New Zealand.'

Mr Garret nodded. 'That would be worth a visit.'

'It certainly is. There's a lovely walk running alongside the castle grounds around the lake and through the meadow too. And if that interests you, you may like to visit the wetlands in Chapel Hornton which are run by the World's Wetlands Trust and protects lots of endangered bird species. It's beautiful there and is normally quite quiet too as it's off of the normal tourist track.'

'Chapel Hornton, you say?'

'That's right. Here, I'll draw you a map.' Pulling a pen from behind his ear, he picked up one of the serviettes from the middle of the table and began drawing a simple map, talking Mr Garret through every turn and roundabout as he did so.

'We also have a Roman Villa five miles down the road, and a little further afield a sculpture foundation which is quite stunning.' Biting the tip of his tongue, he scribbled down a list of other local attractions. 'Here, I've written a list. I'd definitely recommend this one and this one if you're looking for some hidden gems.'

'Thank you. I appreciate this. It's the local knowledge of the owners which distinguishes a Bed and Breakfast.' Standing up, he picked up the serviette, folding it twice and carefully slipping it into his shirt pocket. 'I shall let you know which I choose to visit.'

'I look forward to hearing about your choices.' Nodding, Danny waited until Mr Garret had gone back upstairs and winked at her. 'It looks as though I'm going into partnership with you then.'

'Umm, nice try. Seriously though, thank you. I wouldn't have had a clue where to recommend. We've literally only visited this part of the country once and that was when we came to view this place apart from coming camping as a kid, but that was somewhere miles away.'

'Wow, that sounds very spontaneous.'

'Yes, well, we both needed a fresh start, and this place seemed perfect.'

'I'm sure it will be. And for one, I'm glad you chose to move here.'

Kim shook her head. 'I still can't believe that I've managed to move into a place which you're working on. I mean, what are the odds?'

'Probably a few million to one.' Laughing, Danny stood up. 'I'd better let you get to bed. You look shattered.'

'Thanks. I feel it too, although I think some of it is due to stressing over making breakfasts for the guests tomorrow. I'm not exactly the most natural of cooks.'

'I'm sure it will be fine. They'll no doubt just want a cooked breakfast and I'm sure you've made a fair few of them over your time.'

'Umm.' He really had no idea how their life had been. She'd always been too busy worrying about work or slaving over some document or other to either have the time or the inclination to cook very much, not properly cook. That was another thing she was worried about, what if he resented her for not only not telling him he was a father, but for the rubbish job she had done in bringing his daughter up? Yes, she was trying to make up for it now, but she'd been blind to what she was doing to Mia for so many years, what if now wasn't good enough?

'Are you sure you're okay?'

'I'm fine. I was just thinking how much mine and Mia's lives are changing.' And will only change more when you find out the truth.

'Change can be a good thing though, remember?'

'I know. And it is. This change is good, really good, but it's still a bit scary.' Pushing her chair, back she followed him to the front door. 'Thank you for helping Mr Garret.'

'My pleasure.' Pulling the door open, he looked back at her and paused.

'Did you get it?'

'Get what?' Danny frowned.

'What you came back for from the extension? You've not left it again, have you?'

Looking down at his feet, he cleared his throat before looking back up. 'I kind of made that up. I didn't forget anything, I just wanted to come back and see you.'

'Oh, right.'

'Do you forgive me?'

'Forgive you?' There would probably always be a part of her that wouldn't be able to forgive him for letting her down, whether he had known what was at stake or not.

'Yes, for lying and saying I'd forgotten something.'

She shook her head, of course. 'I suppose I could try.'

'I'd like that.' Placing his index finger underneath her chin, he gently lifted it until they were looking into each other's eyes. His lips gently hovered next to hers, barely a millimetre away. 'May I?'

With the slightest nod, Kim closed her eyes and tilted her face until their lips met. They were as soft and warm as she remembered. Running her hand through his hair, she pulled him closer. He felt like home.

'Right, I'd better be off.' Mumbling against her lips, he pulled away, his hand slipping down to hold on to hers. Turning away, his fingers gripped hers until neither of them could reach any further.

Shutting the door behind her, she lifted the palms of her hands to her cheeks. She could feel the heat radiating from her skin. How was it even possible for a little kiss from him to have stirred so many buried emotions? She could still feel his lips upon hers, could still feel the energy and passion between them. It was as though nothing had changed, all those years apart living their separate lives had just melted away in that one moment.

What had even happened between them? Had it just been a venture into the past? A flitter of reminiscing? Or was it something more serious? Did he want to pick up from where they had left off? Or had he just been teasing her? Had it meant absolutely nothing to him?

And should she tell him about Mia? She could tomorrow. At least then it would be out in the open and he wouldn't be able to accuse her of withholding that from him. Or should she wait and see what the kiss had meant first? After all, if he did what to rebuild their relationship, then her telling him about Mia may ruin all possibilities before anything had even begun. Even worse, he might build a relationship with her, stay with her, out of duty and regret for not returning after travelling.

No, she couldn't tell him now. She would. Of course she would. Just not in this instant. She'd give them a few days to figure out what was going on between them before telling him. At least that way she'd know for sure if he wanted a future with her or not.

Switching off the downstairs lights, she climbed the stairs, her mind whirring with the impossible decision she had just made.

10

Rolling over, she hit the alarm clock for the third time. Its neon green lights flashed back at her, mocking her: 6:15am. She had to get up. She had breakfasts to do. Yawning, Kim threw back her duvet and forced herself out of bed. Lifting her fingers to her lips, she could still feel Danny's kiss, could still feel the warmth and gentleness of his touch.

* * *

Plaiting her damp hair, she threw her towel into the laundry bin and looked in on Mia before heading downstairs.

She switched the oven on and filled the kettle. Looking at the breakfast ordering sheets, she read through them again. Mr Garret wanted a Full English Breakfast, but with a poached egg instead of the traditional fried, and he would be down at seven. He was obviously planning to make the most of his time away and had no doubt devised a full day's itinerary to keep himself busy. Mr and Mrs Towbridge, on the other hand, had chosen to eat at the latest time possible and had ticked that they would be down for half past eight.

Stirring the boiling water into her mug, she breathed in the strong aroma of bitter coffee. Taking a deep breath in, Kim closed her eyes. She shouldn't even be tired. If they hadn't moved here, she'd be grabbing a cereal bar before heading to work.

The trill of the doorbell pierced the silence, and she forced her eyes open. Taking a gulp of coffee, she swilled it around her mouth hoping the caffeine would kick in. Who on earth could it beat this time? Maybe Jane and Bill had their milk delivered and had forgotten to cancel.

'Morning.' Swinging the front door open, she took a step back, her cheeks warming. 'Danny?'

'Morning. I thought I'd swing by and give you a hand with the breakfasts.' Grinning, he walked past her, taking his coat off on the way to the kitchen.

'You didn't have to do that. I can cope, you know. It's only a case of cooking three breakfasts.'

'Four now.' Switching the kettle on, he helped himself to a mug, spooning coffee and sugar in. 'I don't think there's a red-blooded male who can resist the smell of a cooked breakfast.'

'Seriously though, everything's under control. It's only Mr Garret who is coming down for seven, the other two don't want theirs until half eight anyway. Plus, I've got the sausages in already and the oil's heating up for the bacon.'

'I can see. Well, I'll be your moral supporter sitting on the side-lines drinking coffee.'

'Okay, thank you.'

'You are more than welcome. What are your plans for today?'

'Umm, after cleaning the rooms, I thought I might take Mia to the beach and maybe drive by the local schools to check them out before we go and visit them on Monday.' She wouldn't mention that to Mia, they'd enjoy a nice day out and then just happen to pass them on a scenic route home. She knew how Mia was feeling about visiting them next week so familiarising her with the idea could only help.

'Sounds fun.'

'Hopefully. How about you?'

'I need to travel to Plymouth to check a job out this afternoon, but apart from that, I thought I'd mill around here, help Dave and the crew out a bit. Oh, I've got those samples for the floor tiles in the van, I'll grab them in a bit. The quicker you choose those, the quicker we can make a start laying them.'

'Okay cool.' Flipping the bacon, she tilted her head. 'That sounds like Mr Garret coming down the stairs now.'

'Right, let's get this show on the road then! I'll do the drinks, you serve the breakfast.'

* * *

Twenty minutes later, Kim was loading the dishwasher while Danny continued discussing the local nature reserves with Mr Garret before seeing him out.

'Well, I think that went quite well. He seemed to enjoy your cooking anyway.' Walking back into the kitchen, Danny switched the kettle on and leant against the work surface.

'I'm just glad I didn't burn anything. Fingers crossed he doesn't come down with food poisoning and we'll be fine.' Laughing, Kim slumped onto a chair. It had gone well, at least better than she had expected. She had been able to strike up enough conversation so that it hadn't felt awkward, although it had helped Danny being there.

'I'm sure he won't. And if he does, we can blame wherever he decides to eat his lunch.'

'Thanks!' Shifting in her seat, she straightened the coaster in front of her. She needed to know what last night's kiss had meant. It was fine if it had just been a spur-of-the-moment thing. Absolutely fine. But, still, it would be nice to know one way or the other. Taking a deep breath, she asked the question. 'Last night, when you kissed me, what did it mean? I'm guessing it didn't mean anything. And that's fine. Of course, it is. It was just a "can't believe we've met up again" thing, wasn't it?'

Placing a fresh coffee in front of her, Danny sat opposite. 'We can say that if you want to put a tag on it. I'm not sure. To be honest, it *was* in the heat of the moment and it was amazing to discover you've moved here, but it wasn't just that. I'm not that shallow.'

'What was it then?' Taking a sip of her coffee, she inhaled the strong earthy aroma and looked at him.

Clearing his throat, he wrapped his hands around his mug. 'I guess it just felt like the natural thing to do. Seeing you again brought so many feelings back up to the surface.'

'So it was just because we'd met each other again then?' Why had he said it wasn't? The kiss had obviously been to test to see if he held any feelings for her still and clearly he didn't.

'Yes, no. You make it sound so trivial and it didn't feel trivial, not for me anyway.'

'How did it feel for you then?' She watched as he ran his hand through his hair, revealing his eyes, intense and searching.

'Like I said, it felt natural, comfortable, normal. Believe it or not, I have actually thought about you a lot since we last saw each other.'

'You must have done, the number of times you got in touch.' Rolling her eyes, she took a sip of coffee. Maybe she shouldn't have said that. Maybe she'd been too harsh. 'Sorry, I shouldn't have said that. It was a long time ago, and we were different people back then, young and…'

'I did try to contact you. On numerous occasions. I continued to write to you even though I didn't get any replies. I told you this. Then after a while, I kept thinking something had happened, so I kept ringing your house only to be told that you'd met someone else and moved out when your dad eventually answered.' He shrugged, frown lines framing his eyes. 'Don't get me wrong, I don't blame you for moving on. I left to go travelling; I had no right to expect you to wait for me.'

'Sorry. I hadn't met anyone else, and they didn't tell me you had rung or pass on any letters.' How could her parents have kept this from her? They'd known Danny had been the father, why on earth wouldn't they want him to get in touch? To know he had a baby on the way? She looked down at her coffee. 'We didn't see eye to eye over something and I had to leave. I just assumed you'd not bothered to get in touch.'

'What was it then? Why won't you tell me what made you fall out with your parents? You were always so close.' Reaching across, he laid his hand over hers, his warmth transferring to her.

'It's a long story and we haven't really got the time to go into it now.' Looking up at him, she forced herself to make a promise. 'But I will, soon. I promise.'

'Okay. It all sounds very mysterious. Tell me when you're ready.'

'Thank you.' He had practically told her not to tell him yet. Had he guessed that Mia was his, and he really didn't want her to tell him yet? To make it official? Maybe he wanted to get to know Mia before springing it on her. It had always been a gift of his, to read her like an open book, so maybe he did know. Smiling at him, she pushed her chair back. 'I guess we'd better get the breakfasts on for Mr and Mrs Towbridge. They'll be down in a few minutes.'

'I guess we should.' Standing up, he made his way around the table until they were standing face to face. 'But first, there's something I need to do.'

As he stepped closer, she knew exactly what he needed to do, and she stepped forward, letting his arms wrap around her. Leaning her head on his shoulder, she breathed deeply, breathing in his spicy aftershave and the familiar smell of him. One which she had always remembered and had comforted her in the middle of the night many times, in the hospital alone after she had given birth, during the sleepless nights when Mia had suffered with colic, the time she had slept sleeping in a chair by Mia's bedside as she was kept in hospital for observation after hitting her head during a gymnastics event. Unconsciously, she had kept the memory of their relationship alive long after she had given up hope of ever being reunited.

'Come here.' Lifting her chin up with the crook of his finger, his lips met hers for the second time in as many days.

Closing her eyes, she felt the warmth of his skin against hers. The force of his kiss was firmer this time, surer than the tentative touch yesterday. The ringing of the alarm from her mobile pierced through the silence. Pushing her hands against his chest, she stepped back and reached out to her mobile on the table. 'Sorry, that was to remind me to start the next breakfasts.'

'I really have missed you, you know.' Leaning against the table, he crossed his arms.

Looking up from her mobile, she smiled. 'It's good to have run into you again.'

'Run into me? You make it sound like something mundane and ordinary. To me, us meeting up again after all these years, after being on almost opposite sides of the world for so long, is nothing short of miraculous. Or fate.' Running his hand through his hair, he grinned.

'Don't tell me you believe in all that stuff.' Glancing across at him, she laid the bacon in the frying pan.

'You used to.' He shrugged.

'Umm, well that was a long time ago when I was young and naïve. There's no such thing as fate, you make your own way in this world.'

'We certainly both made our own way in the world, but here we both are. If that's not a sign of fate, I don't know what is.'

'Not fate. It's called a coincidence.' If there was anything such as fate, it surely would have pulled them back together all those years ago, or come to think of it, at any point in the last thirteen years when she'd needed his support and Mia had needed a father figure in her life. Nope, it was a coincidence, that was all. And a cruel coincidence at that, putting her in an almost impossible situation. They had moved here to rebuild Mia's confidence and to change their lives for the better, not to be thrown into more changes, more upheavals.

'What happened to the Kim I fell in love with? The one who lived for fairy tales and happy endings?'

'She grew up. Now make yourself useful and go chop up some tomatoes.' Chucking the tea towel at him, she stared at the bacon, the oil dancing and jumping around it in the pan. If he had really missed her like he said, why hadn't he tried harder to try to contact her? Yes, after what he'd said she now realised that her parents wouldn't have told him her whereabouts, but what about Miriam's parents? He could have contacted them. Even going through what they had, they had remained a constant support to Kim throughout her pregnancy and had taken on the role of grandparents to Mia. They would have told him where to find her, and he had known them. She shook her head; he had obviously not missed her as much as he kept saying. If he really had at all.

'You've gone very quiet.' Placing his hand on the small of her back, he held up the chopping board, letting the tomatoes slide off into the pan.

'Sorry, I was just thinking.' Tilting her head, she listened as Mr and Mrs Towbridge came down the stairs. 'Here they come. Are you okay getting their drinks while I finish off the food, please?'

'Of course.'

11

'So what did you think?' Shaking her coat off, she hung it on the dining chair and slipped into the seat.

'What did I think of what? The beach or the schools we drove past on the very scenic way home?' Slipping into the chair opposite, Mia opened the bag on the table in front of her and picked at the candyfloss inside.

'Both.'

'The beach was nice. The schools were okay. I guess.'

'I thought the second one looked really good.'

'Only because it was newly built. It doesn't mean the people are going to be any nicer than the one that looked crummier.'

'That's true. We can find out tomorrow anyway.'

'Tomorrow? I thought you said we were going to look round them both next week?' Scrunching the bag shut, Mia glared across the table.

'I know, but I had a phone call from the second one this morning asking if we could change days because the head teacher had a course booked up for next Monday and I'd asked to be shown around by the head.'

'Can't we just keep them until next week? It doesn't matter who shows us around.'

'It does. I want to speak to the head teachers before we make our decision.'

'Mum, really?'

'Yes, really. I hadn't met your old head before you started at the old place, and if I had maybe I would have been able to get a better feel for the place.'

'You wouldn't have, Mum. It doesn't matter what the head's like or the other teachers. It matters what the kids are like.'

'I know, but if they've got some good policies in place, then I'd feel happier knowing that the school was as safe a place as possible.'

'You mean you're going to ask what they do to stop bullying?'

'Well, yes.' Reaching across the table, Kim placed her hand over Mia's.

'It doesn't matter what stupid policies they have. If I'm going to get bullied again, I'm going to get bullied. They can't stop it. Not really.'

'Yes, they can. And besides, you won't get bullied. It was only because of Amelia and she's not here.'

'There are always Amelias in schools.' Rolling her eyes, Mia pushed her chair back and stalked out of the kitchen, the half-eaten bag of candyfloss forgotten on the table.

Things would be different. This was their new start. She just had to try to get Mia to start at the school with as much confidence, fake or real, as she could and things would be fine. Rubbing her temples, she stood up and switched the kettle on before reaching for the pile of post she'd left on the table before they'd gone out.

Rifling through them, she set aside three for Jane and Bill, one which was clearly from an advertising campaign and two for herself, well, one addressed for her and one for the Berry Grove itself.

Opening the letter addressed to her, Kim grimaced, it was a letter from Mr Pinnel expressing his disappointment in her leaving the firm and asking her to let them have the first refusal if she decided to return to the corporate world.

Taking a pinch of candyfloss, she let it dissolve in her mouth and ran her finger across the thick, expensive paper. She had assumed she'd burnt her bridges with the company after she'd abandoned them so close to closing the deal with Mr Hitches. She smiled; it was nice to know that they had thought highly of her.

Pulling open the second envelope, she braced herself. For it to be addressed to Berry Grove it must be a bill or something official.

'Mum, I'm sorry.'

'Mia.' Looking up, she smiled as Mia walked back into the kitchen. 'It's okay. I know you're feeling nervous about starting your new school.'

'Have you been eating this?' Holding the bag of candyfloss up, Mia stared at her mum.

'I may have had the tiniest amount. Do you want a hot chocolate?' Placing the letter back on the table, she pushed herself to standing.

'Okay. I've been thinking, I think it will be good to go and see the schools tomorrow.'

'Oh yes?'

'Yes, I know I can't just stay at home and not go, so if we have a look tomorrow, it means I can enjoy the rest of the week without worrying about it.'

'That's a good way to look at it. Once we visit you'll see that there's nothing to be worried about.'

'I won't have to start until next week though, will I? Even if we decide on a school tomorrow, I won't have to start straight away, will I?'

'No, of course not. You need a bit of time to settle in here first. Here you go.' Placing Mia's mug down on the table in front of her, Kim slid back into her chair and took a long sip of coffee.

'What if I don't like either of them?' Looking down into her mug, Mia dipped her finger into the whipped cream before wiping it on the tea towel strewn on the table.

'Then we carry on looking. As I said, this move is for you. I won't be pushing you into joining a school where you don't feel comfortable.'

'Okay.' Tapping her finger on the pile of letters, Mia looked at Kim. 'You've had post here already?'

'Yes. From Mr Pinnel, believe it or not. He wrote to thank me for all the years I put in at his firm and to ask me to let him know if I look for work back in the City again.'

'You're not going to, are you? I thought...'

'No, I'm not.' Placing her hand on top on Mia's, she grasped it. 'I'm not going back, but it was nice to hear that he'd have me back. Does that sound silly?'

'No. It means that he realises what you did when you were working for him.'

'Exactly.'

'How about this one?' Picking up the unopened letter addressed to Berry Grove, she tapped the edge against the table.

'I've not opened it yet. I'm assuming it's a bill of some kind, but it's exciting getting our first piece of post for Berry Grove, isn't it?'

Shrugging, Mia took a sip of her drink. 'Not if it's a bill.'

'No, well, there's only one way to find out, I guess.' Taking the envelope from Mia's hand, Kim gently tore it open. 'Ooh, it's from the events management company who book rooms for their clients. Do you think they want more rooms this upcoming season?'

'Really? Maybe. If they do, do you think we'll make enough to go on holiday somewhere nice?'

'Why not? We deserve a treat, don't we?' Shaking the letter open, Kim narrowed her eyes. Something wasn't right. It didn't make any sense.

'Do they? Do they want to book more rooms?' Leaning forward, Mia peered over the top of her mug.

'Hold on.' Having read it once, Kim's eyes flicked to the top of the letter again. 'They don't want any.'

'What do you mean?'

'They're cancelling. They're writing to thank us for our hospitality, and by the sounds of it, Jane and Bill knew they were cancelling before they sold us Berry Grove. Listen, "We wish to thank you again for your kind hospitality towards our clients and are writing to confirm the severance of our contract."'

'Why wouldn't they want to use Berry Grove any more?'

'I'm not sure.' Tapping her fingers against the table, she closed her eyes. There must be a reason. 'Unless, unless they knew it was being sold and maybe they need to enter a new contract with us. I bet that's it. I bet the previous contract they had was specific to Jane and Bill. It would make perfect sense that they'd have to enter a new contract with us.'

'So what now? Are we going to lose out on money?'

'No. I'll give them a call. I'll find out where the closest branch is and we can go up there and sign a new contract. I just hope it manages to get sorted sooner rather than later.' She didn't want to lose out on income. Even if it took them a few weeks to sort the contract out it would have a massive effect, especially being as their old home hadn't sold yet.

'When will we go?'

'Hopefully this afternoon or tomorrow. The sooner we can get it sorted, the better.' Pulling her mobile from her back pocket, Kim tapped in the phone number printed at the top of the letter and reached across to the work surface to grab a pen.

'Good afternoon, Adventurers Limited. Amanda speaking. How may I help you?' Amanda's nasally voice floated down the line.

'Good afternoon. I'm calling from Berry Grove Bed and Breakfast. I have just received a letter confirming the termination of a contract between yourselves and Berry Grove. I am the new owner and wondered when we could come in to sign a new contract.'

'Please repeat the name of your establishment.'

'Berry Grove Bed and Breakfast.'

'Please hold.'

'What's happening?' Mia mouthed across the table.

'I've been put on hold.'

'Thank you for waiting. I can see here that we did send out a letter confirming the termination of your contract, but we will not be renewing.'

Not be renewing? That didn't make any sense. Berry Grove relied on the money Adventurers Limited brought in, without it they'd be competing for the same customers as all the rest of the Bed and Breakfasts lining the streets of Aranel. 'I understand that as the new owner of Berry Grove I will need to sign a new contract, but surely it can be business as usual once I've done that?'

'Your property is no longer required. Thank you for your time.'

'No, wait. Don't put the phone down!'

'Is there anything else I can help you with today?'

Taking a deep breath in, Kim lowered her voice. 'Your custom, the contract, was a condition of the sale between myself and the previous owners. I don't understand how you can say you no longer need our services?'

'I'm sorry to hear that, but it is of no relevance to Adventurers Limited. I'm afraid that is between yourself, the previous owners and your solicitors. The branch in your area is closing down at the end of the month, so as you can see, we literally no longer require your hospitality.'

'Closing down?'

'Yes, closing down, shutting, no longer operating.'

'What? Why?'

'Simply put, the market has been saturated. The business has been losing money for the past year. Now, is that everything?'

'No, yes. Can I just ask one more question?'

'Of course.'

'When did you tell Jane and Bill?'

'I'm assuming they were the previous owners? I'm afraid I do not have those exact details, but quite likely when we found out ourselves, six months ago. At the very least three months ago as written in the contract.'

'I see.' Pressing the End Call button, Kim lowered her phone to the table.

'Well?'

'They don't need us any more. The local branch of the company is closing.'

'Oh no, does that mean we have to move back?' Mia stiffened her jaw.

Shaking her head, Kim lowered her head to her hands.

'It's okay, Mum. We tried. I'm old enough now to know that we need money to live off.' Reaching out, Mia stroked Kim's arm.

'What do you mean "we tried"?' Lifting her head, Kim looked at Mia. Her delicate features suddenly looked grown up, too mature for her age.

'We can go back home. We tried to have a new life, and it's not your fault it's turned out like this. Just promise me you'll make a bit more time for us, please? Maybe you could try to come home early on a Friday or something? I could take the bus to a different school. It might be okay.'

'Mia, no. Our new life isn't over. Berry Grove is our home now. We're not going anywhere.'

'But I thought most of the money came from the events company? How will we keep this place running if we can't get any customers?'

Forcing a smile, Kim hoped it would reach her eyes. 'That's for me to figure out, not for you to worry about. I'll find a way. Now, why don't you go up to the flat and try on those new clothes we bought while I tidy up down here and have a think?'

'Okay. I won't blame you if we have to go back though.'

'I know, sweetheart, but I'm not that easy to break. We'll find a way.' Standing up, Kim watched Mia carry the bags out of the kitchen before switching the kettle on and rooting around the top drawer for her notebook.

Opening up the notebook, she took a long sip of coffee; she'd ladled two spoonfuls of sugar into it hoping the quick hit of energy would help her think. Is that why they had been in a rush to sell? It must have been. Jane and Bill must have known about the cancellation of the contract, they must have wanted to sell before it had finished.

There probably hadn't been another offer on the place. She had been well and truly played by them and she didn't have a leg to stand on. Technically, they had sold with the contract running. What they had done had been legal, even if not moral. She should have checked the contract more thoroughly. And she would have if they hadn't been pushing for a quick sale and if she hadn't been so desperate to move, to change her and Mia's life.

'Did you have a good trip out?'

'Danny!' Twisting around, she jerked her cup and watched as

coffee dripped onto her notebook, blurring the ink on the open page.

'Sorry, did I surprise you?'

'Yes, just slightly.' Using the tea towel she dabbed at the paper. 'Sorry, I'm still not used to people lurking around my home.'

'Here, let me help you with that.' Taking the tea towel, Danny patted the notebook dry. 'There you go, no harm done.'

'Thanks.' Standing up, Kim took her mug over to the kettle.

'You sit down, I'll make it. It's the least I can do after making you spill that one.'

'Okay, thanks. Can you shove a couple of sugars in there too, please? Get yourself one if you want.'

'Stressed, hey?' Taking a mug out of the cupboard, he turned around, leaning his back against the work surface.

'Do I look that frazzled?'

'No, but the two sugars give it away.'

'You remember?' Leaning back in her chair, she tucked her hair behind her ears.

'Of course, I do. Two sugars when you're worried about something and three before an exam. Is that right?'

'You know it is.'

'Do you want to talk about it?' Placing the coffees on the table, he slipped into the chair opposite. 'I might be able to help.'

'I bought this place on the understanding that we had a contract with an events company which booked up a lot of the rooms for its clients and brought in the majority of the customers and profit. Well, I've just got off the phone with them confirming that the branch is closing and the contract is up.'

'You're kidding?'

'I wish I was. I would never have bought this place if I'd known.' Wrapping her hands around her mug, she took a deep breath, the warm steam enveloping her.

'So you didn't know about it finishing before you brought it?'

'No, I bought it on the understanding that the contract was still running. Jane and Bill told me to my face that the company brought most of the money in and that the business was secure because of them. They lied to my face.'

'But I thought that's why they were having the extension built? Something to do with the company?'

'Yes, that's the impression I got. The profit coming from the extra rooms being booked was certainly paying for it anyway. I just can't believe how stupid I've been.' She took a big gulp.

'You weren't stupid. You just trusted them.'

'No, I really was. I didn't get my solicitor to look through the contract with the company.'

'It's still not your fault.'

'I'm normally so thorough, but with everything that was going on with Mia and my job, and Jane and Bill contacting me to say they'd had a higher offer and were going to have to take it because the potential buyers could move in earlier, I just wasn't thinking straight.' Leaning back, she ran her hands through her hair. Why hadn't she had her solicitor look through the contract? The number of contracts she'd written up and looked over with a fine-toothed comb for her job, she should have realised what was going on.

'Do you think it was all an act then? You don't think there was another buyer?'

'You tell me. You were here doing the extension.'

Danny shifted in his chair. 'Well, I wasn't here half as much as I am now.'

'Sorry, I didn't mean to snap. I'm just so angry at myself. Of course you weren't, I'm assuming you leave Dave and the crew to it when it's at the beginning of a job.'

'That's not entirely true. I'm here more now because of the present company.'

'Right.' Allowing a small smile to grace her lips for a second, she breezed over his compliment. Compliments weren't going to pay the bills, or the big extension for that matter.

'Can you get your solicitor to have a look over everything now?'

Shaking her head, she lowered her chin to her hands. 'There's no point. I signed the contract to buy this place. I guess I might be able to take them to court for not disclosing everything but then they'd probably argue that I should have taken more notice of the contract, that I should have contacted Adventurers Limited to double-check everything anyway. Plus, there's no way we can move back. No, it was a stupid oversight on my part and it's me who needs to sort it out.'

'How are you going to do that?'

'I have no idea. It doesn't help that our old house hasn't sold yet so I can't even rely on the profits to keep us ticking over until I figure something out.'

Standing up, Danny came behind her and placed his hands, strong and heavy, on her shoulders. He pressed his fingers and thumbs into her shoulders, circling his thumbs. 'I can probably swing it so you don't have to pay out for the extension until it's completed, or a bit later than that.'

'No, it's okay. Thank you though, but I'll sort it.' Leaning back, she circled her neck and stretched her back. 'I'd forgotten how good you are at giving massages.'

'They're my speciality.' Dipping his head, he kissed her on the forehead.

'They certainly are.' Closing her eyes, she allowed her mind to empty, focusing instead on his touch and imagining her muscles relaxing.

'What happened back home? I'm a very good listener. You can't have forgotten about that, surely?'

'Back home?'

'You said you couldn't go back, and you wanted to leave quite quickly?'

Opening her eyes, she fixated on the kitchen clock in front of her. 'I was too involved at work. I took my eye off the ball big time with Mia and then I found out she was being bullied. We needed to get away and get a fresh start.'

'There you go again.'

'There I go again what?'

'Blaming yourself. You're blaming yourself for the contract ending, and you've just blamed yourself for Mia being bullied. Kids can be cruel. Do you remember Melissa and her gang? I'm pretty certain Mia being picked on wasn't your fault.'

'Oh, yes, I remember that group and their vile tongues. But it was my fault with Mia. Maybe not that she was being bullied, but I was to blame for the fact that she didn't feel she could come to me.' Pulling away from his touch, she twisted around and looked at him. 'I was at working all of the time.'

'You're too hard on yourself. You were only trying to pay the bills and, besides, I'm sure all you did was for Mia.'

'No, you don't understand. I could have had any job, a part-time job even, and still provided for her, but instead I felt I had something to prove. I felt I had to climb the stupid career ladder, prove myself to my parents. Show them that I could become someone even after having a baby so young. It wasn't for Mia. It was for my parents and I haven't even spoken to them in thirteen years.' Wiping her face dry with her fingers, she shook her head. Why was she even crying? 'Sorry, I don't know what's got into me. I haven't cried for years.'

'Hey, don't apologise. Sometimes a good cry is a good thing.'

Laying his hands on her shoulders, he waited for her to stop shaking. 'You don't need to prove yourself to anyone.'

'I know that now. Things have just been so hard.' Pinching the top of her nose, she took a deep breath.

'I bet they have. I can imagine it's no easy task to bring up a child by yourself. When did Mia's dad leave?'

Jumping up, Kim pushed past him and hung the tea towel on the oven door. 'Sorry, I need to get on now.'

'Was it something I said?'

'I can't do this right now.' Putting her head down, she walked quickly out of the room. She shouldn't have said anything. She shouldn't have spoken about Mia or about her parents. Or anything.

Glancing behind her, she checked that Danny hadn't followed before sinking down onto the first step of the stairs. Leaning her forehead against the cool of the wall, she steadied her breathing. She could have told him then. She could have told him that Mia was his. Why hadn't she? Digging her nails into the palms of her hands. She reminded herself why they had moved here, to get Mia away from the drama of those bullies, to spend more time together. If she told her now, it would only produce more anxiety, more worries and questions for Mia. No, Mia needed space, time to settle into her new life. She needed the best chance of a new start at her new school, not to be laden down with problems and truths she shouldn't have to deal with.

12

'So, what are your first impressions of Tadbury High, Mia?' Resting her hands on the desk in front of her, Mrs Silverman, the head teacher, smiled at them.

'I really like it. I especially like the science lab. I can't believe we can actually do experiments every week.'

'That's right. We believe that our students learn best when they have practical experience and are able to investigate what they are learning. We also offer half-termly subject days in all of our subjects, including science, where students can choose their preferred subject and participate in a day of activities tailored to that subject or go on a subject-specific trip.'

'Wow, that sounds really good. When will the next one be?'

'Two weeks' time, on the Friday. Do you think you may be interested in coming back tomorrow and attending a trial day here?'

Leaning forward in her chair, Kim cleared her throat. 'I don't think...'

'Yes, please.'

Jerking her head to the side, Kim looked at Mia. Her eyes were glistening as she nodded enthusiastically. She hadn't seen her this excited in ages, years perhaps. But was she ready? After her experiences at her old school, was she rushing too quickly to get back into the education system?

'Is that okay with you, Mum?' Mrs Silverman looked directly at Kim.

'Yes, I guess so. I'm just concerned that she's rushing into it all. I think she may be better off having some more time to settle into our new life here.'

Smiling kindly, Mrs Silverman looked over her glasses. 'I understand your concerns, Ms Reynolds, but often in cases where students have been through what your daughter has and who may be feeling disillusioned with the schooling system, we find it best if there is not such a long break between establishments. It can lead to further anxiety and a feeling that all schools will be the same.'

Nodding, Kim smiled at Mia. It made sense.

'I can assure you that here at Tadbury High, we do not tolerate any form of bullying or antisocial behaviour at all. If there are any such incidents, I have an open-door policy and every single student of mine are welcome to share their worries, school or home, with me or one of our dedicated school counsellors at any time of the school day.' Turning to Mia, she slid a prospectus across the desk. 'There are some lovely girls in your year group, which I think you will get on very well with.'

'Okay.' Mia nodded.

'Now, unless either of you have any other questions, I shall see you at nine o'clock back here in my office tomorrow morning and I shall introduce you to your tutor group. If you think of anything else you want to ask or anything that is worrying you then jot it down and we'll go through it tomorrow. Does that sound okay?'

'Yes, thank you, Mrs Silverman.' Taking the prospectus, Mia

turned to face her mum. 'Is that okay, Mum? Can I really come in for a trial day tomorrow?'

'Yes, of course, you can. I think that would be a good idea. Does she need to be in school uniform?'

'No, not for a trial day. We like to give prospective students the chance to get a real taste of the school before committing to buying the uniform, so jeans and a T-shirt will be fine for tomorrow.'

'Okay, thank you.'

* * *

'She seemed nice, didn't she?' Pulling the car keys from her pocket, Kim clicked them towards the car.

'Yes, she did, and the other people in my year group seemed nice.'

'They sure did. So, are you looking forward to tomorrow then?'

'Yes. I mean, I'm a bit nervous, but I think it's probably best I just jump in and go so I don't build it up and worry about it.' Pulling her seatbelt across, Mia wound down the window.

'I think that's a great way of looking at it. It looked like a really good school and they obviously care about the students there. Plus, the subject days sounded great, didn't they?'

'I can't wait. I'm going to choose science. Definitely.'

Danny had always been good at science. Mia must have got her passion for the subject from him. Kim shook her head and put the car into reverse. She'd never compared Mia to him before. She'd never even thought about him and Mia at the same time since she was about three when Kim had decided it would just be her and Mia for the foreseeable future.

'Are you okay, Mum?'

'I'm fine, thanks, sweetie.'

'You've just gone very quiet. Do you not want me to go? Did you prefer the school we looked round this morning?'

'No, I didn't. I think this is a great choice, the right choice. I was just thinking about how much our lives are changing at the moment, that's all.'

'Are you sure? Because it's further than the other one. I don't mind going to the other one if it's going to be easier for you to drop me off and pick me up?'

'No chance. It wasn't a patch on this one. What's an extra ten minutes in the car when I know you're happy? Hey?' Turning to face Mia, she grinned. It was definitely the right choice. Hopefully Mia could be happy at Tadbury High. And once she had settled in and made a good group of friends, then she'd be able to tell her the truth about her dad. It was definitely the best thing waiting though. It was definitely the right choice for Mia's welfare and happiness. Plus, it wasn't as though she wasn't ever going to tell them both. She was just postponing it a couple of weeks, that was all.

13

'Are you sure this T-shirt looks okay?'

'It looks fine. You look lovely.' Glancing across at Mia, Kim smiled before pulling up against the kerb. 'Everything will be okay, you'll see. You never know, you might even enjoy it.'

'I know. I *am* looking forward to it, but I'm really worried about acting weird with the other girls in class.'

'What do you mean?'

'I don't know. I just don't want to come across as shy or scared of them. I don't want to give whatever impression I did to Amelia and the others at my old school.'

'Hey, what happened with Amelia and the others wasn't down to whatever impression you gave them. What they did says more about them than it does you.' Turning to face Mia, she held on to her hand. 'You are beautiful, wonderful and strong. This school will be a good thing and you'll make loads of new friends.'

'But if it isn't, I don't have to come back, do I? I mean, it is just a trial day.' Looking down, Mia pulled at the hem of her T-shirt.

'Yes, it's just a trial day. It's just one day to see how you like it. If you don't, for whatever reason, then we can try another school.'

'Promise?'

'Promise.' Undoing her seatbelt, Kim twisted behind her to pick up her handbag. 'Right, let's go.'

'Umm, do you mind staying here and I'll go in on my own? I just don't want to stand out by having my mum take me into school.'

'Right, yes. Of course. Do you remember where to go?'

'Yes, to the head teacher's office and she'll take me to my tutor group.'

'And I'll meet you out here at half past three?'

'Okay. Thanks, Mum. You don't mind, do you?'

'Not at all. I wouldn't have been seen dead walking in with my mum to secondary school. I do remember being your age, you know.' Kim grinned and slipped her bag back behind the driver's seat.

'Okay.'

'Go on then, or you'll be late. Remember, you're my girl, you can get through anything. Smile and everyone will see how amazing you are.'

'Mum.' Mia rolled her eyes and grinned before getting out of the car.

'Love you.'

'Love you too.' Smiling, Mia shut the door behind her.

Resting her hands on the steering wheel, Kim watched as she walked towards the double doors to the entrance. Turning the radio on, she leant back and waited for ten minutes until she was sure Mia wasn't going to come back out and then indicated to pull out.

* * *

Hefting the vacuum down the stairs, Kim paused and wiped the sweat from her brow.

'Morning. I've got those floor tile samples if you want to come and have a look?' Danny called up the stairs and swung his jacket over his shoulder.

'Danny. Hi.' Dipping her head, she tucked a loose strand of hair behind her ear before lifting the vacuum down the final few steps. 'Yes, that'd be good. I'll be through in a few minutes.'

'Okay, do you need a hand?'

'Nah, I'm okay. Thanks though.' Smiling, she pushed the vacuum into the understairs cupboard and closed the door as she watched him disappear into the kitchen. Wiping her hands down the front of her jeans, she checked her watch. It was eleven fifteen. Mia would probably be having break now. For the tenth time that hour, she checked her mobile. Still no call from the school. Hopefully that meant she was having a good time.

* * *

'Which one do you like then? I can always get some more if none of these are jumping out at you. I could get some samples from this place if you like?' Sliding a dark blue catalogue across the table, Danny frowned.

'No, it's fine. There's plenty of choice here.'

'Are you sure? You don't seem to be very impressed by them.'

'Sorry. I've just got other things on my mind. Mia's gone into school for a trial day. I'm just worried about how she's getting on.' Shifting her weight to her other leg, Kim shuffled the sample tiles around on the table. 'Plus, I'm still not a hundred per cent sure what I'm going to use the room for now.'

'I'm sure she'll be fine. Kids are resilient to change, aren't they?'

'Umm, I hope so.' Standing back, she watched as he collected the tiles together, neatly stacking them into a pile.

'Look, why don't you let me take you out for lunch? Take your mind off everything for a bit?'

'I don't know...'

'You've been cleaning and tidying all morning now. You must be due a break. Come on, I know this lovely little café in Seahampton right on the beachfront. It'll be good for you.'

'Okay. I don't have much of a choice, do I? Not if I don't want you on my case all afternoon.' Circling her shoulders, Kim smiled. He was right; she could do with a break. She felt as though she hadn't stopped since moving here. A couple of hours at the beach wouldn't hurt, would they?

* * *

'I told you it was lovely here, didn't I?'

'You certainly did.' Looking across the table at Danny, Kim smiled. She hadn't realised how much she'd needed to get out fora bit. She took a deep breath, letting the salty warm air fill her lungs and looked past the railings on the patio. The tide was out so the expanse of sandy beach seemed to stretch for miles before it met with the brilliant blue of the ocean. 'This looks good too.'

'They're the best cream teas I've found, and I've tried a fair few in many places.' Taking a bite of his scone, he lowered it, revealing a trickle of jam on the corner of his lip.

'Come here, you're wasting the jam.' Leaning forward, Kim wiped him clean with the tip of her index finger.

'Thank you.' Grinning, he gently held her finger and licked the jam off.

'Oi!' Pulling her hand away, she laughed and wiped it on the napkin in front of her.

'That was supposed to be romantic.' Pulling his mouth down at the corners, he laughed.

'Well, I'm just not a very romantic person then.'

'Oh you are, just in ways you seem to have forgotten. Do you remember we used to pack a bag and just walk out of the village and camp up for the night?'

'Yes, I remember being chased off fields by various farmers on numerous occasions. They didn't take too kindly to us trespassing and lighting campfires on their land.'

'Ah, but you must remember cooking teacakes and roasting marshmallows before falling asleep under the stars?'

'You mean on the occasions we didn't end up running for our lives?'

'Yes. On those occasions. Now, that was romantic, you've got to admit.'

'Yes, it was very romantic.'

'So you have got it in you then?'

'Maybe. Maybe I've just been disillusioned over the years.'

'I think you must have been. Luckily for us though, I haven't been, and so can reignite your romantic side.'

'Umm.' Bringing her teacup to her lips, Kim looked over the edge at him. What was he looking for? And did she even have a romantic side any more?

'What's that for?'

'What?'

'That "Umm"?'

'I don't know.' Lowering the flowery teacup, she shook her head. 'I was just wondering what your game was?'

'My game?' Looking up from buttering his second scone, he frowned.

'Sorry, that wasn't the right word. I mean, I was just wondering what you want from me, from this, I guess.' Was he after a relationship or a quick trip down memory lane? Not that she was sure she was ready for either. The kisses, the massage, what had they been about? Was he playing with her or being sincere? He hadn't really given her a real answer when she'd asked him after their first kiss.

'Nicely put. I thought it was obvious?'

'No, not to me anyway.'

Clearing his throat, he shifted in his seat. 'I'd really like it if we could give our relationship another go. I know it's been years since we went out with each other and that we were only young back then, but I had been serious about you then, and I still feel as though we've got a special connection.'

Focusing on him, the background of the beach and the quiet murmurings of the other diners around them melted away. She realised then that it had always been him. No one else had stood a chance of competing with the memory of him. What if that was all it was though? A memory? What if she had built him up into this wonderful person, her soulmate, in her mind and in reality he wasn't who she believed he was? What if by falling into a relationship with him, it made him less perfect in her mind? What if it spoilt the memories she had carried around in her heart?

'Do you feel the connection too?' Leaning forward on his elbows, Danny took her hands in his.

'I do. I'm just worried it will spoil things.'

'In what way? We've only just met up again, don't we deserve a chance to find out? After all these years of being apart, don't we deserve a chance at finding our happiness again?'

Closing her eyes, she reopened them and looked out towards the sea. There were so many questions swimming around in her head, so many reasons not to give things another go. It had been too long since they were last in a relationship to pick off where they had been, too many things had happened. There were too many secrets between them, too many events in their pasts to talk about and overcome.

'I'm sorry. I've scared you away, haven't I? I shouldn't have said anything.'

But what about Mia? If this worked, she could have both her parents back together, back in her life. 'I guess we don't know what's going to happen until we try.'

'Really?' Jerking his head up towards her, a slow grin spread across his face.

'Yes. You only live once, as they say.'

'Perfect. We can take it as fast or as slow as you want. I'll keep pace with you.'

Kim nodded. Maybe if they could fall back in love with each other, then when Mia had settled in at her new school and she told him about her, they could finally be that happy family she'd yearned for.

Picking her sandals up from the ground, Kim sank her toes into the soft warm sand, letting the millions of grains wash over her feet with every step. Slipping her hand into Danny's, they effortlessly found their 'comfortable spot' as they used to call it, their fingers interlocking around each other's. 'It really is beautiful here.'

'It sure is.'

'When did you move down here?' There was so much that she didn't know about him any more.

'Last year, when my ex-wife and I split. We had been living a few miles inland. I'd always wanted to move closer to the beach, but she had family in a town a few miles inland where we lived so...' Shrugging, he turned his face towards the ocean, his hair waving in the wind. 'And when we split, I thought "Why not?" and moved down here.'

'Are you amicable?'

'Yes, we're waiting for the two years to be over before we get the divorce. It's just easier that way, plus, we don't have to lay the blame with either of us if we wait. We speak occasionally, usually to discuss the financial settlement and details of the divorce, boring stuff like that, but I help her out as much as I can and she does the same. We're still friends, we're just not in love any more.'

'In what way do you help each other out?' Should she be asking questions like this? 'Sorry, you don't have to answer. I'm just being nosy.'

'No, it's fine. You're just trying to fill in the blanks of my life since we knew each other last. I feel the same; I want to find out everything about your past, too. Of course, I'll wait until you're ready. I'm not going to push you, but I'm happy to answer your questions. She's an accountant, so she helps me out if I have a financial query about the business, and I help her out around the house.'

'Oh, okay. When was the last time you saw her then? Not that it matters, I think it's lovely you're still friends and help each other out. It says a lot about who you are as a person.'

'About two-and-a-half weeks ago. Just before you moved into Berry Grove.'

'Ah okay.' Pausing, she looked out to sea, tucking her hair behind her ears.

'Here, come here.' Taking Kim's other hand, he gently circled her back around to face him. Placing his hands in the small of her back, he brought her closer, their breath warming each other's faces. 'I really want this to work.'

'Me too.' And she did. There was more at stake than he knew. Lifting her chin, she met his lips and sank against his body.

14

'It really was great, Mum. There's this one girl in my tutor group and she chose to show me around. She chose! She wasn't asked by the teachers, someone else was, but she was kind of rubbish. Nice still, but rubbish. She kept getting distracted by her boyfriend. Yuck. He was okay though, he kept reminding her she was supposed to be showing me around, but in the end, Tilly, the girl I said about, came up and asked if she could show me around instead. I said "yes" and the other girl agreed, so Tilly showed me around.' Throwing her bag onto the kitchen floor, Mia turned the kettle on. 'Do you want one of our special hot chocolates, Mum?'

'That would be lovely, thank you.' She grinned, Mia had been buzzing the moment she'd got into the car after school and then had been on her mobile with this Tilly girl all the way home only saying their goodbyes when they had pulled up outside Berry Grove. 'I'm so pleased you had a lovely day. What were the lessons like?'

'They were great actually, which I never, ever thought I'd ever say about lessons at school! We had double science and did an experiment. It was great, we had to mix all these chemicals and things together and then it puffed up and kind of exploded. But it was supposed to, that was what was meant to happen. Can you ever imagine me being allowed to do an actual experiment in my old school? I mean, we did do experiments, but they were normally with the whole class watching and the teacher doing them mainly and asking some kids, normally the popular ones, to add bits and bobs.'

'Wow, that does sound fun. Do you think you want to start there then?' Sitting down at the table, Kim took the mug of hot chocolate from Mia. 'Yum. This looks nice. Thanks.'

'Yes, definitely! Can I? I'd really really like to start. We've got art tomorrow and PE, and I think they're doing netball in PE and I love netball.'

'Okay, yes, you can. I don't know about tomorrow though, we'll need to get the uniform and I'm not sure what time the shop closes.'

'No, that's fine. Mrs Silverman caught up with me this afternoon and she's said I can just go in non-uniform for the rest of the week. She said she's going to email you all the forms and information and that, but I can start. I gave her your email address, is that okay?'

'Of course it is.' Mia was acting and sounding like a completely different child. She was brimming with confidence and excitement at going back to school. The move had definitely been worth it. One hundred per cent, just to see her smile again.

'Oh, and Tilly said she's going to ask her mum if we can car-share. Her mum works and struggles to get there on time to pick her up. Anyway, I said about you having to jiggle around the times with doing the breakfasts and she said, 'Why don't we ask them to car-share?' Her mum can take us and you can bring us both home. What do you think? It will make your life easier, won't it? And it means I can walk in with Tilly every day and not on my own. What do you think?'

'I think it sounds like a great idea. I'd like to meet her before I let her pick you up though.'

'Yes, don't worry that's what I said to Tilly and Tilly said her mum is the same, so we thought we could meet up at the weekend? That way you can both see that the other one isn't an axe murderer and we can have fun too. She was saying that there's a nature reserve we can walk around and even row a boat on the lake. And, of course, there's a little café which sells ice cream too.'

'The nature reserve by the castle? I think that sounds like a lovely idea.'

'Brilliant, shall I go and ring her and arrange a time then? So will you take me and pick me up for the rest of the week and then when you and Tilly's mum have met we can car-share from next week?'

'Yes.' Standing up, Kim held her arms out. 'Come here.'

'Aw, Mum.'

'Hey, you're never too old for a hug from your mum.' Wrapping her arms around her, she breathed in the coconut fragrance of Mia's shampoo. 'I am so so proud of you, Mia.'

'Okay, can I go and ring her now then?'

'Yes, go on then.' Laughing, she watched as Mia ran out of the room, already ringing her new friend.

'You look happy.'

'Danny! Stop doing that would you?' Laughing, she twisted around as Danny came through from the extension.

'Sorry.' Grinning, he offered her a mint before laying some paperwork on the table. 'I've been having a look at my business accounts and if it's going to help you, I'm happy to take on the costs until the end of the tax year?'

'What? No!'

'Oh, okay. It was only a thought because of what you said about the contract ending and you struggling to cover the bills with the profit.' Frowning, he looked down at his pile of paperwork.

Glancing at him, Kim swallowed. She'd coped this far in her adult life without any support, she certainly wasn't going to start becoming indebted to people now. 'I'm sorry, I didn't mean to snap. It's just I don't need anyone to help me fight my battles. I've always coped by myself and I'll find a way to sort this.'

'No, I'm sorry. I must have sounded very condescending, but it doesn't hurt to let people help you. You'll still be paying me, just a little later than you would have done.' Shrugging, he picked up his stack of papers. With his head down, he turned away.

'Wait.' Watching as he paused and looked back at her, Kim could see by the downturn of his mouth that she had offended him. It wasn't him. Not really. It was her. She knew it was her. When the two people who she had truly thought she could rely on, her parents, had turned their back on her when she'd been pregnant with Mia, she'd promised herself she'd be more careful in who she entrusted. And then, when she had fallen for Max and he'd turned out to be married, she'd vowed to never depend on anyone. And it had worked. It had got her to where she had been in her career.

'What?' Putting his hand against the wall, he shifted his weight from one foot to the other.

Clasping her hands in front of her, she narrowed her eyes. It had started with him if she was completely honest; her distrust in people had begun with him. He had supposed to come back for her, and although she knew now that he had tried, at the time, struggling with a newborn baby whilst learning to live on her own, she had believed he too had abandoned her. She shook her head. He hadn't known. None of it was his fault. And, besides, now he was just being kind. 'I kind of find it hard to accept help from others. I really do appreciate your offer though.'

'It's okay. It was just a thought. Have you had any more ideas about how to fill the rooms yet?'

'Not really. I mean, I've thought about it, but everything just seems a long way off and pretty impossible without ploughing a ton of money into the business first. I did think I could market the extension as the perfect place to have wedding receptions and offer the rooms at a discount hoping the wedding party would stay, but for that to work I think the rooms would all need updating.' Kim shrugged. She knew the extension would be an amazing place for a small wedding party. She could probably quite easily get a drinks license to have a bar too, but while the extension would be perfect, the bedrooms were so tired looking it would put a lot of people off.

'That's a good idea though.'

'Umm, I've also thought about using my old contacts and reaching out to some of the businesses I used to work with, maybe some of them would want somewhere regular to hold conferences, but it's just a little way out, not being anywhere close to London or anywhere.'

'No, but there are still a couple of big towns and cities close by, remember.' Scrunching up his nose, he took a deep breath in. 'You know you could even team up with a couple of local tourist attractions and offer it with excursions. That way you're not only offering conference space but also team-building and self-care time. A lot of these big businesses are into staff well-being nowadays.'

'Ooh, I like that idea! You're not just a pretty face, are you?' Kim grinned. Danny might just have something there. She remembered that Pinnel's had tried to force her to attend a team-building weekend a few years ago. If they were doing them, there would surely be a lot more businesses who might be interested. And being close to the seaside too might just give Berry Grove an edge over a more local establishment.

'I sure am!' Danny patted the papers in his arms. 'So am I forgiven now?'

'Yes, you are.' Smiling at him, Kim stood up and kissed him on the cheek before switching the kettle on.

'Is that all I get for single-handedly saving your business?'

'No, I'll make you a coffee too.' Taking the mugs down from the cupboard, she spooned in the coffee granules. 'Oh, I had some positive news about my house too. There's a couple coming back for a third viewing soon, so fingers crossed if it sells then I'll have enough to keep us going until I can turn Berry Grove around.'

'I shall keep my fingers and toes crossed for you then.'

'Why thank you!' Smiling, she handed him the coffee.

Taking the mug, Danny looked over at her and smiled sheepishly. 'Thank you for giving us another chance. I really think this could work.'

Glancing down at the floor, Kim allowed her hair to cover her face before looking him in the eye. 'Me too.' Once Mia had settled in at her new school, they'd be able to be the happy family they all deserved.

'Shall we go and get a bite to eat tomorrow lunchtime again?'

'Yes, that'd be nice.'

'We could even make that little café on the beachfront our regular, unless you wanted to explore somewhere else that is?'

'No, that café was perfect.'

15

'Okay, I know we'd arranged to go back to the little café on the beach, but I thought we could do something a little different, if that's okay?' Standing by the front door, a wide grin spread across Danny's face.

'Right...' Tilting her head, she watched as he bounced from foot to foot. 'What do you have in mind?'

'Ah, I'd rather not tell you until we're there.'

'Why?' What was he up to? Dressed in shorts and a T-shirt rather than the usual trousers and shirt, he was definitely up to something.

'Do you trust me?'

'I guess so.' Squinting, Kim laughed. She did trust him, one hundred percent. Of course she did, but she also remembered when he had taken her bungee jumping as a surprise when they had been teenagers, and she was sure she remembered him acting like this then. 'You do know that I'm too old for bungee jumping, don't you?'

'Of course! What do you take me for?'

'Oi, you're supposed to say I'm not too old for anything!'

Punching him on the arm, she pretended to frown.

'So, you want to go bungee jumping then? That can be arranged. One moment.' Holding up his index finger, he pulled his mobile from his back pocket.

'No, no. Although I'm most definitely not too old for bungee jumping, we've been there and done that.' Pulling his mobile away from his ear, she laughed.

'It's agreed then, you trust me.'

* * *

'Come here.' Holding her hand as she jumped from the pavement to the beach, he laced his fingers through hers.

'This is lovely. No wonder you wanted to come here.' Turning her face up towards the sun, she took a deep breath, letting the salty warm air fill her lungs.

'Yes it is, but that's not why we're here.' Holding her by the shoulders, he turned her to the right. 'This is.'

'You've got to be kidding!' Standing still, she took in the white van to her right with a huge cartoon picture of a jet ski emblazoned across it. 'No, no chance!'

'Come on, we're booked in for half twelve.'

'Oh no.' Groaning, she held her head in her hands. 'I don't think I can.'

'Of course you can. You were always up for an adventure, a new experience.'

'Yes, well, I'm not seventeen any more.' Rubbing the back of her neck, she looked across at the brilliant red jet skis lined up in front of the van. 'I'm a completely different person now.'

'Don't be daft. You're still the Kim I know. You've just got to allow your adventurous side to come out again. It's been hiding behind that corporate adult front for too long.' Standing in front of her, he took her hands in his. 'Will you just give it a go? Five minutes, and then we can go and find a café somewhere?'

Grimacing, she shook her head. 'Five minutes, and then I'm getting off.'

'Deal. I've done this so many times before, you're in safe hands.'

* * *

Nodding as the instructor gave a mini tutorial, Kim gripped Danny's hand, the shallow waves rolling around her ankles. Was she actually going to get on one of those things? She needed to shake off the stuffy old Kim that she had turned into. Year after year of stress and adulthood had taken its toll and if she wanted to become the 'fun mum' Mia deserved she knew she had to take risks.

'Thank you, mate.' Shaking the balding instructor's hand, Danny pulled the straps tighter on her life jacket before holding her hand as she climbed onto the back of the Jet Ski bobbing up and down in front of them. 'You okay?'

'I will be in five minutes when it's all over.' Gripping hold of his waist, she could feel the heat of his skin through his T-shirt.

Twisting around, he grinned at her before turning back and revving the engine. 'Hold on tight.'

'Oh, I will. Don't worry about that.' Licking her lips, she closed her eyes, immediately opening them again. Was it best to see what was coming or not?

With the Jet Ski vibrating beneath them, they bobbed up and down with each wave and inched forward, quickly gaining speed.

Looking behind her, she could see the beach quickly fading in the distance as they sped through the water. With her hair flying out behind her, she could feel her heart pounding in her chest.

The spray of water soaked her light fabric trousers as they hopped and soared over waves. Laughing as the air rushed past her, she could feel her shoulders relax. Maybe he knew her better than she knew herself. Maybe the old Kim was still inside waiting and ready to resurface.

Bringing the Jet Ski back around, the beach came back into view. Slowing down, they coasted. 'So, do you want to go back now?'

'No way. Let's find some more waves first.'

'Really?'

'Really.' Leaning forward, she kissed the back of his neck, the salty, fresh taste tingling her lips. 'Thank you for making me do this.'

'You're very welcome. I knew you'd enjoy it.' Twisting to face her, his lips briefly met with her, strong and intense before he turned back to the sea ahead of them. 'Let's go and find those waves!'

* * *

Twenty minutes later, Kim handed her life jacket back to the instructor and thanked him before turning to Danny. The sand beneath seemed to dip and lurch underneath her much as the waves had out at sea.

'Hey, careful, you've still got your sea legs.' Wrapping his arm around her he settled his hand into the small of her back, supporting her as she walked.

'It was worth it though. I haven't done anything that fun in years!'

'That's because I haven't been about.'

'Ha-ha, very funny.' Turning to face him, she looked up into his eyes which were still glistening with adrenaline. Moving closer, she tried to still the fluttering in her stomach. With their open lips millimetres apart, she could feel his warm, minty breath on hers. Slowly leaning forward, she kissed him, slowly and gently this time, his skin soft against hers. Wrapping her arms around his neck, she pulled him closer still, until she could feel the heat from his body against every inch of hers. Their kissing became more frantic, stronger and deeper. She really had missed him. He really did feel like home. As though they truly were meant to be together. She should have tried harder to track him down all those years ago. He should have tried harder too. They had so much time to make up for.

Gently pulling his lips away, Danny held on to his grip around her waist. 'I never stopped loving you, Kim.'

'Me neither.' Closing her eyes, she felt his hand run up her spine, his fingers in her hair, as his lips met hers again. The quiet hubbub of the beach on a weekday, the pensioners chatting, the parents appeasing toddlers with ice cream and the occasional dog walkers strolling by, their dogs running excitedly out into the shallow waves and bringing back with them a fur full of sand, melted away. All Kim could focus on was Danny, his lips against hers, the touch of his fingers, his hands, his body. Nothing else mattered.

16

'Bye, have a good day.'

'You too, Mum. Remember me and Tilly have that Book Club meeting after school today, so are you still okay picking us up at half four?' Throwing her rucksack over her shoulder, Mia took her lunch money from Kim's hand.

'Yes, of course. I'll see you in the usual place at half four then.' Waving and mouthing 'Thank you' to Tilly's Mum, she watched as Mia slid into the backseat, immediately turning to chat to Tilly.

Fiona, Tilly's mum, smiled and waved as she turned the car around. She had seemed really nice when they had met up at the nature reserve and Kim had surprised herself by inviting her to pop round for coffee later in the week. It would actually be nice to have a friend now she had more time to socialise.

As Mia turned back to her and grinned, Kim blew her a kiss. Shaking her head, she could hardly picture the timid, scared Mia she had been just a couple of months ago. They should have made the move sooner. Much sooner. Rubbing her hand over her face, she reminded herself that she had promised to look forward instead of regretting past mistakes.

Closing the door behind her, she made her way back into the kitchen. They had only had one guest last night, but he hadn't wanted breakfast until eight o'clock so she still had to tidy up.

Slipping the plates and frying pan into the dishwasher, she wiped the surfaces down. She really needed to start reaching out to more of the local attractions and try to set up some meetings to discuss the conference and team-building mini-breaks. The castle had seemed to like the idea, probably because they were eager to fill the gap in their own profits caused by the closure of the excursion company's branch, and there was a paintball centre whose boss had sounded keen over the phone.

Drying her hands on the tea towel, she pulled her notebook off the shelf and sat down. She had three and a half hours until Danny was taking her out for lunch, although he'd probably pop in for a coffee when he arrived with the extra tile samples.

Riffling through the notebook, she found the list of companies to ring to discuss the business idea. Pulling her laptop towards her, she opened it up before clicking through to her emails.

'Yes!' Pumping a fist in the air, Kim grinned. Her old boss from Pinnel's had replied to the email she'd sent out yesterday. They would be interested in staying at Berry Grove once she'd got the conference and team-building project up and running. If Pinnel's were definitely interested, then it was a good indicator other corporate companies would be.

Now, all she needed was enough money to complete the extension and to renovate the bedrooms. Even if she just gave them a cursory lick of paint to begin with, it would brighten them up no end.

Poring over the list in her notebook, she cleared her throat and picked up her mobile.

* * *

'Morning.' Striding in with a pile of tile samples, Danny placed them on the table before leaning down and kissing her. 'How's it going?'

'Good. Very good actually. Pinnel's, the company I used to work for, have shown an interest in the conference and team-building mini-breaks and the estate agent should be ringing later to let me know how the third viewing went for that couple I told you about.'

'The couple who wanted to go back again to check the size of the utility room or something bizarre like that?'

'Yep, that's them. So fingers crossed they make an offer.'

'I've got those extra samples you asked for, if you could do with a break from that stuff?'

'Okay, cool. Thanks for bringing them.' Linking her fingers and stretching her hands out in front of her, she rolled her neck from side to side. 'Do you want a coffee?'

'I would love one, please. I'll get it though.'

'No, don't worry. I could do with getting up, I've been hunched over my laptop since Mia left for school.'

'She's really enjoying it there, isn't she? She was telling me yesterday after school about the science experiment they'd been taught. I'd have loved being able to do that kind of stuff as a kid. What year did you say she was in again?'

Standing up, she rolled her shoulders back and switched the kettle on, keeping her eyes fixated on the mugs on the work surface. She cleared her throat. 'I know you would have. You used to enjoy science, didn't you?' Turning around, she forced herself to smile. 'So, you say you've brought the tile samples?'

'Yep, right here.' Scrunching his forehead, he indicated to the pile of tiles next to her laptop and shook his head.

'Brilliant. Thank you. Now I know I'm definitely going ahead with turning the extension into a conference room; it should make it a bit easier to choose.' Turning around, she passed him a mug. 'Here you go.'

'Thank you.' Leaning forward, he kissed her before settling in the chair next to where she had been working.

Sitting down, she pushed her laptop and notebooks out of the way and wrapped her hands around her mug, letting the boiling steam rise to her face. The time for telling Mia and him the truth was fast approaching now that Mia was happy and settled at school. She wanted to speak to Mia first though; it was only fair on her. Staring at the dark brown liquid in her mug, she closed her eyes. She'd already told Mia she would take her to the nature reserve for a picnic on Saturday. She'd tell her then, nice and calmly over a special picnic. Mia would understand why she hadn't told her straight away, why she had let her get to know Danny bit by bit first and why she had given her time to settle in at school before ripping the rug out from underneath her again. She was a mature girl, wiser than her years, she'd understand. She'd forgive her for keeping secrets.

'Hey, are you okay?' Rubbing her on the back, Danny frowned.

Opening her eyes, she smiled. 'Sorry, yes, I'm fine thanks. Just worrying about what the estate agents will say.'

'Try not to worry. There's nothing you can do. You can't change what other people are thinking.'

'No, I know. Right, let's have a look at these tiles then.' Pulling the pile towards her, Kim glanced at Danny. He'd understand too, wouldn't he? He wouldn't have wanted her to rush into making a big disclosure like this. He'd understand that she was only looking out for Mia and that she was putting their daughter's welfare first. Leaning back in her chair, she nodded. As he talked her through the pros and cons of the different tiles, his words washed over her as she tried to suppress the sick feeling churning in the pit of her stomach. She didn't want this to be over; she didn't want to ruin what she had with him.

But it was a chance she had to take. For Mia and Danny's sake.

'So, what do you think?'

'I like those ones.' Pointing to a white tile with black trim, she tried to focus on what he was saying.

'But they're the ones I was telling you about. The ones that would make the room appear smaller than it actually is, due to their size and the trim around them.' Crossing his arms, he looked at her. 'Did you hear a word I said?'

'Yes.' Kim shook herself. 'I'm sorry. I'm listening now. I really am.'

'Umm, I believe you.' Grinning at her, he picked up another tile, repeating what he had told her.

'So these would probably be best then? They're neutral and will go with a neutral colour scheme whilst maximising the light?'

'Ahhh, you listened that time then!' Laughing, he threw his head back.

'I told you I would.' Grinning, she placed her hand over his. 'Thank you.'

'You're very welcome.' Leaning in, he kissed her on the nose. 'I like to satisfy all my customers.'

'Not like this I hope?' Circling her arms around his neck, she laced her fingers behind his head, pulling him towards her. 'How long have you got until you've got to get back?'

'Umm well, I've got to put the order in for your tiles so we can get cracking, but if you don't mind a delay, I can spare a few minutes.'

'Good, because there's a leak I need you to look at in the flat.' Standing up, she held out her hand and waited for him to take it before leading him out of the kitchen.

'I'd best have a look then in case it jeopardises the success of the extension.' Lowering his voice and grinning, he followed her.

'That's what I thought.'

* * *

'That's amazing news. Only two thousand under the asking price, is that right?'

'That's correct, Ms Reynolds. They are currently in rental accommodation so are eager for a quick exchange too.' The estate agent's young voice floated down the phone line.

'As you know, a quick exchange would suit me too. Thank you.' Putting the phone down, Kim jumped up out of her chair. It was sold! The house was finally sold! All being well, she'd have the money to pay the remaining bill on the extension and to renovate the bedrooms within the next couple of months. It should all be complete and the corporate business breaks up and running for the end of the summer season, just as the holiday makers disappeared. There'd be enough money to get them through the summer even if she couldn't drum up more customers than had already booked.

Running into the extension, she picked her way through some tools lying on the ground and looked around for Danny. She knew Dave and the crew had gone to the builders' yard but Danny should be about somewhere. Making her way out onto the patio, she saw him measuring something or other around the side of the extension. 'Danny! Danny, guess what?'

'Hey, what? What's happened?' Standing up, he turned to face her, tape measure in hand.

'My old house has sold! They're living in rented at the moment so want a quick exchange!'

'Wow, that's great news! The utility room was big enough in the end then?'

Laughing, Kim walked towards him. 'I guess it must have been.'

'We should celebrate.'

'Yes, definitely. I've got to go and pick the girls up in a bit but there's nothing stopping us from celebrating with coffee and a slice of cake in the sun.'

17

'Yes, of course. I'll go and get them now.' Smiling at Mrs Thompson, Kim gently closed the door and made her way to the linen closet.

Standing on her tiptoes, she reached up to the top shelf and pulled down two pillows before slipping them into freshly washed pillowcases. Mrs Thompson had apparently been coming here for the past eleven years. Hopefully she'd approve of the modernised bedrooms when they were completed.

Walking back to Room 1, Kim carried a pillow under each arm. Maybe she should keep a few rooms, perhaps the ground floor rooms, in a more traditional style for returning guests like Mrs Thompson. Obviously, she would still modernise them, they needed that as much as the other rooms, but if she weaved more traditional elements into the room design or used more chintzy accessories then she wouldn't end up alienating Berry Grove's loyal, repeat customers.

Knocking on the door, she waited until Mrs Thompson opened up. 'Here you go, Mrs Thompson.'

'Thank you, love. It helps with my aches and pains if I sleep a bit more upright in bed.'

'You're welcome. Is there anything else I can help you with?'

'No, I don't think so, love.' Smiling, she shut the door.

* * *

Placing the key to the linen cupboard back behind the desk, she locked it and made her way towards the kitchen. She could hear Mia talking, her voice dipping and soaring with excitement. She must be on the phone to Tilly. She shrugged. It amazed her how long they could chat for after school after spending the day together. How did they find so much to say to each other?

Tilting her head, she paused. There was another voice floating through the hallway now, a male voice. It was Danny. She checked her watch. What was he still doing here? And why was he talking to Mia?

Slowing down, she stood in the doorway, resting her head against the doorframe. They were both sat down, their elbows on the table, plates in front of them. Watching, she stood as they both picked up a slice of toast from their plates and pulled the crust off, making sure they kept the crust in its perfect square, not pausing for fear of breaking it, before carefully holding it by the edge and eating it. Mia must have made the toast, she never cut the bread, preferring instead to dissect it and save the centre for last.

Shaking her head, she blinked. She had forgotten how Danny had eaten his toast. She remembered now. She remembered how she used to make fun of him for it. How hadn't she ever realised Mia had been eating like him for all of these years? She'd always assumed she'd picked up the habit from someone at nursery or from one of her childminders. Surely the way someone ate couldn't be in the genes? Could even the preference to save the best until last be? She shook her head, laughing at herself under her breath; she most likely had eaten her toast like that when Mia had been smaller. During her toughest times, she used to pull Danny's old hoodie over her clothes and hug herself to sleep, she must have unconsciously eaten her toast in the same way to try to feel closer to him.

'Hey, you okay?'

'Mum! Danny was just suggesting we have a BBQ for my birthday party! What do you think?' Still holding her toast, Mia twisted around and grinned.

'Your birthday? Danny, you know when her birthday is?' Holding her breath, she wiped her hands, clammy from sweat, down the front of her jeans. He knew. Mia had told him her birthday. He knew she was his.

'Yep, the middle of June, isn't that right, Mia?'

'Sure is. The perfect time for a BBQ. Or that's exactly what Danny's just said.'

'So, what do you think, Kim? A BBQ in the sunshine for Mia's birthday?'

'Great idea.' Swallowing, she made her way towards them and slipped into the chair next to Mia. Why did he look so... normal? So calm? He must be brimming with questions, with regret, and maybe even blame. Squinting her eyes, she watched as he spoke to Mia about whether to offer burgers or chops, chicken wings or sausages.

'Of course, we could always throw a mixture on the BBQ, make sure everyone is catered for.'

'Oh yes, that's a good idea because I'm not sure what people would prefer. Oh, but there's this girl in my class, Freya, who is vegetarian. Is there anything that could be cooked on the BBQ for her? Would Quorn sausages work, or would they just burn and taste weird?'

'I should think they'll be fine. We could always do a test run though? Now the weather's so nice, maybe we could arrange to have a BBQ sometime and test out those Quorn sausages? What do you think, Kim?'

Nodding, Kim looked from Mia to Danny and back again. Their cheeks were glowing with excitement as they grinned at her, waiting for her to answer. They both had dimples on the right side; their eyes were a similar green too.

'Mum?'

'Sorry. Yes, good idea.'

'Awesome. I'm just going to get my notebook. Do you know where it is, Mum? You know the one I've started writing my birthday present list in? The purple sparkly one with the lock and fluffy keyring?'

Kim blinked. 'Umm yes, it's on the coffee table. It might be under my magazine so you might have to move something.'

'Okay thanks. Stay here, won't you, Danny? You won't go anywhere, will you? And then we can tell Mum what else you said.'

Danny nodded and gave her the thumbs-up before picking up his next piece of toast.

'Thanks!' Pushing her chair back, Mia jogged out of the room.

Was he going to say something now? Was he going to give her the interrogation she expected? Narrowing her eyes, she watched as he picked apart his toast again.

'Are you okay, Kim?'

She nodded, her eyes fixed on his.

'Are you sure? You don't seem yourself. Have I overstepped the mark by helping Mia come up with ideas for her birthday? It's just she started talking to me about it and I just thought I'd throw some suggestions her way. I can back out if you want? I can make up some excuse to rush off now?'

She cleared her throat. 'No, that wouldn't be fair on you.' He had every right to be a part of her birthday celebrations, especially now.

'Okay.' Frowning at her, his tugged his right earlobe. 'It's just that because it's an important birthday, I thought I'd throw a few suggestions her way.'

'An important birthday?'

'Yes. I remember feeling as though I was truly becoming a teenager when I turned thirteen. It was a big deal.'

Breathing out through her teeth, she laid her hands on the table, palms down. He thought she was going to be thirteen. He hadn't realised. He still didn't know.

'I'm back!' Waltzing into the kitchen, Mia hugged her notebook to her chest.

'You were quick!' Turning around, Kim smiled at her.

'I ran!' Slipping back into her seat, Mia opened her notebook and flipped through to a page already entitled 'Birthday!!!!' in large bubble writing.

Clearing his throat, Danny stood up, his chair scraping against the tiles. 'I'm going to head off now.'

'Oh no, I thought you were going to help me arrange my party?' Looking up at him, Mia frowned, biting down on her pen.

Standing still, he ran his fingers through his hair.

'Yes, why don't you stay? Maybe we could order a pizza or something to properly celebrate our old house being sold?' Smiling at him, Kim nodded.

'A takeaway? You mean we can get a takeaway?'

Looking at Mia, she laughed. 'Yes, a takeaway. Why not? Mrs Thompson is our only guest tonight, and she's already here.'

'Awesome. I'll go and grab a menu. I think there's one by the desk in the hallway.' Grinning, Mia raced out of the room.

'Hey, please don't feel you have to go. I'm sorry if I seemed a bit weird earlier, I just didn't feel right.'

'Are you feeling okay?' Sitting back down, Danny leant forwards and grasped her hands in his.

'Yes, I think I'm just hungry.'

'Are you sure you don't mind me helping Mia out with organising her party?'

'No, no, not at all. Thank you.'

'Okay.' Stroking the back of her hands with the pads of his thumb he whispered to her. 'I love you, Kim Reynolds.'

'Love you too.' Smiling, she tried to push the niggling dread of telling him the truth out of her mind. He would still feel the same about her when he found out about Mia, wouldn't he? It wouldn't change anything, would it? It would make them stronger. It would. Rolling her shoulders back, she bit down on her bottom lip. She knew they wouldn't suddenly become the instant perfect family, she wasn't daft, but it would make them stronger. It would.

* * *

With the pizza ordered, Mia turned her attention back to her notebook. 'Okay, so I've written BBQ down. Oh, Mum, Danny said he's got a karaoke machine he can bring. What do you think? It would be awesome to have a karaoke party, wouldn't it? Do you think my new friends would like it?'

'Karaoke? Yes, I would never have thought of that but I think it's a great idea.'

'Cool. I'll write karaoke down then. It will be awesome, won't it? I mean, like, really awesome. And so funny. Can we get some Hawaiian decorations and have it as a Hawaii themed party too? Can we? You know, like, those flower necklace things and stuff?'

'Yes, okay.' Kim hadn't thrown a party for Mia for years. Scrunching her nose she tried to remember the last party Mia had had. Had she been five? Yes, she had. She had asked for a party for her sixth birthday too, but Kim had been snowed under at work and had said that she'd had a big party for her fifth and invited the whole class so they'd go bowling, just the two of them, to celebrate her turning six. They hadn't gone though, had they? No, she was sure Mia's birthday had fallen on the weekend before a big meeting with a new client and Kim had been stuck in the office. Pinching the bridge of her nose, she realised Mia had spent her sixth birthday with a new babysitter. Kim had only just arrived home in time for bath and bed. Mia hadn't asked for a party the following year, or any year until now.

'Can we get some coconuts or something to decorate the place too? Maybe we could even crack them open and have them after the BBQ? Oh, and some bunting, could we? That would look so pretty, wouldn't it?'

'Yes, it would. We'll get lots of bunting and balloons too. And you can choose your own cake.'

'It's going to be so amazing! And Danny, are you sure you don't mind doing the BBQ?' Mia looked over at Kim before whispering loudly. 'I think Mum would just burn it.'

'Oi! I heard that!'

'I don't mind at all. As long as I can have a go on the karaoke machine, of course.'

Giggling, Mia held her notebook up in front of her face.

* * *

'I can't believe you're still eating pineapple on your pizza!' Laughing, Danny tore another slice from the box and plonked it onto his plate before picking every last piece of pineapple off his pizza, making a neat tower of discarded pineapple chunks.

'There's absolutely nothing wrong with eating pineapple on pizza. When was the last time you tried it? You might find you like it now.' Taking her slice of pizza between her fingers, she held it towards Danny and laughed.

'Yuck! No thanks!' Leaning back in his chair, he pulled a horrified face. 'Everyone knows it's just not right to have fruit cooked on pizza.'

'It's lovely.'

'But, Mum, you wouldn't eat orange or apple on your pizza, would you? You wouldn't ring up and ask for extra orange or strawberries on your pizza!' Mia held her thumb and index finger up to her ear and mouth pretending it was a phone. 'It's just the same with pineapple, it's weird and disgusting.'

'Oi. Don't take sides with him!'

'Yes, do take sides with me.' Winking at Mia, he grinned before turning back to Kim. 'I'm afraid it's two against one. You're not going to win on this one. We...' Pointing between himself and Mia, he grinned. '...obviously have a more sophisticated palate than yours.'

'So, I'm assuming neither of you want any pudding then? I mean, chocolate covered pizza base is hardly sophisticated.'

'Yes, yes, we do!' Laughing, Mia grabbed the box of chocolate pizza and held on to it.

'I think we can just about manage chocolate pizza.' Nodding, Danny grinned before squeezing the last of his pizza slice into his mouth. 'See, sophisticated.'

'Very.' Pausing, Kim lowered her slice of pizza. This is what it should have been like for all those years. Danny, Mia and her joking around and having fun as a family. They were getting on so well, Danny and Mia, and yet they had missed out on so much time together. Narrowing her eyes, she looked at Danny tucking into the chocolate pizza with Mia and felt her eyes welling up. Swallowing, her stomach suddenly felt uncomfortably full, her throat tight, he should have found them. When he had gotten back from traveling, he should have made sure he'd found them. It wouldn't have taken long. Miriam's parents had known where she had moved to. He'd given up at the first hurdle; he had spoken to her parents and given up. She hadn't been in hiding.

'You all right, Kim?'

Momentarily closing her eyes, she shook her head. She wasn't being fair. And yet... Opening her eyes, she looked at him. 'I'm fine. Absolutely fine. Although it is getting quite late...' Pausing, she looked at the clock.

Frowning, Danny cleared his throat before pushing his plate away. 'That's me stuffed. I'd better get off.'

'Oh.' Laying her chocolate pizza back in the box, Mia looked up at Danny.

'See you tomorrow, Mia. Are you going to show me out, Kim?'

'Yes.' Standing up, Kim followed him through the hallway to the front door. As he turned to face her, she forced herself to smile.

'Are you sure everything is okay?' Taking Kim's hands in his, Danny pulled her closer.

'Yes.' She shook her head. 'No, well, yes, but can I ask you something?'

'You can ask me anything, you know that.'

'Why didn't you try harder to find me? When you came back from your travels?'

Blinking, Danny stepped back and ran his hand through his hair. 'What? I did. We spoke about this. Your parents...'

'I know my parents were no help, but why didn't you ask around? Why did you just stop there? If you had really wanted to get back in touch with me, you would have found me.'

'I did ask around. All our old friends just said that you'd disappeared. Left without a forwarding address.'

Kim shook her head, of course they had. They had all been Danny's friends really anyway, and after Miriam had died, she'd kind of been forgotten about. Everyone had distanced themselves from her. Looking back, she knew they had just been nervous, uneasy around her, unsure how to support her while she was grieving, but at the time she'd felt let down, dropped, and so she hadn't bothered contacting them when her parents had kicked her out. 'All you needed to do was to ask Miriam's parents. They knew where I lived.'

'Are we seriously having this conversation? It was years ago. We were both so young. I'd just been travelling, and I wanted more.'

'More than us? So, that's how it was then.'

'No, no, not more than us. Us is all I've ever wanted.'

Stepping back, Kim avoided Danny taking her hand.

'I'd just been to Australia, Thailand, the Philippines. I had the travelling bug. I wanted to travel more. I was young, carefree, with no responsibilities. We both were. And, I guess it just didn't occur to me to ask Miriam's parents. I didn't think you'd have been in contact with them still, not after...' Danny looked down at his shoes.

'Not after Miriam passed away, you mean?'

'Exactly.'

'Well, I was. I still am in contact with them. They're actually coming to visit over Mia's birthday. They've been my rock. They're the only people who stuck by me throughout everything.'

'Look, I'm sorry. I was a kid at the time.'

'And so was I.'

'Exactly. We were kids. We needed to live before we settled down.'

Covering her mouth, a strangled laugh escaped her throat. He had no idea. Literally no idea.

'Look, Kim, what's going on here? What's the point in dragging up the past? Yes, maybe I should have thought about contacting

Miriam's parents to ask where you were, but I had just got back from months away to find that my girlfriend had done a disappearing act and one of my closest friends had been killed in a car crash. I quite possibly wasn't thinking straight.' Turning his back on her, he rubbed his face with the palm of his hand.

What was she actually doing? He hadn't known about Mia. It hadn't been his fault. None of it had. Twisting her hands in front of her, she watched as he turned back to face her, his face pale and his eyes bloodshot. 'I'm sorry, Danny. I don't even know why I brought it all up. I guess I've just been feeling a bit insecure. I mean, if you didn't want me back when we were younger, why would you want me now?'

'Come here.' Stepping forward, he drew Kim into his arms. 'I wanted to be with you back then, but unfortunately, circumstances kept us apart. Yes, we can argue about whose fault it was, mine for not thinking to ask Miriam's parents, yours for not leaving a forwarding address, but that won't change anything apart from make us both feel insecure and rubbish. We just need to leave the past in the past and move forward, be thankful that we've found each other again and enjoy this relationship.'

'That makes sense.' Leaning her head against the warmth of his shoulder, she let herself be pulled in tighter, his arms safe and strong around her. 'Sorry.'

'No need to be sorry, the conversation was bound to come up sooner or later. Let's just enjoy the now.'

'Umm.' Kim let her shoulders relax and smiled. Once she'd told Mia Danny was her father on Saturday, she could break the news to Danny and they could finally be the happy family they should have been. Tipping her head back, she looked up at him. He'd be so happy when he found out Mia was his. He was acting like her father already, helping her plan her party and just the general way he interacted with her.

'Look, I'll let you get some rest now, but how do you fancy going out somewhere tomorrow?'

'Don't you need to work?'

'I've got a couple of sites I need to pop to, but I should be done by eleven if you're free then?'

'Okay, that'd be nice.'

'Great. Oh, I'm hoping the tiles will be delivered tomorrow, so I might be about first thing before I go out to the other sites. Night.' Lifting her chin, Danny kissed her, his lips warm and soft against hers.

'Night.'

Watching as he disappeared around the back of the building to the carpark, Kim slowly closed the door. Why had she even brought all of that up? Why was she trying to jeopardise their relationship when they were this close to being a proper family? Sinking down onto the bottom step, she leant her head against the wall. She should be looking forward to telling Mia the truth about him. And she was. She was, but if she was completely honest with herself there was that small niggle of a doubt in the back of her mind that kept whispering to her. What if Mia wasn't as accepting of the situation as Kim thought she would be? After all, she hadn't asked any questions about her biological father for at least five, maybe six years. What if she had just accepted it was the two of them and that was that?

And Danny. What if he resented the fact that she hadn't told him straight away? What if he didn't understand why she had left it until Mia had settled at school? He would though, she was sure of that. He would understand that she was only putting Mia's feelings first.

One more day and it would all be out in the open. She just had to carry on as normal tomorrow, and then on Saturday she'd take Mia up to the nature reserve and tell her.

18

'Mum, have you seen my homework planner?'

'Have you looked in the living room?' Looking around the flat's small galley kitchen, Kim moved a mountain of Mia's magazines from the kitchen table. 'Found it. It was under your magazines.'

'Thanks. Remember Book Club has been cancelled today, so are you okay picking me and Tilly up at half three?'

'Yes, of course.' Passing Mia her water bottle and break-time snack, she smiled at her. 'I was thinking we could take a picnic over to the nature reserve tomorrow, what do you think?'

'Yes, okay, that sounds nice. Can I invite Tilly?' Stuffing her bottle and bag of crisps into her rucksack, Mia looked up.

'Umm, do you mind if it's just us? I thought it would be nice to spend a bit of time together.'

'Oh, okay. You mean "Mummy and Daughter Time"?'

'That's it, "Mummy and Daughter Time". You can always invite Tilly over in the afternoon, though. Does that sound okay?'

'Okay cool. Sounds good. Can I grab a croissant for breakfast? We haven't got anything up here.'

'Of course you can. There's a couple left over from the breakfasts earlier. They're still on a plate on the work surface, I think. I'll be down in a moment.'

* * *

Sweeping her hair back as she walked downstairs, Kim bundled it up in a messy bun and made her way into the kitchen just as the doorbell rang.

'Mia! That'll be Tilly.' Where was she? She'd obviously had her croissant, or so the crumb-filled plate left on the table suggested. 'Mia!'

'Coming.' Mia walked through from the extension, hoicking her rucksack onto her shoulder as she did.

'Where have you been?'

'Just talking to Danny, that's all. See you later, Mum. Remember there's no Book Club.'

'Right, no Book Club.' What had they been talking about? 'Have a good day.'

'Will do. Bye.'

Ten seconds later the front door slammed shut. Kneeling down, Kim opened the cupboard under the sink and reached towards the back. Feeling around between the pipes and bleach bottles, she pulled out an old tattered tin. Slipping onto a chair, she placed the tin in front of her and ran her hand over the cold metal. She hadn't looked inside it for years. In fact, she had meant to put it in the attic along with all of her old business books and Mia's old school books she couldn't bear to get rid of, but after Mia had pulled it out of a box when they'd moved in, she'd had to pretend it was where she kept a collection of spare nails and screws, which is how it had ended up under the sink.

* * *

Taking a long sip of coffee, she waited until the strong bitter taste hit the roof of her mouth and gently lifted the lid. Slumping back in her chair, she carefully pulled out one thing after the other: old cinema tickets, three beer splattered Glastonbury tickets (their first, and last, festival), a poem Danny had scrawled on the back of a serviette at the greasy café they used to frequent to cure their hangovers after a full night of drinking and dancing, and a line of photo booth photographs, grainy and discoloured compared to the memories that could now be now be snapped.

Spreading them out in front of her, she picked up the photographs, delicately holding them between her fingers, careful not to touch the images grinning back at her. The day they had captured slipped easily into her mind's eye. They had been at the shopping centre, grabbing last minute essentials for Danny's impending travelling trip and, after a wine-soaked lunch, Miriam had dragged them into a squat, white photo booth inside the pharmacy. In the first three photos they had just been goofing around, sticking their tongues out, Danny circling both their necks with his arms and drawing them in closer, pulling the silliest faces they could. Kim smiled before finally letting her eyes settle on the third picture. She remembered that moment so clearly, the overwhelming feeling that life was about to change for the three of them. The next day Danny would be flying off on his adventures, the following week Miriam and Kim would be heading up to Durham to study, marketing for Kim and psychology for Miriam. Or that's what should have happened. In reality, the following week Miriam was dead and Kim had found out she was pregnant with Mia.

Laying the photographs down on the table, Kim pinched the top of her nose before wiping the tears cascading down her cheeks.

'Hey, Kim, do you want to come and see these tiles?'

Covering the spilt memories in front of her with her arms, Kim twisted around just as Danny appeared in the kitchen. 'Sure thing. Just give me a moment and I'll be right there.' Grinning as wide as she could, she watched as he slipped back into the extension before letting her smile fade.

Carefully lifting each precious item, she replaced them back in the tin and snapped the lid shut. She would take these on the picnic. If she could show how happy she had been with Danny, it might help Mia accept the news she was to hear.

* * *

'So, what do you think? Do you still like them?' Holding up a white floor tile boasting a barely visible swirling flower design, he grinned.

'They're beautiful. Really lovely.' Reaching forward, Kim traced her index finger along the design, the flowers looked as though they might be lilies or daffodils. She shook her head, she wasn't a gardener, she had no idea, but they were pretty.

'They are the ones you wanted, right?'

'Umm. Yes.' Avoiding his gaze, she looked behind him at the huge stack of tiles standing in the corner of the extension. Laying all of them would take hours, days, a week even.

'You okay?'

'Of course.' Finally looking him in the eye, she smiled. His whole world was going to change tomorrow and he had no idea. Biting down on her bottom lip, she stopped herself from blurting out the truth. She owed it to Mia to tell her first. 'Why was Mia in here this morning?'

'She came in asking if I was serious about helping her out with her party, but she ended up talking about school.'

'Oh. Is everything okay?' Surely Mia would have confided in her if something was wrong at school?

'Yes, everything's fine. She seems to really be enjoying it, actually. She was telling me about her old school and how things used to be for her though.'

'Right.'

'It sounds awful what she was put through thanks to that little shrimp, Amelia. Some kids can be downright nasty.' Frowning, he shook his head.

Glancing at her shoes, she nodded. It was strange hearing Danny getting so emotional over what had happened to Mia. It was as if he already knew. 'I know.'

'She also told me what you had said to her, what had got her through it all.'

'What had I said?' She hadn't said anything that would have made a jot of difference to the situation. Damn, she hadn't even noticed something had been up until the day she'd taken her out of school. He must have gotten it wrong.

'Yes, she told me how you had always told her that when she had any problems to look up at the night sky and find Orion's Belt and to remember that whatever was happening at the moment was just a tiny stepping-stone on her journey. That it wouldn't last forever and that she had her whole life ahead of her to look forward to.'

'She said that?'

'She sure did. She told me that every time Amelia or her sheep were horrible to her, she'd look up at the sky and imagine Orion's Belt looking down on her. She used to draw the constellation in the back of her exercise books to flick back at in the classroom.'

'Really?'

'Really.' Touching her forearm, Danny's eyes searched hers.

'You remembered and told her what I had told you? You remembered that trick, for all these years?'

Blinking back the tears that were threatening to spill, she frowned. Had he guessed?

'I think it's really sweet that you told your daughter something I'd said to you.'

'Right, yes.' He hadn't guessed. Of course he hadn't. Why would he presume Mia was his just because she had spoken about Orion's Belt? One more day of the lies to get through. Just one more day.

19

'It was so unfair. I mean it was obviously just one person who had stolen the mobile and yet we were all punished. All of us. And, I mean, how do they actually know it was a Year Nine who had taken it? Yes, we were in there last, but the Year Ten's had been in there before us. Maybe they just hadn't noticed it had gone then.' Rolling her eyes, Mia pulled the visor down and smoothed her hair whilst looking in the small mirror.

'I don't know. They must have thought they had proof it was someone in Year Nine though, I should think. Apart from that, how was the rest of your day?'

'It was good, thanks. Art was amazing. We had a supply teacher who taught us how to do this Andy Warhol printing stuff.'

'That sounds fun.' Pulling into the small car park, Kim slowed the car to a stop.

'It was. It really was. Tilly was saying that she'd heard the supply teacher, Ms Hanlope, might actually be taking over from our normal teacher when she goes on maternity leave which would be awesome.' Opening the car door, Mia threw her rucksack over her shoulder.

'Fingers crossed she does then. You go on in and get yourself a snack, I've just got to sort something and then I'll be in.' Smiling, Kim waited until Mia had closed the front door behind her before she slipped out of the car and opened the boot. Pulling a small canvas bag towards her, she opened it. Inside was the tin she had been looking through earlier and a thin photo album holding photographs of her and Danny as teenagers. She would collect the bag on the way to the picnic tomorrow, that way she could show them to Mia once she'd told her Danny was her father. Letting her fingers run over the embossed photo album, she reminded herself that everything would be okay. There was no reason it wouldn't. Mia got on really well with Danny, she'd be so happy to learn that he was her dad.

Closing the boot, she turned her face up towards the sun, letting the warmth from the rays soak into her skin. Life would be perfect. She wasn't sure whether to tell Danny at the weekend or to wait until Monday when Mia had gone back to school. Circling her shoulders, she tried to relieve some of the pent-up tension. She'd probably just go with the flow and see what felt right. See what Mia wanted to do. There was no point worrying about it now.

* * *

Letting herself inside, Kim picked Mia's rucksack up from where she had discarded it on the floor. How many times did she have to remind her that they were now sharing their home with guests who didn't want to have to run an obstacle course every time they went up to their room?

Hanging it on the coat hooks by the bottom of the stairs, she paused. She could hear Mia chattering away excitedly in the kitchen. Surely she wasn't on the phone to Tilly already? They'd only just dropped her off at her house, and she was due to come round to collect Mia before going to the Youth Club in the village later. Rolling her eyes, she remembered how she and Miriam had been the same. Only it had been house phones rather than mobiles which had always annoyed her mum who would fret in case someone had been trying to call or there was a family emergency.

'...and they basically accused one of us of stealing the mobile. There was no suggestion that Mr Flynn may have left it somewhere or lost it. Oh no, they marched us into the hall but they...'

No, no, she wasn't on the phone. Why would she be telling Tilly about the mobile? Tilly had been there. It must be Danny she was talking to. Kim couldn't imagine Mia talking to one of the guests so openly. She must be talking to Danny.

Picking up speed, Kim ran the final few feet to the kitchen.

'...only blamed the Year Nines. They only kept *us* in over lunchtime.'

Pushing the kitchen door open, Kim burst through. 'How is the tiling going?'

Glancing across at her, Danny frowned and looked back at Mia. 'What year did you say you were in?'

'Year Nine. Like I said, they only blamed us. It could have been anyone though, couldn't it? I mean, maybe it was even another teacher, but then, I guess they wouldn't blame another teacher, would they? Oh no, teachers can do no wrong.' Huffing, Mia picked at a crust of paint on her sleeve.

'Year Nine?'

'Yes, exactly, Year Nine. We're old enough to know that stealing is wrong.'

Standing still, her hand on the door handle, Kim watched. She could almost see Danny processing the information, working out what it meant. The colour from his face had disappeared, highlighting his ashen lips and green eyes. He knew.

Sensing the atmosphere changing, Mia looked from Danny to Kim and back again. 'What's up? You agree with me, right? It was completely unfair?'

The shrill tone of the doorbell echoed through the kitchen.

'That'll be Tilly. She said she'd come over straight away so she can help me choose what to wear for Youth Club.'

Nodding, Kim waited until she heard both girls head upstairs before looking across at Danny. 'Danny?'

'She's in Year Nine? I thought she was going to be thirteen?'

Walking towards the table and standing opposite him, she gripped the back of the chair in front of her, her fingertips quickly turning white. 'No.'

'You said...'

'No, I didn't say.'

'You didn't correct me though.' Grasping his hands in front of him, he wound them around and around each other before slumping into the chair in front of him, his hands lying limply in his lap.

'No, I...'

'Is she?'

'What?' Why didn't she just answer him? She couldn't. She couldn't admit what she had kept from him. But she had been going to tell him. Tomorrow, she would have told him.

'Mine? Is she mine?'

Ungrasping her fingers, she pulled out the chair, slid in and lay her hands, palm down on the table in front of her. 'Yes. She's yours.'

Opening his mouth and closing it again, Danny rubbed his hand across his chin.

'Danny, say something.'

'What the hell do you want me to say, Kim?'

The tone of his voice, low and clipped, made Kim jump. He had never spoken to her like that before. 'I... I don't know.'

'I mean, literally, what the hell were you thinking, Kim?' Standing up, he pushed his chair back under the table with such force that the vase in the centre shook violently before somehow steadying itself. 'Were you ever going to tell me? Were you playing with the idea of being happy families, the three of us spending time together, before you decided to tell me or not?'

'No, I...'

The sound of laughter and footsteps floated through the hallway, both Kim and Danny fell silent, the air between them charged and cold.

'I'll be back just gone seven then, Mum, okay?' Mia pushed the door open and stood still looking at them both. 'Everything okay here?'

Clearing her throat, Kim twisted around and smiled. 'Everything's fine. Just a mix-up with the floor tiles, that's all.'

'Oh, okay. Well, I'm sure whatever Danny has chosen will be nice anyway.'

'Yes, you're right. I should think they will be. You have a lovely time then. Is Tilly's mum still okay dropping you off after?'

'Yes, see you.' Turning on her heels, Mia shut the door behind her.

Twisting back around, Kim watched as Danny crossed his arms and set his jaw.

As soon as they heard the front door click shut, Danny looked up. 'More lies?'

'What? About the floor tiles? What would you rather? Would you really want me to break the news to her like that?'

Shaking his head, he laughed, a shallow, hollow laugh which sounded as though it was forced from his throat.

'I was going to tell her. I was going to tell you both. I just wanted her to settle in at school first. She told you about the bullying, didn't she? I needed to let her settle, to be happy. I was going to tell her tomorrow and then I'd have told you. I had it all planned.'

'Sure you did.'

'I did. I swear. I was going to take her to the nature reserve for a picnic tomorrow and tell her then. I've even got all of our old photos and that ready to show her.'

'Right.'

'I was. I promise. I was going to tell her. The only reason I left it was so she could settle into her new life first. So she would feel safe, secure.'

'Even if that's true, even if you had planned to tell her who I was tomorrow, what about me? Why didn't you tell me?'

'She's my daughter. I owed it to her to tell her first.' Wringing her hands in front of her, she stared at Danny. He must understand that, surely?

'But it's been weeks. We've... I thought we had something between us? Was it just to give Mia a family? Did you feel nothing for me? Is it all part of this... I don't know? This lie?'

'What? No. I love you, Danny. You know that.'

'You don't lie to someone that you love. You don't keep it a secret that they've got a daughter. I'm a father, for goodness' sake. A father, and I had no clue. How? Why? Why would you keep it from me?'

'I didn't. I mean, I did, but I was going to tell you this weekend. I swear I was going to tell Mia and then you. It's been killing me, keeping this from you both.'

'Well, that could have been easily been avoided.'

'Look, I was going to tell you. Mia's just been through so so much and I didn't want to just throw this at her. I needed to make sure she was in a better place first, that she would be able to handle it. You've got to see that, surely?'

'I understand why you didn't tell her straight away, of course I do. I'm not a monster.' Pulling the chair out, he slumped down on it again, slamming his elbows onto the tabletop and dropping his head into his hands. 'But why not me? Why couldn't you have told me? I would have understood not to say anything to her. Why did you lie to me?'

'I didn't lie...' Catching Danny's eye, she looked down at her hands. 'I'm sorry. I just, I needed to know what was going on with you first I guess.'

'What do you mean?'

'Well, between us. I needed to know you wanted to be with me for me, not because I was Mia's mum.'

'That's just...' Danny shook his head. 'So you didn't tell her about me? At all? I mean, all these years, you didn't tell her about me? Who her father was? No photos? Nothing?'

'No, I did. In the beginning, when she was really little, I used to tell her about you all the time, but then...' Kim closed her eyes. 'You wouldn't understand.'

'Try me. Please tell me how and why you've kept this from my daughter for all of these years. For her whole life. What? Did you just tell her that her dad didn't want to know her? What did you say?'

'No, of course not. I told her that her dad loved her but just couldn't be with us.'

'How come she hasn't recognised me from photos?'

'I showed her photos when she was little but I haven't for a long time.'

'How long? How long have you kept me a secret from her?'

'It wasn't like that. You're just twisting my words.'

'Tell me then, what was it like?' Laying his hands on the table, he drummed his fingers.

'It wasn't a case of me making a decision to stop talking about you, to stop telling her about you, it just happened. I got into a bad relationship, a really bad relationship, and after that, I guess I just wanted to put men in general out of my head. I threw myself into my work and it just didn't come up again.'

'That literally makes no sense at all, Kim. You had a bad relationship, so you pretended your daughter didn't have a father? Can you actually hear yourself?'

'Danny, please?'

'Don't 'please' me, just help me understand why you kept my very existence a secret from my own daughter because what you've told me makes no sense.'

'I blamed you. Okay? I blamed you!' Pushing her chair back, Kim stood up, the wooden chair slamming against the tiles as it fell behind her. 'I blamed you for my bad relationship. I blamed you for the way my life turned out. Is that what you want to hear? You left me. You went off into the sunset travelling, living your dream while I was left alone.'

'You can't...'

'I was completely alone. Alone. Alone. Alone. I found out I was pregnant in hospital the same day that Miriam had died in my arms. I had lost you, I had lost my best friend in the whole world and then my parents disowned me.' Scrubbing her hand over her face, she sank to the floor. 'I was young. I was petrified and then I let this guy into our lives and... and it went wrong. I couldn't cope, I couldn't. I had to stop thinking about you. I had to stop talking about you.' Sobbing, she tried to catch her breath. 'You left me. You left us. It was you, not me.'

'Kim, Kim, look at me.' Kneeling down beside her, he laid his hand on her shoulder.

Looking up at him, she noticed his face was red, his cheeks glistening with tears. What had she done? She'd made a terrible mistake. She should have put Mia first; she should have forgotten about her feelings and made sure she had kept the memory of Danny part of their lives. She should have carried on talking about him, made sure Mia knew who her father was. 'I'm sorry. I'm so sorry.'

And then he was gone. She watched him grab his jacket from the table, turn on his heels and disappear through the door. Holding her breath, she listened to the hollow tap, tap, tapping on the hall floor as he made his way out. She listened as the front door was shut quietly behind him. He was gone.

Rocking her body forwards and backwards, she drew short breaths in and out, her body shaking and numb. She had done this. She had handled everything badly. She had been wrong, so wrong. She should have told Mia as she was growing up. She should have told him straight away.

'You left me. You didn't come and find me.' Her voice, hoarse and shaky, echoed in the empty kitchen. He hadn't come back for her. He had left her back then and now he had left her again.

Closing her eyes and drawing her knees to her chest, she sobbed. She sobbed for all the mistakes she had made, all the wrong decisions she had believed were right, all the wrong paths she had led her and Mia's lives down. She sobbed for what should have been. She sobbed for what they had missed out on with Danny all those years ago, and she sobbed for what they were missing out on now.

* * *

Hearing the rattle of keys in the front door, Kim pushed herself to sitting and wiped her tear-soaked cheeks. Was it Danny? Had he realised that she hadn't meant to hurt him? Had he come back to them?

'Mum. I'm back.'

Mia. It was Mia. Youth Club must have finished. It was Mia. Gripping hold of the leg of the upturned chair next to her, Kim pulled herself to standing, her legs stiff and cold from lying on the hard tiles. Straightening her back, she took a deep shuddering breath, her throat sore from crying. Quietly lifting the chair, she tucked it back under the table before running her hands through her hair.

Running the tea towel under the cold tap, she patted her face, hoping the chill from the water would soothe her puffy eyes.

'Mum?'

Twisting around, Kim took a deep breath and smiled. 'Did you have a good time? What was it like?'

'Have you been crying?' Balancing her bag on the back of a chair, Mia tilted her head and looked at her.

'What? No, I've just got a bit of a headache, that's all.'

'No, you've been crying. Where's Danny? Have you two been arguing about those floor tiles?'

'Floor tiles? Everything's okay. Honestly, I've just got a headache.'

Frowning, Mia stared at her before shaking her head. 'Okay. It was great actually. There were a couple of other girls from school and we all played pool.'

'That sounds fun.'

'Yes, it was. Are you sure you're okay, Mum? You really do look like you've been crying.'

'I'm fine. I think I just need an early night, that's all. Why don't you go on up and I'll do my checks and be right up.'

'Okay. I love you, Mum.'

'Love you too, Mia.' Standing still, she waited until Mia had gone upstairs before checking the plugs and turning the light off.

In the guest sitting room, Kim switched off the two lamps either side of the fireplace and sank onto the overstuffed sofa. Pulling her mobile from the back pocket of her jeans, she stabbed in Danny's number. Leaning her head back against the cushions, she listened to the empty ringtone. He wasn't going to pick up, was he?

'Danny, please? Please pick up.' Nope, it rang through to voicemail. Resting her chin on her chest, she ended the call. What was the point of leaving a message? He probably wouldn't listen to it, anyway. He would probably delete it as soon as he realised it was from her.

Shaking her head, she gritted her teeth. She had to try. If she left a message, he might ring back. He might. Calling him again, this time she took a deep breath and waited for the familiar voice instructing her to leave a message. 'Danny, I'm sorry. I'm so sorry. I should have told you when I first saw you again. I should have told you the truth. I was just confused. It was such a shock, and I didn't know what to do. Please, please forgive me. Please, Danny, please come back and we can talk about this properly. We can tell Mia together. Please?'

Letting her mobile fall onto the sofa, she caught her breath. She'd ruined it. She'd ruined everything.

20

'Mum?'

'In here.' Spooning baked beans onto the two plates lying on the work surface, Kim turned to face Mr and Mrs Cheringham who were helping themselves to toast and juice on the far table. 'Here you go, two full English breakfasts. Is there anything else I can get you?'

'Just some tomato ketchup if you have any, please?'

'Yes, of course. Sorry, I normally set them on the table.' Reaching into the fridge, Kim grabbed the ketchup and placed it in front of Mr Cheringham. 'I'll let you enjoy your breakfast. If you need anything, please just give me a shout.' Stepping into the hallway, she strode to the desk and routed around in the top drawer for her mobile. She'd hidden from herself there so she couldn't check it every two minutes.

'Mum?'

Jerking her head up, she smiled at Mia. 'Yes?'

'I know we're supposed to be going on this picnic and spending some time together and I want to, I really do, but I was just wondering...'

Pinching the bridge of her nose, Kim looked at Mia, her cheeks were covered in a rosy glow and she was grinning back at her. 'Where is it you want to go instead?'

'Well, the Youth Club are having a BBQ on the beach. I'd said I wasn't going to go because of our picnic, but now Tilly really wants to go and I thought it would be a nice way to get to know everyone.'

'You can go.'

'But, what about our picnic? I feel bad letting you down.'

'You're not letting me down. Come here.' Pulling her in for a hug, Kim breathed in the coconut fragrance of her shampoo. The picnic idea was redundant now anyway. She couldn't very well tell Mia about Danny before he came back to talk, could she? 'You go and have some fun, make new friends. We can have our picnic another time.'

'Are you sure?'

'Of course, I'm sure. That is unless you want to stay here and change Mr and Mrs Cheringham's bedding?'

'Yuck! No, it's okay. I'll go.'

'Have fun and I'll see you later. Ring and let me know what time you'll be back when you know, please?'

'Will do. Love you, Mum.'

'Love you too, Mia.'

Waiting until Mia had closed the front door behind her, Kim looked down at her mobile. Nothing. Not even a text. Nothing.

'Thank you. Breakfast was lovely.'

Looking up, she smiled as Mr and Mrs Cheringham emerged from the kitchen. 'You're very welcome. Have you got any nice plans for today?'

'Yes, we're going to have a stroll on the beach before exploring the castle.'

'Lovely. Have a wonderful day.'

'Thank you.'

'See you later.' As the door clicked shut behind them, Kim turned and leaned her back against the desk before sinking to the floor. Gripping hold of her mobile, she rang Danny's number, holding her breath as the familiar beeps rang through to the voicemail. 'Danny, please let me explain.'

Letting her mobile slip from her fingers to the floor, she leaned her head back against the wooden drawers and closed her eyes. Her body ached from lying on the sofa all night, her eyes stung from the tears she was constantly trying to hold back and her mouth ached from forcing a smile. She could barely think through the fog and pain in her head but at the same time she knew there was no point in trying to sleep, she couldn't escape the thoughts of guilt and stupidity that were tearing through her mind. Why hadn't she told him straight away?

Opening her eyes, she focused on a small crack in the wall by the ceiling in the far corner. What actually gave him the right to take the moral high ground? If he had tried properly to find her all those years ago or returned her phone calls or letters, then he would have known about Mia from the very beginning. It wasn't as though she hadn't tried to tell him; she had.

As she picked up her mobile again, she could feel her muscles tensing. How dare he lay all the blame with her? Pressing his name, she waited until the wishy-washy voice instructed her to leave a message. 'Actually Danny, you have absolutely no right to blame me for everything. The way that you spoke to me yesterday and the way you're completely ignoring me today is completely unfair. Do you really think I didn't try to tell you when I found out I was pregnant? I did. I left messages with your sister asking her to get you to call me, I wrote letters and letters and sent them to the last address I had for you. I tried everything. Short of getting on a plane and flying out to find you, there was nothing else I could have done. So please…'

'If you wish to re-record your voicemail, please press one…'

Damn phone. Who decided on the length of time to give someone to leave a message anyway? Signing off from the call and ringing him again, she took a deep breath. 'So please, if you think you're the one who has been wronged or hard done by, just remember that it was me, me, who was left to bring up our daughter for all of those years alone, without any acknowledgement from you whatsoever. So, if anyone should be feeling pissed off right now, it should be me!' Ending the call, she threw her mobile across the floor and watched as it bounced, coming to a rest face down on the stone tiles. She shrugged, she'd be lucky if it hadn't completely smashed, even with the so-called indestructible case on, the hard tiles must surely have won.

Leaning back against the desk and clenching her hands into fists, she told herself she would not cry. Why would he just not pick up? Or ring back? She had been going to tell him. Tell them both. He had no right to act like he was.

Pulling herself to standing, she picked up her mobile, running her finger across the newly acquired crack in the right-hand corner of the screen. Wandering through to the kitchen, she switched the kettle on. If she couldn't sleep, she would need caffeine to get through the day's chores.

Walking through to the extension, she went to the stack of tiles and ran her hand over the blue cardboard boxes balanced on top of one another. At least he would be back. He'd have to come back on Monday. He'd said something about some checks he had to do on the floor before the tiles were laid. He'd be there on Monday. Maybe she should just leave him be over the weekend. Let him cool off. He was bound to come round to her way of thinking and understand why she hadn't said anything straight away. He'd realise that she'd tried her best to contact him all those years ago.

Everything would be okay between them, and then they'd be able to tell Mia. It was only a matter of time.

He'd even left his clipboard. Picking it up from the window ledge, she smoothed the front page down. Replacing it, she turned around and headed back to the kitchen. She'd speak to him again on Monday. She'd make him understand.

21

'Just go and knock.' Tapping the steering wheel, Kim looked across at Mia sitting in the passenger seat.

'But we're early. Tilly doesn't normally pick me up until later. She probably won't even be ready yet.'

'But she might be. Plus, if you go and knock she's bound to hurry a little.'

'Mum, seriously? We're fifteen minutes early. Why did you even want to leave early? We'll be waiting around for ages outside school if we go now.'

'No, you won't. You can go into the canteen. They open the doors at half past eight anyway.'

'I know, but no one gets there early.'

'Please, Mia? Just this once. I need to get back in time for something.'

'For what? You've already done the breakfasts for this morning. You made sure people booked in early when you knew you had to take us.'

'I've just got someone coming to look at the extension, that's all.' It wasn't a lie, was it? Danny dealt with the extension.

'Who? Danny? Why didn't he pop in over the weekend? He's been spending so much time round ours recently, and then nothing? Have you two fallen out or something?' Looking at her mum out of the corner of her eye, Mia frowned.

'We're not joined at the hip, you know.'

'I know, but you were both acting weird before I went out on Friday, and then he's not been round.' Mia shrugged. 'I just thought… Everything's okay though, right?'

'Everything's always okay. Now, are you going to go and knock, or shall I?' Unfastening her seatbelt, Kim placed her hand on the door.

'I will. I'll go and knock. It's embarrassing enough getting here so early without you going to hurry her up.'

'Thank you.' She watched as Mia walked up the short garden path towards Tilly's cottage. Hurry up, hurry up. Come on, Tilly, please be ready. Looking across at the small digital clock on the dashboard, it blinked from one minute to the next. Looking back up, Mia must have gone inside. How long did it take to put some shoes on? She needed to get back to Berry Grove. She couldn't risk missing Danny.

'Morning, Tilly. Right, jump in, let's get going.' Turning the key, she let the engine tick over as rucksacks were piled in and seatbelts clicked on.

'Morning.'

'Right, off we go. Have you two got anything nice happening at school today?' Twisting her head, she pulled out into the road.

'Not really. I just hope the Mrs Silverman's going to apologise for keeping us in all lunchtime on Friday.' Turning to look at Tilly, Mia bit her bottom lip. 'You don't think they'll keep us in again this lunchtime, do you? Because no one owned up, did they?'

'I'm sure they won't.' She hoped the head teacher had her mobile stolen. If it hadn't been for her keeping the Year Nine's in at lunchtime, none of this would have happened. Danny wouldn't have found out like he had. She would have taken Mia on that picnic and told her that Danny was her father, and then she would have told Danny and he would have accepted it. Gripping the steering wheel, her fingertips began to turn white. She couldn't miss Danny. She had to speak to him today.

* * *

'Bye then, girls. Have a great day and make sure you go into the canteen. I don't want you standing out here alone.' Rubbing the back of her neck, she watched as Mia and Tilly slowly made their way in through the school gates before she started the engine and began the journey home.

Opening the side windows, she turned the radio up to full blast, trying to drown out the 'what if's' floating around her mind.

'It will all be fine. It will all be fine.' Even just repeating the mantra over and over again seemed to calm her nerves. And it would. It would all be fine.

* * *

Spooning another heap of coffee into her mug, Kim watched as it dissolved in the boiling water, turning it an even darker shade of brown. Taking it to the table, she slumped into the chair and pulled the mug closer. Wrapping her hands around the blue ceramic, she bent her head low, breathing in the strong aroma.

He hadn't shown up yet. The breakfast dishes had been tidied, the beds changed, the bathrooms cleaned, and he still hadn't turned up. She'd been careful to pop back downstairs and check he wasn't here every few minutes but, no, nothing. Dave, Barry, and John hadn't even turned up yet.

Lifting the mug to her mouth, she let the burning liquid scorch her lips as she sipped. Drawing her notebook closer, she doodled along the margin, swirling circles and jagged triangles. She should be trying to organise day trips and experiences for the corporate team-building exercises, but she just couldn't focus. Even with the realisation that she needed to get the ball rolling and that she should already be taking bookings for after the summer season, she just couldn't concentrate. Nothing mattered more now than her family.

Tilting her head, she lowered her pen to the table; she could hear voices. One was Danny's, she recognised that, but the other she was sure she hadn't heard before. The deep smooth voice floated through from the extension again. It definitely wasn't Dave or any of the other builders. Who could it be and why would Danny have brought them here?

Standing up, she pushed her chair back and watched as her mug juddered with the force, a stream of coffee poured from the rim, leaving a pool of murky, brown liquid at its base. What if it was a solicitor? Was Danny going to try to get custody? Could he do that being as he had only just found out he was her dad? What about Mia? She wouldn't be able to deal with something like that. Not going through the courts and everything. And what if he won? Would they really just take Mia away from all she had known?

She was being daft. She was. This was Danny. Her kind, passionate, thoughtful Danny. He may be annoyed with her, but he would never do something like that. He would never hurt her, or Mia, intentionally. There must be another explanation. There must be.

They were coming. Their footsteps heavy on the concrete of the extension, on the tiles in the utility area. She'd find out now. She'd find out who he was talking to.

A man, tall and bearded, dressed in a deep blue suit entered the kitchen carrying an almost identical clipboard to Danny's. Danny, a step behind, came through next.

'Danny...'

'Ms Reynolds, this is Mr Charles. He will be overseeing the building work on your extension from now on.' His voice, low and firm, was purposeful and professional, no hint of anything else.

'Pleased to meet you, Ms Reynolds.' Leaning across the table, Mr Charles stuck his hand out towards her.

Looking from Danny to Mr Charles and back again, she took his hand, allowing him to envelop hers, his handshake a strong and heavy grip. 'Hello.'

'I'm sorry, would you mind if I were completely unprofessional and asked to use your cloakroom? I fear I've had too many coffees this morning.' Laughing at himself, Mr Charles grinned and laid his clipboard on the table.

'Of course. It's just down the hallway. Near the front door.'

'Thank you.'

Kim watched as he strode out of the kitchen before turning to Danny. 'What's going on?'

'I need to take some time off. Elliott, will do a good job. He'll get the extension finished.'

'I don't want him here. I want you here. You can't just run away from this, you know. Did you get my messages?'

'Yes, thank you. I did. Not that I can say I agree with what you said.' Shuffling his feet, he looked down at his clipboard.

'Just let me explain. Maybe we could go for lunch or just stay for a coffee and I'll explain everything. I'll tell you what happened. You'll understand.' Striding towards the kettle, Kim switched it on before taking a mug from the cupboard above.

'Kim. I don't think I'll ever understand why you kept the fact that I had a daughter from me.'

The stilted, cold way he spoke made her pause, and she carefully placed the mug back in its place. 'I tried. I tried so hard to contact you.'

'Clearly not hard enough.'

'Danny, please? Danny, I love you. Don't do this.' Walking towards him, she placed her hand on his forearm.

Clearing his throat, he looked up as Elliott returned from the toilet and stepped back, forcing her to remove her hand. 'Right, well, I'll be off then Elliott.'

'Righto. I just had a quick question about the tiles before you go, if that's all right?'

'Lead the way.' Waiting until Elliott had made his way back into the extension, Danny stood still and looked at Kim before turning on his heels and leaving her.

Covering her face with her hands, she tried to steady her breathing, tried to slow the battering of her heart. Was that it? Was that really the end for them, for their family? What about Mia? Was he really not bothered about seeing her, about telling her who he really was? He must be. Her old Danny would have been. He would have taken fatherhood seriously. He wouldn't have just walked out on them.

* * *

Pouring the pasta into the sieve, Kim watched the misty water stream out and hit the bottom of the sink. Blinking as the steam hit her face, she couldn't believe a week had passed since Danny had found out the truth. Four days had gone since she had seen him last.

'Mum, did I tell you that Tilly has already bought my birthday present?' Looking up from her mobile, Mia took a sip of her orange juice.

'No, you didn't. Wow, I wonder what it is. Has she told you yet?'

Placing the pasta back in the saucepan, she took a jar of carbonara, twisted it open and covered the pasta.

'No, she's refusing to.'

'Oh well, at least it will be a nice surprise for you on your birthday.'

'I know, but still...'

'It will go quickly. It'll be your birthday before you know it.'

'It's only two weeks and then I'll be fourteen. Can you actually believe it? I'll soon be as old as you.'

'Oi, you!' Laughing, Kim turned to face Mia and placed a bowl of carbonara in front of her.

'Will Danny be doing my BBQ and helping with the party still?'

Pausing, Kim slowly picked up her bowl and rummaged in the cutlery drawer. 'I don't think so, no.'

'Oh.' Placing her mobile down, Mia pulled her bowl closer to her.

'Don't worry. I can sort your party out.' Slipping into the chair opposite, Kim passed Mia a fork.

'Not all of it. Danny was going to bring his karaoke machine and sort the BBQ.'

'I can do it.' Reaching across the table, Kim took Mia's hand. 'Granny and Grandpa Epin are coming to stay too, so they'll help.'

'Are they? Cool, I haven't seen them for months.'

'I know. They've been wanting to come and stay ever since we moved, but they've been sorting things with their house and redecorating.'

'That's okay then. Grandpa can sort the BBQ, can't he? He always does BBQs in the summer for us.'

'Exactly. It will be great.'

'I guess we don't need karaoke, do we? We can just chat and

things anyway.' Forking a piece of pasta, she scraped it off on the side of her bowl.

'No, you don't need karaoke. You're a group of teenagers. All you'll be doing is talking anyway, but I can pick up a karaoke machine if you like?'

'No, it's cool. Are we going to decorate the garden like Danny said?'

'Yes, yes, we will. Just let me know what you'd planned and I'll get the bits.'

'Okay, thanks. I'll run and get my notebook and we can go through it all.' Pushing her chair back, Mia stood up.

'Eat your dinner...' Too late, Mia was already out of the room. Why did she feel as though she'd let her down? It had been Danny who had promised her everything and then ran off, so why did she feel like this? Stirring her pasta, Kim promised herself that she'd make this the best party she could. She could do just as well, if not better, than what Danny had promised her. She would not let her down. Not again.

22

'Are you sure they're straight?'

'Yes, I'm sure. Now hop down before you fall.' Eric held his hand up to her.

'Thanks.' Holding Eric's hand, Kim stepped down from the bench and surveyed her work. The pale pink and green bunting strung across the gondola looked really good. Mia had a good eye for design. She hadn't wanted balloons or streamers in the end, worrying that they would look too childish, and so had chosen a mixture of pastel-coloured bunting and pompoms to decorate the patio. 'Thanks again for all your help getting this ready.'

'You're most welcome. You know it brings both me and Diane great comfort being a part of yours and Mia's lives.' Looking at the floor, Eric shook his head. 'I know I've told you this before, but I really don't think Diane would still be with us if you hadn't shown up on our doorstep all those years ago. You and Mia gave her something to live for again. You two are the ones that helped us, not the other way around.'

'I miss her. Really miss her.'

'I know you do, love. We all miss her. She'd be proud of what you'd accomplished though. Miriam would have loved the thought of you running a Bed and Breakfast. You'd have done well not to let her move in with you.'

Kim smiled. 'She would have done, wouldn't she? I'd have been more than happy to have her live here. We could have run the place together.' Wiping her eyes with the sleeve of her jumper, Kim could just imagine what life with Miriam living with them would have been like. Wine would have flowed freely day and night and the place would have been covered in flowers. It would have been wonderful.

'Hey, you're doing a good job. More than good, a great job here. And your friend will be back. Just give him time.'

'Danny? He won't ever forgive me. He thinks I kept Mia a secret from him on purpose.'

'Have faith. Things will work out. Now, I need to go and start that BBQ. Why don't you go and get yourself and Diane a nice cuppa and have a rest before the crowds of young people get here?'

Nodding, Kim watched as he hobbled across the garden to the BBQ. She literally didn't know where she would be now if it hadn't been for them taking her in and treating her as one of the family. But he was wrong, and she didn't like to think that of Eric, but this once, he was wrong, Danny wouldn't be back. She could feel it. She had well and truly messed it up with him. Completely.

* * *

'Here you go.' Placing a mug of tea on the table, Kim smiled at Diane. 'It's so great to have you both here.'

'It's wonderful to be here, love. I'm just sorry it's so overdue.' Placing the last of the plates away, Diane closed the dishwasher door and sat down at the table.

'Right, that's the BBQ set up. I just need to light the thing now. Have you got any matches, Kim?'

'Alright, love?' Diane tipped her head back as Eric leaned down to kiss her forehead.

'Never better. Nothing like a good BBQ to look forward to.'

'Yes, I think they're in here.' Opening the cupboard above the kettle, Kim pulled out a small box of matches. 'Do you want a coffee too?'

'Oh, that sounds like a plan. Thanks, love.'

Pouring the water, Kim smiled to herself. Mia was going to have a great time today, despite Danny letting them down. 'Here you go, Eric, one coffee and a box of matches.'

'Thanks, love.'

'Eric, why don't you sit down for two minutes and we can tell Kim our good news.' Diane patted the chair beside her.

'Now? I thought we were going to wait until after the party?'

Diane shrugged. 'Let's tell her now. Kim, sit down, love.'

Sliding into the chair opposite, Kim sipped her coffee.

'We've put the house on the market. We're moving down this way, if you don't mind us cramping your style, that is.'

'What? Seriously?' Placing her coffee mug down, Kim looked from Diane to Eric and back again.

'Yes, seriously. The house has got a couple of second viewings this week coming and we've lined up a couple of places to view while we're here. Diane has always wanted to live by the coast and when you moved down here, we didn't have any excuses left to stay where we were.' Patting the back of Diane's hand, Eric smiled sadly.

'Wow, that's great news.' Looking at Diane, Kim could see what a hard decision it must have been. They still had Miriam's room set up the way it had been left that day.

'It's what Miriam would have wanted for us. Can you imagine what she'd have said if we didn't take this opportunity?'

'Exactly. And it will be wonderful to be able to be a proper part of yours and Mia's lives again.' Eric smiled and drank some coffee.

'That will be amazing. If you need any help with anything, just let me know.' Kim wrapped her hands around her mug. It really would be lovely to have them closer. 'Mia will be so excited.'

'Excited for what?' Mia and Tilly came into the kitchen, giggling and holding armfuls of clothes.

Twisting around in her seat, Diane smiled at her. 'We're moving down here, Mia, love.'

'Really? That's awesome! It'll be great you guys being here. We can go for picnics at the nature reserve and go to the beach together.' Leaning down, Mia hugged Diane and Eric in turn before straightening back up. 'Hey, Mum, we could even all have Christmas dinner on the beach! You know, like they do in Australia? Grandpa, you could do a BBQ on the beach!'

Eric chuckled. 'We'll see what the weather's like for that, shall we?'

'Awesome!'

'What have you girls got there then?' Pointing at the clothes now heaped on the table, Eric grinned. 'Going camping, are you?'

'I'm trying to decide what to wear for my party. What do you guys think?' Picking top after top from the heap on the table, Mia shook them out and held them up in front of her.

'Which do you like best?'

'Well, I like the blue one and this frilly one best. What do you guys think?'

'Ooh, I think the frilly one is lovely, but they're both nice.'

'Okay cool, I'll wear that one then. Come on, Tilly, let's go and get ready.' Clutching her chosen top, Mia headed towards the hallway.

'Mia, take these up with you, please? Remember, we're trying to keep it tidy for your party.'

'Okay, Mum.' Bundling the pile of clothes in her arms, Mia grinned at Diane and Eric. 'It's epic you're moving down here!'

'We think it's pretty epic too.' Eric retorted and laughed before pushing himself to standing. 'Right, I'm going to start the BBQ now. Make sure it's hot enough to start cooking when all those wayward teenagers start arriving.'

'Thanks, Eric. I'd best get on, too. I've still got to finish making the punch and get the nibbles ready.'

'The punch is done and in the fridge, and I'll help you with the nibbles in a moment. First though, sit back down and finish your coffee. You don't look as though you got much sleep last night.'

'Thanks.' Kim slumped back in the chair and pinched the bridge of her nose. 'I think I barely got two hours last night.'

'I thought as much. Now, is it everything that's happened between you and Danny that's playing on your mind?'

'How did you guess?' She smiled across at Diane. She'd always had a knack for knowing what was wrong.

'It doesn't take a genius to work out what's troubling you.'

'I just feel so guilty about it all.'

'Guilty? What have you got to feel guilty about?'

'Well, that I've taken away the final chance Mia had of meeting and getting to know her dad.'

'You didn't do that. You didn't tell him to disappear on you both.'

'I know, but I could and should have handled it all better. I should have told him as soon as I saw him here. I shouldn't have left it. Hey, maybe there *was* something I could have done to get news to him when I was pregnant with her.'

'You tried. You sent messages asking him to get in contact through his sister and you sent letters to the last address he'd given you. What else could you have done? He was travelling around the world, it wasn't as if you could have just jumped on a plane, and even if you had, you had no idea of his whereabouts.'

'I know, but I still can't help thinking there was something else I could have done.'

'No, there really wasn't, love. It wasn't your fault he didn't reply to your messages.'

'Did I tell you he tried to find me when he got back?'

'No, you didn't.'

'He called in at my parents and asked where I was. They told him they didn't know. Plus, he said he carried on sending letters to my parents' place. They must have known who had sent them and they didn't send them on.'

'That's tough, love, but it's not your fault.' Diane shrugged. 'It's not really their fault either. They had all these plans for your future and were probably in shock from the pregnancy news. I'm sure they regret what happened now.'

'Maybe, but it still doesn't excuse how they treated me and how they behaved.'

'Shock does funny things to you, remember.'

'I know, but I'd never turn Mia away, whatever happened or whatever she did.' Leaning her elbow on the table, Kim rested her head on her hand.

'We all react differently. Have you thought any more about trying to get in contact with them?'

Kim squirmed in her seat. Ever since Diane had suggested it last Christmas, she had thought about it. Maybe they did deserve a second chance. Kim frowned, nothing would make up for how she had been treated, but maybe it was time to try to build some bridges. 'I have. Maybe when things have settled here, I will.'

'Good. I'm glad you're thinking about it. Now, back to Danny, give him time and I'm sure he'll get in contact again. It must have been such a surprise for him to find out he had a daughter, and a teenage daughter at that.'

Kim nodded. She knew Diane was right. Danny would probably ring her at some point, even if it was just to say he didn't want anything else to do with them but still… 'I just miss him being around. When we moved, and he was here it was lovely, we just sort of picked up from where we left off. I just thought it was meant to be, you know? And, now, I've lost him all over again.'

'Oh, love. Give him time. You don't know what the future holds.'

'I guess.'

'That sounds as though Mia and Tilly are coming back downstairs, although the amount of noise they make, you'd have thought it was a herd of elephants!' Diane tilted her head to the side, listening. 'Now, finish your coffee and put your game face on. Today is going to be a happy day.'

Kim nodded, drained her mug, and grinned. Today *would* be a happy day. All thoughts of Danny could wait. Today was Mia's day, and she was damn sure she'd make it a good one for her.

23

'She's having a great time, isn't she?' Eric sidled up to where Kim and Diane were perching on a wall to the side of the patio, close enough to keep an eye on the party but far enough away to 'not be embarrassing' as Mia had worried.

'She certainly is. You've done a good job organising this, Kim.'

'To be honest, it was Mia and Danny who came up with the idea.'

'It's you who's pulled it together though.'

Kim smiled and watched Mia and her friends laugh and joke as they tucked into their burgers and hot dogs. Mia was the centre of attention and seemed to be revelling in it. Watching the way she interacted with her new group of friends was a stark contrast to how she had behaved with people she had known from her old school. 'I'm just so relieved she's happy again.'

'Ay, definitely. She's like a different girl.' Eric drank from his can of cola.

'I say this every time I see you, but I'll say it again, you've done a marvellous job bringing her up, love.' Diane patted her on the knee.

'Umm, I'm not sure about that, but I'm determined things are going to be good from now on.' She laughed as Mia turned up the music and encouraged others to join her in dancing under the gondola.

'Kim?'

Jerking her head around, Kim steadied herself on the low wall as she came face to face with Danny.

'Sorry, I didn't mean to startle you. I saw the side gate was open and...'

'Hello, Danny, love. Good to see you after all these years.' Eric turned and slapped him on the back, drawing him in for a hug.

'Eric? Diane?' Looking from Eric to Diane and back again, Danny's cheeks flushed a pale crimson.

'That's right, love. You've grown a bit since I last saw you.' Diane smiled before turning back to Kim. 'We'd best go and sort the desserts out. Come on, Eric.'

'You came back.' Looking up at Danny, Kim watched as he switched his attention to her.

'I came to see how the party was going?' Standing still, he looked down at her.

'Of course.' Wrapping her hands around her icy glass of lemonade, Kim watched the teenagers dancing and giggling in front of them. 'Mia seems to be enjoying it.'

'You didn't get a karaoke machine?'

'No, but she said it was fine.'

'Sorry.'

Looking up at him, Kim saw his jaw clench.

'For not getting the karaoke machine, I mean.' Danny cleared his throat.

'Right. Like I said, she was happy enough.'

'Good.'

'Danny!' Having spotted him, Mia pulled away from the group and skipped across the patio. 'You came!'

'Happy birthday, Mia.' Pulling a small present and card from behind his back, he passed it to her.

'Oh wow! Thank you!' Taking the present, Mia tore the pink wrapping paper off to reveal a small fluffy blue photo album. 'Thank you. It's great.'

'I thought you could put photos from your party in it.'

'Ooh, good idea. Thank you, Danny.'

'You're welcome, there's a voucher in the card too.'

Opening the card, Mia pulled out a voucher. 'One hundred pounds! For Top Fashion! Wow, that's awesome. Thank you!' Leaning forward, Mia hugged him before running back to show her friends.

'That was very generous. Thank you.'

'It's not really, is it? It's not nearly enough to make up for all the lost years.'

'I guess not.' Biting down on her bottom lip, Kim watched as the voucher was passed around Mia's friends, gasps of delight and hidden envy flowing through the group. 'Are you…'

'You still haven't told her then.' It was a statement, not a question.

'I… I didn't want to spoil her birthday.' She'd used the wrong word. 'Not spoil it. I didn't mean that, but I just wanted her to be able to enjoy her birthday without any worries.'

'So when is a "good time"?' Using his index fingers, he wrapped his words around quotation marks, the sarcasm rolling off his tongue.

'I don't know.' Closing her eyes, she took a deep breath. 'I'll tell her tomorrow.'

'Right. Sure.'

'I will.' She watched as Mia pocketed the voucher and began dancing with her friends again, jumping up and down to some band Kim hadn't heard of before. 'I promise.'

'Thanks.' Nodding, Danny ran his fingers through his hair. 'Look, I still don't know what to think.'

Kim nodded. 'I did try to contact you as soon as I found out I was pregnant. I really did.'

'I believe you.' Keeping his eyes facing forward and a polite smile etched on his face, he spoke so quietly Kim had to lean towards him to hear. 'What I don't understand though, is why you never tried to contact me again at any point during the following fourteen years.'

Taking his lead and keeping her voice low and her eyes forward, she blinked back the tears threatening to spill. 'I picked up the phone and wrote numerous letters addressed to your parents' house. I just didn't have the courage to send them. I figured that if you had actually decided to return to England, you would have started a new life, got married, probably had kids even, and if I had then dropped a bombshell like that on you it would have made things difficult for you. I guess I was trying to do the right thing.'

'Don't you think that should have been my decision to make? That I had a right to know I had a child out there?'

'Yes, I do, but I was young. I didn't know what to think.'

'You grew up though. What about then?'

'I guess, I thought the time had gone. I mean, how was I supposed to have told you about her when she was already four, seven, ten? And, plus, life kind of got in the way. We were used to it being the two of us. I was busy at work, running a home, looking after Mia. It kind of went to the back of my mind.'

'Telling your daughter's father she existed "went to the back of your mind"?' Smirking, he shook his head.

'No, yes, yes it did. I know how awful and shallow that sounds…'

'You do? That's a relief.'

'…but it did. We got on with life. You got on with your life too.'

'I didn't know about her! You can hardly blame me for getting on with my life! Unless you're still annoyed with me for not finding you when I got back? That's it, isn't it? You didn't contact me to tell me about Mia because you thought I should have found you first.' Shaking his head, he narrowed his eyes.

Taking a short intake of breath, Kim pushed her hands against the wall and stood up. Dipping her head down, she made her way through the crowds of giggling teenagers and pushed her way into the house.

Running upstairs, she ignored Diane's calls and shut the door firmly behind her as she entered the flat. Sinking down to the floor and leaning her head against the cool wood, she closed her eyes. She didn't recognise this Danny. Her Danny would never have even thought a thing like that, let alone voiced it.

She didn't blame him. Not really. How could she? It did sound shallow – her getting on with her life and 'forgetting' to track him down to tell him he had a daughter. But what had she supposed to have done? Continually try to ring him? They hadn't had mobiles back then so was she supposed to have stalked his parents' house? That would have gone down well, wouldn't it? Yes, she supposed she could have, maybe should have, told his parents that she had been pregnant and asked them to get a message to him, but she had been young, scared. Her university plans had been thrown up into the air, she had been kicked out of her home and, above everything else, her best friend had died. She had been grieving. She hadn't been thinking straight, not then, and probably if she was honest for a long time after giving birth. It hadn't even occurred to her to break the news to Danny's parents and not him.

Shaking her head and digging her nails into the palms of her hands, she reminded herself that she had done what she had thought was right for Mia at the time. Yes, maybe she should have handled things differently, but it was in the past. However angry Danny was at her, however she felt about her past mistakes, that's what it was, the past, and they now had to find a way to move forward. Together. However that may be.

'Kim, love. It's time for the cake.' Diane's voice floated through the thin wood as she gently tapped the door. 'Are you there, Kim?'

Taking a deep breath in, Kim wiped her eyes and stood up. Opening the door, she forced a smile.

'Oh, Kim, love. Was it that bad?' Holding out her arms, she waited until Kim stepped towards her before wrapping her arms around her. 'He'll come round, love. As I said, it's a big shock he's had. He just needs a bit of time to process it all, that's all.'

'I don't think he will. He's never going to forgive me for not telling him about Mia.' Laying her head on Diane's warm, familiar shoulder, she relaxed into the hug. 'I don't blame him either. I don't blame him for feeling and acting the way he is. It *is* my fault. I should have tried harder to find him.'

'Hey, now you listen to me.' Gently pushing Kim away from her, she looked her in the eyes. 'This is not your fault. Yes, it's not the best of circumstances to be in, but you didn't make it this way. You did try to find him. Do you remember that day Eric drove you up to his parents' house? You sat there all day until someone finally got home and it was a complete stranger. They had moved.'

'I remember, you made us a picnic, and we each had a flask of tea.'

'That's right. Have you told him that?'

'No, he wouldn't listen to me. He probably wouldn't even believe me.'

'Well, make him. You did what you could, and when you couldn't find him, you raised his child. You couldn't have done anything else. Mia had to be your priority.'

'He doesn't see it that way. He doesn't understand.'

'Well, maybe you need to make him understand. Maybe you need to tell him what it was like for you back then, what you went through to have Mia and to raise her into the wonderful young lady she is today. Now, go and freshen up and come and do the cake.'

'Thanks.' She watched as Diane turned on her heels and made her way back down the stairs before going into the bathroom.

Splashing water on her face, she let the cold liquid cool her flushed cheeks. Patting herself dry, she breathed in the familiar cherry blossom and sweet pea fragrance of their fabric conditioner and looked in the mirror. Replacing the towel, she traced the deep dark circles under her eyes with her finger. How had her life turned out like this? She'd gone from successful career woman in control of her life, or at least thinking she was, to someone desperately trying to build a guest base for a failing Bed and Breakfast and, more importantly, trying to protect her daughter from a truth she knew she had to tell.

How would Mia react? She'd never had a father figure in her life. Would she be pleased? Or would she find it all too overwhelming?

Kim dotted foundation across her nose and cheeks before rubbing it in. Mia liked Danny, liked him a lot, she'd be fine. She'd probably love the idea of having her father in her life. She'd find out tomorrow anyway.

* * *

'Happy birthday to you, happy birthday to you...' Kim shifted the cake tray in her arms as she walked towards Mia who was standing expectantly on the patio, her friends swarming in a group around her, everyone singing at the top of their voices. '... happy birthday dear Mia, happy birthday to you!'

Dipping her head down and holding her hair back with her left hand, Mia blew the silver and black stripy candles out, their flames disappearing as a raucous cheer rang through the garden.

'Make a wish! Make a wish!' Tilly clapped her hands in time to her chanting, looking around and grinning as the other teenagers joined in.

'Okay, okay, I know what I'm going to wish for.' Holding up her hand to silence her friends, Mia looked across to Kim and then to Danny who was stood at the back of the small gathering and closed her eyes. 'Okay, done. Who's for cake?'

Standing there counting the waving hands of the teenagers desperate for cake, Kim tried to keep her eyes focused on the task rather than be pulled towards Danny who was stood opposite, his arms crossed and a fake smile on his face.

'Hey, don't worry counting, love. We'll cut it all up and bring it out on a plate. Those who don't want any, don't have to take it.' Placing her hand on Kim's forearm, Diane gently turned her towards the door.

* * *

'Damn, I've only cut it into sixteen.' Holding the knife above the cake, Kim tried to steady her shaking hand. This was supposed to be a good day. A day to celebrate not only Mia's birthday but also to celebrate their new life, the new life that had given Mia her confidence, her smile back. And now, all she could think about was Danny and how much she had seemingly messed up both his and Mia's lives.

'That's okay. Here, just slice this row in two. Nobody will notice.' Taking the knife from Kim's hand, Diane passed her the pile of napkins and deftly sliced the cake into more pieces.

'Right, where did we put those giant marshmallows? The kids are ready to toast them over the barbie.' Coming in from the garden, Eric rubbed his hands together and scanned the room.

'Umm, I think we put them in one of these cupboards. Here, Kim, you take the cake out and I'll find the marshmallows.'

Taking the plate of sliced cake through into the garden, Kim was soon surrounded by a hungry swarm of teenagers.

'Can I have a slice please, Ms Reynolds?'

'Of course you can, Tilly, and it's Kim, not Ms Reynolds.' Being called Ms Reynolds reminded her of her great aunt, who had taught at the local primary school. She had always seemed to have to prove she wasn't favouring her niece by being that bit stricter with Kim, always picking up on the slightest whisper exchanged behind an open book or making her rewrite her work due to a single spelling mistake or unconscious doodle on the page. Kim shook her head. No, she really didn't want to be likened to her. Peering over the heads of munching teenagers, Kim scanned the garden for Mia. 'Tilly, have you seen Mia?'

'Umm...' Wiping her lips, Tilly placed her cake back on the napkin in her hand. '...Yes, she was talking to your friend, Danny, I think. Round there.'

'Thanks.' Laying the almost empty plate down on a nearby garden table, Kim picked up her pace as she walked towards where Tilly had pointed. Nearing the side of the wall, she slowed down and stopped. She could see them now, standing by the side of the house, deep in conversation. Mia had her arms crossed and her shoulders slumped while Danny spoke to her quietly. Had he told her? Was he telling her now? Mia was facing away. Kim couldn't see the expression on her face but her body language suggested she was listening intently. Would he really do that? She had said she'd tell her tomorrow. Wasn't that good enough?

'Mia.' Clearing her throat, she called again, louder this time. 'Mia.'

'Mum.' Twisting around to face Kim, Mia turned back to Danny and waved as he retreated through the side gate.

'Is everything okay?'

'Yes. Why didn't you tell me?' Looking at her mum, Mia grinned.

He had told her. Frowning, Kim watched as Mia approached her. She looked happy enough. Maybe she had been worrying about telling her for no reason at all. 'I... I just hadn't found the right time. I'm sorry, Mia. I'm so so sorry. I should have told you when you were younger.'

Scrunching her forehead, Mia tilted her head and looked at her. 'That's okay, but you didn't need to be embarrassed or anything. I'm fourteen now. You can tell me stuff.'

'I know, and I should have. I wanted to, I really did, but I just didn't know how you'd react.' Digging her nails into the palms of her hands, Kim bit her lip. Was Mia really not angry with her? Not annoyed in the slightest that she hadn't told her before?

'Mia, your favourite song's coming on!' Tilly's delighted shout broke the conversation.

Looking across at Tilly and her friends, Mia shook her head before running towards them, turning her head briefly, she called to Kim. 'It's cool, Mum. I think it's sweet that you and Danny used to date when you were teenagers. I guessed as much anyway.'

'What?' Too late, Mia had been welcomed back into the centre of the throng of teenagers dancing along to Mia's favourite pop song. Date? He hadn't told her. Surely he hadn't. If he had, Mia would have said something about him being her father, not about them having dated, surely? Wiping her forehead, she lowered herself onto the small wall separating the garden from the small carpark and wiped her hands down the legs of her jeans. He hadn't told her.

24

'Where's Granny and Grandpa?'

Putting the last of the plates into the dishwasher, Kim closed the door and turned it on. 'They've popped out for a drink and a bite to eat. Has Tilly gone home?'

'Yes, her mum just picked her up.'

'Oh good, it's too late for her to be walking on her own. Here, come here.' Holding out her arms, she waited until Mia had stepped closer before enveloping her in a hug and kissing the top of her head. Breathing in, she could smell the smoky aroma of the earlier BBQ. 'Did you have a good time today?'

'Yes, it was awesome. The best party ever! Thank you, Mum.'

'You're welcome. Granny and Grandpa helped a lot.'

'I know, Tilly helped me make a Thank-You card, and I thought I could make them a cake tomorrow. Is that okay?'

'Yes, I think that's a lovely idea. What flavour were you thinking?'

'Chocolate?'

'They'd like that, you know how Grandpa loves his chocolate!'

'That's what I thought. I thought I could get some KitKats to go around the edge of the cake and then put Maltesers or chocolate buttons on top?'

'Sounds yummy.'

'Cool. Do you mind if Tilly comes round again tomorrow, please? She said she can help me if it's okay?'

'Of course, that's fine. I want us to have a bit of "Mother and Daughter Time" tomorrow too though, please?'

'Okay, cool. Thanks, Mum.' Lifting her head from Kim's shoulder, she rubbed her eyes.

'Why don't you go upstairs to the flat and put a film on? I'll just set up the breakfast things and then I'll be up.'

'Okay.' Turning around, she paused by the door. 'What did you mean when you said you were sorry you hadn't told before?'

'Sorry? What for? When did I say that?' Placing the breakfast dishes on the table, Kim arranged them ready for the following breakfast. Even though she'd made sure she hadn't booked any guests to stay tonight, she'd still cook a proper breakfast for Diane and Eric. They deserved to be treated, it was the least she could do after all the effort and work they had put in for the party.

'After I'd spoken to Danny, he went and you kept apologising.'

'Oh, that.' Standing still, she patted a plate against the palm of her left hand and cleared her throat. 'Well, I meant that it should have been me who told you about me and Danny dating when we were younger.'

'That's what I thought, but you were acting really weird, and you're acting weird now.' Crumpling her brow, Mia looked at her mum.

'Weird? No, I'm not.'

'You are. You really are, and you kept saying that you should have told me earlier.' She shifted on her feet. 'You said you should have told me when I was younger, but I hadn't even met Danny then and you didn't know I would ever meet him back then, did you? You didn't know we would end up moving here and he would be building our extension when I was younger.'

'No, no, I didn't. I just meant I should have told you before he did.' Laughing, Kim turned around to get the cutlery. She bit her bottom lip, she shouldn't have faked that laugh, it had sounded hollow and forced even to her own ears. Please, Mia, please, drop it. She couldn't spoil today for her.

'No, that's not it.' Crossing her arms, Mia lifted her chin. 'You said when I was younger. I didn't think anything of it until after the party, but you definitely said that you were sorry and that you should have told me when I was younger. It makes no sense, Mum. Why would you have been sorry that you didn't tell me you went out with him when I was younger?'

'Mia, sweetheart, I don't remember what I said. I was in the middle of giving out cake and I was busy.' Turning back around to face her, Kim smiled, her lips pulling her cheeks awkwardly too high.

'Okay, but why would you have been worried about how I would react?'

'Well, I...' The cold metal of the cutlery in her hands was a welcome distraction. '...I don't know, I just...'

'Unless. No, it can't be that.' Frowning,Mia looked at the floor and back up to her mum. 'You're not hiding something from me, are you? I know we always promise to be honest with each other, and that's what I told Tilly when I was talking to her about how weird you had been after I'd spoken to Danny, but she'd said maybe...' Shaking her head, she walked closer towards Kim.

'Why don't you go and put a film on? We can talk about things tomorrow. You're shattered.'

'No, Mum. Tilly said that maybe Danny was...' Narrowing her

eyes, she stared at Kim. 'She's right, isn't she? You've been lying to me! Both of you have!'

'What? I think you're just tired. We can talk about whatever you want tomorrow. You've had a lovely day today, let's not spoil it.'

'I want to talk about it now, Mum. Danny's my dad, isn't he?'

Looking at Mia, Kim watched her daughter as her lips wobbled and her eyes glistened. Slowly laying the cutlery onto the table, Kim made her way towards Mia.

'He is, isn't he? Just tell me.'

'Mia,' Placing her hand on Mia's forearm, Kim momentarily closed her eyes, taking in a deep breath. She couldn't protect her any more. She couldn't lie. She had to tell her the truth. 'Yes, he is.'

'Danny's my dad.' Stepping away from Kim, she slumped into a chair and placed her hands on the table in front of her.

'Yes, Danny is your dad. I'm so sorry I didn't tell you before.' Pulling out the chair next to Mia, Kim slowly sat down. 'I should have told you as soon as I found out he was working on the extension, but I wanted you to start school first, get settled. And then, when you were in school and were settled, you were so happy, happier than you have been in such a long long time, and I didn't want to rock the boat. I didn't want to jeopardise that.'

'What about before? Before we moved here? Why hadn't you told me about him then? You never spoke about who my dad was and when I asked you, when I was younger and I started to realise it wasn't just normal not to have a dad at all, you told me it didn't matter and you'd change the subject. Why? Why didn't you tell me? I was the only one in my class who had to make Fathers' Day cards for my mum. You could have told me then that I did actually have a living, breathing dad.'

'I was protecting you. I thought I was protecting you. I didn't know where he was. He didn't know about you.'

'What? You didn't tell him you were pregnant with me?'

Looking at the tabletop, Mia ran her fingers around the plate placed in front of her.

'I tried to. He went travelling before I even knew I was pregnant. I tried my hardest to get hold of him. I sent messages through his sister, I wrote letters addressed to the last place I knew he had been.'

'So, he didn't miss out on my childhood because he didn't want me?'

'No, not at all. He didn't know anything about you, but I did try my best to get hold of him and tell him. I really did. You need to believe that I tried my best. I always wanted to tell him.'

'Okay.' Mia looked up at Kim. 'I believe you, but I still don't understand why you didn't tell me about him when I was growing up?'

'I don't know really. It just sort of happened. I guess life just carried on. You grew up, I threw myself into work and trying to support us and...' Looking down at her hands, it all sounded so shallow now. They were feeble excuses, that's all they were. Nothing, nothing should have come before telling Mia about her dad. Closing her eyes, she coughed before looking at Mia. 'To be completely honest, I think I just found it all too hard, too difficult to deal with.'

'Me? I was too difficult to deal with?'

'No, not you. Never you.' She shifted in her chair. 'Ever since I first saw Danny as a teenager, I fell in love with him. I knew he was the one I wanted to be with, to spend my life with, and then he went travelling and I never saw him again. I guess it was easier to put him out of my head rather than to be honest. I'm so sorry, Mia, I thought I was doing the right thing. I thought if we didn't talk about him, you wouldn't miss not having a dad around.'

'Does he know now? Does he know I'm his daughter now, or

are you still keeping it a secret from him?' Mia stopped circling the plate with her finger and looked Kim in the eyes.

'No, of course not.' Looking down at the table, Kim could feel her cheeks flush. Danny only knew because he had worked it out, she hadn't told him, had she? She hadn't been going to tell him until Mia knew. 'He knows.'

Mia looked down at her hands, now clasped in her lap. 'So why isn't he here now? Is that why you stopped seeing each other? Why he isn't working on the extension any more? Why he hasn't been here recently? He doesn't want me.'

'Mia, no! Danny wants you! He's just angry at me. He thinks I should have told him straight away when we moved here and saw him, but I wanted to tell you first. I had planned to tell you and then to tell him. He's also angry at me for not telling him when I found out I was pregnant but like I told you, I tried.'

'If he had wanted you to tell him when you were pregnant, why does he not want to get to know me now?'

'Oh, Mia, he does. He wanted me to tell you. That's what we were talking about earlier at your party. He wanted to know if I had told you yet.'

'He doesn't want me. He got to know me when he was doing the extension and he doesn't like me.'

'No, that's not it at all. He likes you; he loves you. He's cross with me, not you.' Grasping Mia's hands, Kim looked at her. 'He wants to be a part of your life.'

'Well, he's not here.'

'He will be, when I've told him that you know, he'll come straight back. He loves you, Mia.'

'Umm, well, I can't really believe anything you say any more, can I? You've lied to me all my life. Why would you start to be honest now?' Pulling her hands away, Mia pushed her chair away from the table and ran towards the door.

'Mia, wait! I'm telling you the truth...' Standing up, Kim ran after her.

* * *

'Mia, please just open the door. We need to talk about this.' Kim slid down to the floor and knocked again at Mia's bedroom door. Leaning her head against the wood, she listened to Mia's sobs before the sound of her favourite band drowned out all other noise. She'd messed it all up. She had always messed it up. Ever since she found out she was pregnant, she'd messed up. Danny was right, and now Mia was right too. She'd lied throughout her entire adult life. She'd got it all wrong.

'Mia, please?' It was no good; she wouldn't be heard over the music pulsing through the door. Standing up, she pulled her mobile out of her back pocket, went into the small living room and curled up on the sofa.

Pressing Danny's name, she waited until it rang through to voicemail, the familiar voice filling the room momentarily until the beep of the voicemail kicked in. Why couldn't he just answer it? This wasn't something that should be left on voicemail.

Taking a deep breath, Kim held the phone tight against her ear. 'I've told her. Please come and see her.' Letting her mobile drop to the sofa, she curled her legs up and leaned her head against the arm. Scrunching her eyes tightly shut, she tried to block the thoughts whirring in her mind. Mia had said that she couldn't trust anything she said any more. She couldn't blame her; she had handled everything so badly. Would she ever forgive her?

Pulling the throw off the back of the sofa and covering her legs, she pulled it up towards her chin. They had become so close since moving here, their relationship had been healing. The last few years of Kim's busy work schedule and the effects of Mia being bullied had felt so long ago, a fraught mother-daughter relationship of strangers. Until now. Now she had messed everything up, her only daughter, her best friend wouldn't even speak to her, couldn't even face her to learn the truth, to see things from her point of view.

25

'How are you feeling, love? Did you manage to get any sleep?' Diane placed a plate of eggs, bacon, and toast on the table in front of Kim as she slid into a chair.

Shaking her head, she looked at the breakfast in front of her. 'Not really.'

'How's Mia?' Folding his newspaper, Eric placed it on the table.

'I don't know. She won't turn her music down so I can talk to her.' She'd told Diane and Eric everything when they had returned from their evening out a little before eleven last night.

'Give her time, love. She'll come to understand what happened.'

'No, she won't. She'll never forgive me, and why should she?'

'You did what you felt was right at the time. Everything you did, every decision you made, was for the good of her.'

'That's not how she sees it. I wouldn't blame her if she never spoke to me again.' Picking up her fork, she stabbed the yolk of the egg, watching it seep across the porous surface of the toast.

'It's not you, Kim. She's angry at the world at the moment.' Eric stirred a sugar cube into his coffee. 'She wouldn't even answer

Diane when she tried to talk to her. She just needs time to come to terms with it all. To get it straight in her head.'

'She said that I had lied to her, for her whole life I had lied to her, and she's right, I did. She said that she'll never be able to believe a word I say again.' Pulling the crust off the toast, she dipped it in the small lake of yolk not yet absorbed by the toast before laying it back down on the side of her plate.

'She's probably still in shock, love. She'll come to understand why you didn't tell her before.'

'I don't think she will.'

'Does Danny know that you've told her?' Eric sipped his coffee.

'Yes. Well, I think so. I rang him last night, but it went straight to voicemail so I left a message.'

'Maybe you should try giving him another call? Just in case he didn't get the voicemail for whatever reason, you know what these mobile phones can be like sometimes.'

'I guess so.'

'Mia was getting on with him really well before, wasn't she? She spoke to me enough about him anyway.'

'Yes, she seemed to really like him.'

'There you go then. She'll come round soon enough to the idea of him being her dad. At least she had the chance to get to know him before you told her, she won't need to worry about what he's like or whether she'll like him or if they'll get along.'

'Umm, although now she thinks Danny doesn't want her because he's distanced himself. He was round every day before he found out Mia was his and since then he's even stepped away from overseeing the extension. I tried to tell her that it was me he was angry at, not her, but I don't think she believes me. She's taken it personally, she thinks it's her he's avoiding.'

'Oh, the poor little mite. Why don't you give him another call? See if you can get him to come round and set her straight.'

'Okay.' Standing up, Kim made her way into the hallway. Tilting her head towards the stairs; she strained to hear Mia's music. The thumping bass had stopped. She'd either finally fallen asleep and turned it off or she'd put some calmer, quieter music on. She'd ring Danny and then go up and see if she'd open the door to her. Or at least let her speak through the door.

Lowering herself onto the bottom step, Kim leaned her back against the wall and pressed Danny's name on her mobile. Closing her eyes, she listened again as the monotonous tone rang through to his voicemail. 'Danny, please, please give me a call? Mia is really upset. Can you come and see her, tell her that you want to be part of her life? Please, Danny, I'm really worried about her.'

Firmly placing her mobile on the step next to her, Kim took a shaky breath in. Surely Danny must have got the message from last night? He must know that she has told Mia, so why hadn't he come round? Why was he still staying away when he must know that his daughter needed to know he loved her and wanted to be a part of her life?

She picked at a thread at the edge of the carpet; she had no right to be angry at him. After all, she'd spent the last few weeks trying to keep him away from Mia, she had no right to be angry at him for doing as she had wanted.

Standing up, she made her way upstairs towards the flat. Mia had definitely turned the music off.

'Mia? Mia, can you let me in?' Gently tapping on the door, Kim called quietly. If she had finally fallen asleep it might be best not to wake her. 'Mia?'

Nothing. There was no answer. Not a sound from the bedroom at all. She must have fallen asleep. Trying the door handle, Kim breathed a sigh of relief. The door was unlocked now. Turning her back, she walked into the small kitchen. She'd get Mia a glass of water and a croissant to leave on her dressing table for when she woke up.

Returning to Mia's room, she balanced the plate and glass in one hand and slowly opened the door. Sure enough, Mia's bed was piled high with her usual collection of a duvet and two blankets.

'Mia, if you're awake, it's just me. I'm bringing you a drink and something to eat.' Placing the glass and plate on the dressing table, Kim lowered herself onto the edge of the bed. 'You don't have to talk to me if you don't want to. Just know that I love you and always will. I'm sorry that I didn't tell you more about Danny when you were growing up. I've handled it all completely wrong but everything I did, I did because I thought it was the best thing to do at the time.'

Silence.

'Okay, I'll leave you to sleep now. I love you, Mia.' Patting the duvet, Kim frowned as her hand sank into the mound of duvet and blankets. Twisting around, she pulled the duvet down. Pillows.

Standing up, she yanked the duvet from the bed. It was empty, just pillows. Why would Mia have stuffed pillows in her bed? Why would she want Kim to think she was asleep? She must have got the pillows from one of the guest rooms; she normally only slept with one.

'Mia? Mia, are you in the living room?' Making her way into the cramped living room, Kim scanned the empty room. Where was she? She had said about Tilly coming round to bake a cake for Diane and Eric. Maybe she had decided to go over there instead. That would explain why she had wanted Kim to think she was still in bed, Mia knew the rules, she knew she had to let Kim know where she was going. It was her own fault that Mia hadn't wanted to tell her, she obviously couldn't even bring herself to talk to her.

Lowering herself back onto Mia's bed, she pulled her phone out of her back pocket again. She'd give Tilly's mum a call and ask her to keep an eye on her. It was probably a good thing she'd gone round there. She knew Mia and Tilly spoke about everything and it was nice to know Mia had someone to confide in, someone to help make sense of things.

As she listened to the buzz of the call connecting, she frowned and bent down to pick up a T-shirt from the floor. Shaking it out and refolding it, she pulled open the top drawer of Mia's dressing table. That was strange, the drawer was empty. She sighed, the amount of clothes one teenager could get through in such a short space of time never ceased to amaze her. Placing the T-shirt carefully in the drawer, she twisted around. There would no doubt be a pile of clothes scrunched up on the floor somewhere.

Shaking her head, she ended the call. Did no one pick up their mobiles any more? She couldn't very well leave a garbled message on Fiona's phone. She didn't know her that well. She'd try again later; explain things properly when she could actually talk to her.

Walking around the other side of the bed, she scoured the floor. She couldn't see a pile of clothes anywhere and the room was too small for them to be hidden. Standing still, she looked around. Something wasn't right. Something was missing.

Slowly, she took the few short strides back to the dressing table. Mia had tipped the photo of them both face down. Blinking back tears, she stood the photo frame upright and traced her finger across Mia's smiling, happy face. The photo had been taken down on the beach the day after they'd moved in. They'd been paddling and Mia had insisted they should take a selfie to mark the start of their new adventure. They'd both been full of such hope, such happiness. And now she'd messed it all up.

Something still wasn't right though. Where was the photo of Diane and Eric? Mia always kept a photo of Diane and Eric by her bed. She had done in the old house, and she did here too, but the photo with its home-made frame decorated with brightly coloured stickers that Mia had made in primary school wasn't in its usual place.

Standing still, her hand on the dressing table, she looked around the small room. She couldn't see the photo anywhere and now she was looking other things were missing too. Little things like Mia's hairbrush and the book she was reading. She may have taken her book to Tilly's house but other things, the stuffed bear, unoriginally named Mr Bear which she had had since she was a baby had gone.

Shaking her head, she told herself she was being daft. Nothing was wrong, Mr Bear would be here, Mia had probably kicked him under her bed.

Leaning down, she looked underneath the bed. There was no sign of him. Mr Bear wasn't here, and neither was the photo. And what about the clothes missing from the drawer? What was Mia up to? Where had she put them?

It didn't make any sense. Not unless... No, Mia wouldn't.

Running back out onto the small landing, Kim shouted Mia's name, her voiced laced with an urgency she was trying to deny.

No answer.

Where was she? What had she done with her things?

'Mia! Mia, answer me now. Mia!' Running down the stairs, she held on to the banister as her feet pounded on the garish carpet. 'Mia!'

'Kim, love, whatever's the matter?' Coming out of the kitchen, Diane and Eric rushed up to her.

'She's not there. Mia's not in her room.'

'Okay, she's probably gone over to Tilly's house. I'll give her a ring.'

'No, you don't understand. Her things have gone. She's taken Mr Bear and that photo of you both and some of her clothes. She's not here. She's not here.'

'Kim, love, what are you saying?'

'I think she's run away.'

'What? No, not our Mia. She wouldn't have done that.'

'She has. Her things, she's taken her things.' She could hear the rasp of desperation in her voice. Where was her little girl?

'Listen,' Placing his hands on her shoulders, Eric spoke quietly but firmly. 'Sit down and calm down. She's fourteen, if she has run off she's likely to have gone to a friend's house. Get your phone out and start making some calls. Start with Tilly's mum, Mia's more than likely just gone over there. Me and Diane will have a scout around here and make sure she's not just holed herself up in a room or in the garden for a breather. Okay?'

Nodding, Kim let herself be led to the kitchen and pressed into a chair. As Eric and Diane bustled off to search the building, Kim pulled her mobile out and scrolled through to Fiona's number again.

'Hello?'

'It's Kim, Mia's mum. Is she there? Is Mia at yours or is Tilly out with her? Have you heard from her?'

'She's not here, no. Is everything okay?'

'No, no, it's not. She's not at home. She's taken some things, clothes and things, and she's not here.'

'Hold on, I'll just check and see if Tilly has heard from her.'

Tapping her feet against the tiles, Kim listened as Fiona called Tilly's name. She waited as a conversation between mother and daughter ensued. Just hurry up, just ask her if she knows where my baby is. Please? After what felt like half an hour but was presumably less than a minute or two, Fiona came back on the line, her once sing-songy voice laced with concern.

'I'm sorry, Tilly doesn't know where she is, but she said that Mia rang her last night crying and saying that she'd just found out Danny was her dad?'

'Yes, yes. So she doesn't know where she is then? Is she sure?'

'Yes, I've told her how worried you are and she knows to tell the truth. Is there anywhere else she might have gone? Any other friends you could call?'

'Yes, no. I don't know anyone else's contact details.' She should have taken contact details for all of the friends that had come to Mia's party yesterday. She should have taken their parents' numbers. She would have done if they had been younger. That was the done thing, wasn't it? Parents left their phone numbers when they dropped their children off at parties in case of emergencies but because they were teenagers, all old enough to have their own mobiles, she hadn't given it a second's thought. She should have.

'Okay, we'll be right over. Tilly has most of their phone numbers.'

'Thank you.' Before Fiona put the phone down, Kim could hear her rushing Tilly to get her shoes on, her voice high pitched with urgency.

Pushing the chair back, she stood up. Striding to the front door, she pulled it open and looked outside. Where would she have gone? Think. Think. Jerking her head around she watched as Diane came down the stairs.

'Nothing. She's not in any of the rooms.'

'Where? Where could she be? Fiona is on her way. Tilly has the phone numbers of their friends.'

'Good, good. That's the best place to start. She will be hiding out at one of her friend's houses.'

'But why didn't she go to Tilly's? She's her best friend.'

'She was the first person you called. Mia would have known that she would be, that's why.'

'She's not out the back.' Walking towards them, Eric held his hands out. 'Any luck ringing Tilly?'

'Mia's not there, love. They're coming here so we can contact their other friends. Tilly has their phone numbers.' Walking up to him. Diane placed her hand on his forearm.

'Right, right. Good idea.' Rubbing his face with his hand, he looked at Kim. 'You two stay here and work your way through her friends, I'll go for a drive and see if I can see her. Where are her favourite places around here? Where might she have gone to for the day?'

'Umm, she loves the nature reserve. And the beach, by the pier, that's her favourite part. Although she likes it up by the rocks too, you know the big boulders? Do you know where they are? Shall I come? Maybe I should go out and look too?'

'No, it's best you're here. It's best you contact her friends. Plus, she'll probably come back in a bit, once she's calmed down.'

Nodding, Kim watched as Fiona's car pulled up.

'Keep me updated.' Collecting his car keys from the desk, Eric called over his shoulder as he headed outside.

* * *

'Thank you for coming.' Waving Fiona and Tilly into the kitchen, Diane put her hand on Kim's shoulder. 'Come on, love. Mia's one phone call away, that's all. She'll be back in no time at all.'

Nodding, Kim followed them back through to the kitchen and sat down opposite Tilly and her mum. 'Did she say anything to you, Tilly? Did she say she was going to run away?'

Shaking her head, Tilly looked at Kim. 'She was upset. She kept crying down the phone and I asked if she wanted to come round but she said no, she said that she would be okay.'

'Right, who shall we start with then?' Diane patted Tilly's hand.

'Umm, Jade maybe? We hang around a lot with Jade.'

'Okay, love. Let's have her number. Kim, do you want me to call or do you want to?'

'I will.' Picking up her mobile, she punched in Jade's number.

* * *

Placing her mobile back on the table, Kim blinked back the tears. No one had heard from her. How come no one had heard from her?

'Is there anyone else you can think of?' Wrapping her arm around her daughter, Fiona pulled her closer. 'Anyone else's number you've got from school? Even if you don't think Mia will have gone to see them, it's worth a go.'

'No, that's everyone's numbers I've got.'

Kim watched as Tilly wiped her eyes, her hands visibly shaking. 'Thank you, Tilly.'

'It's okay. I'm sorry I wasn't any help.'

'You were, love. You were a lot of help.'

Standing up, Fiona rubbed Tilly's shoulder. 'We'll have a walk around town, pop into her favourite shops. Someone is bound to have seen her. If there's anything else we can do, please just let me know.'

'I will. Thank you.'

'I'll show you both out.' Standing up, Diane left the room.

Sitting at the table, her hands palm down against the cool wood, Kim tried to concentrate on her breathing. She'd be back. Mia would be back soon. Looking out of the window, she watched the leaves of a nearby tree gently swaying in the breeze. Had she taken sunscreen? Would she remember to reapply? The sun was so bright today, the UV factor would be high and Mia burnt easily. Especially if she was at the beach, the sun would reflect off the sea and double in strength or something. Had she taken her sunhat and sunglasses? Standing up, she made her way out into the hall.

'Yes, I think you're right, love, I'll suggest it. I'll see you in a bit.' Standing by the front door and speaking quietly into her phone, Diane quickly ended the call and walked towards Kim. 'Where are you going, love?'

'I'm going to check to see if she took her sunglasses and hat. You know how quickly she burns in this weather. I need to check the UV factor. She'll need to reapply her sunscreen. Do you think she'll remember?'

'I'm sure she will. She's a bright girl. Come back through to the kitchen.' Putting her arm around Kim's shoulder, Diane rotated her back.

Doing as she was told, Kim sat back down at the kitchen table, her hands clasped in her lap.

'I've just spoken to Eric.'

Kim jerked her head up, searching Diane's face for clues. 'Has he found her?'

'No, I'm afraid not, love. I need to talk to you, but I need you to be strong, okay?' Sitting on the chair next to her, Diane held Kim's hands. 'Both Eric and I think we should ring the police.'

'The police? What? Why? Did Eric find something? Does he think she's been hurt? Or taken?' She couldn't breathe. What if she had? What if something had happened? What if she was hurt, and they'd been ringing round her friends thinking she'd just run off?

'No, no, nothing like that. It's just if we inform the police there will be more people searching. They can help bring her back quicker than if we just look ourselves. Are you okay if I give them a call?'

Nodding, Kim listened as Diane rang through to the police, the words she used whirring around in her head. 'Missing'. Mia was missing.

26

'Kim, they're here.'

Looking up, Kim watched as Diane led two uniformed officers into the kitchen, ushering them to the chairs opposite Kim.

'Ms Reynolds, I am PC Everett, and this is my colleague PC Compton. We understand that your daughter Mia has gone missing? Do you have a recent photograph, please? If we can have one now, we can circulate it to our other officers before going through the details surrounding her disappearance.'

'Her disappearance? She's just run away. She's not disappeared; she'll still be in town. She's not disappeared.' It was Mia. They weren't talking about some poor child on a milk carton. That wasn't Mia. Nothing bad had happened to her. She'd just run off.

'It's okay, love. This is just to be on the safe side. Have you got a photo on your phone from yesterday?'

Kim felt the warmth from Diane's hand on her shoulder and picked up her phone. It was all just a precaution. Mia hadn't been gone long anyway. She wouldn't have got far. She'd be back by dinnertime. 'Maybe I've just forgotten something.'

'What have you forgotten, love?'

'Maybe Mia had something to do with school? A trip? Extra lessons? Maybe she's there. I've been so preoccupied with the party. Maybe I just forgot.' She flicked through the photos on her mobile; Mia's face grinned back at her. She had been so happy yesterday. Someone who had been that happy wouldn't have run away even if she had found out about Danny.

'I'll have some officers go and check the school, but as it's a Sunday, I think we need to distribute the photograph of Mia. The first few hours after a disappearance are the most vital.' Speaking softly, PC Compton tucked her dark hair behind her ears and gently took Kim's mobile from her hand. 'This looks a good one; it's clear and head on. Was it taken recently?'

Nodding, Kim watched as PC Compton passed the mobile to PC Everett who took a picture of the photo before handing it back to Kim.

'Right, that's done. All our officers across the borough will now be alerted to Mia's photograph and will keep an eye out for her. Now, if we can just take a few details surrounding Mia's disappearance...' Taking a small notebook out of his top shirt pocket, PC Everett began scribbling inside. 'Now, when did you first notice she had gone missing?'

'About an hour, an hour and a half ago?' Looking across at Diane, Kim scrunched her forehead. It was about then.

'That's right. Kim, here, went up to talk to her and she wasn't there.'

'Up?'

'Yes, she was in her bedroom.'

'Okay, and when was the last time you saw her?'

Looking at her hands, clasped on the table in front of her, Kim spoke softly. 'Last night. The last time I saw her was last night.'

'So she could have left last night? After you saw her last?'

'No. No, her music was on. It only went off this morning.'

'Okay.' PC Everett looked across at his colleague.

'Was she playing the same album or playlist throughout the night? Or were there any gaps in the music or a change of music?' PC Compton placed her hand on Kim's.

'It was the same playlist. She played it over and over again. It was still playing when I woke up this morning and then when I went back up to speak to her, she'd turned it off.'

'I know this is very hard, but is it a possibility that the playlist was on repeat until the iPod or CD player timed out?' PC Everett tapped his pen against the notepad, dull thuds filling the silence in the kitchen.

'No, no.' Kim sank her head into her hands, shielding her face from the truth he had spoken. Why hadn't she thought of that herself? 'You're saying she could have run off last night? That she could have been out there alone all night?'

'Possibly, although normally iPods and the like time out or go to sleep after four hours or so, so it's more probable that she may have left sometime during the early morning rather than last night.'

'Right, of course.' Kim pushed her chair back, she needed to get out of here, she needed to go and find her.

'Kim, love, where are you going?'

Looking down at Diane, Kim shook her head, trying to clear the thoughts whirring around. 'I'm going to find her.'

'Ms Reynolds, Kim, we have officers patrolling the streets. What we need from you now is a statement of the events leading up to her disappearance.'

'No, I need to go and find her. That's what I need to do.'

'We really do need you to answer a few more questions.'

'Kim, love, listen to them. You need to answer their questions so they can help in the best way they can.' Diane's voice, calm and strong, spoke authority and Kim sat back down.

'Okay.' Nodding, Kim looked across the table at the two police officers. How had life turned out like this? Not in a million years had she ever thought that Mia would run away. Not her Mia.

'Thank you. We understand that you are eager to help with the search and find your daughter, but really the best thing you can do at the moment is to give us information regarding Mia, what she was wearing the last time you saw her, what she may have taken with her and any favourite places she may have gone.'

* * *

With her hands loosely clasped on top of the table and her head tilted, PC Compton nodded as Kim explained how Mia had found out that the person she had come to see as a close family friend was, in fact, her father. 'I see.'

Closing her eyes, Kim breathed out through her nose. She didn't see. She judged. Kim could feel her judgement in every sympathetic nod, in every word of reassurance. She'd brought this upon herself, Mia running away. She'd made it happen. PC Compton was probably thinking that she didn't blame Mia for wanting to get away from this mess. She couldn't deal with this. She couldn't deal with the judgement, the knowing glances between police officers who thought they understood but clearly weren't listening properly.

Opening her eyes, she pushed her chair back and stood up. 'Thank you for listening, but now I must go and find my daughter.' The words and the way she had said them, sharp and authoritative, propelled her back to her career days, it was the clipped, quiet voice she used to use in meetings. Maybe she shouldn't have left. If they hadn't moved, they wouldn't have run into Danny and none of this would have happened.

'I really do advise that you stay...'

'Diane, if she comes back, please ring me.' Turning on her heels, she left the kitchen, leaving Diane to look after the police officers.

27

Out on the street, she blinked as she took a deep breath. She'd find her. She wouldn't have gone far. It wasn't as though she had anywhere to actually go to. Diane and Eric were the only family she knew, besides her and Danny. It wasn't as though she'd have gone back to Hulberry. Amelia had seen to that. She had no one and nowhere to go to apart from her new friends here, and as soon as she got in contact with them, their parents would inform her or the police. No, she'd be close.

Picking up the pace, she turned right at the bottom of their close. Eric had already checked the nature reserve and the beach and was currently scouring the town centre, so if she made her way up to the castle she could check the castle grounds. Mia had been talking about going to see the jousting next weekend. Maybe she had decided to check out what else was there.

* * *

Clambering over the style, Kim slipped, grazing her hand on the worn, rough wood. Wiping the blood down the front of her jeans, she stood back up and looked across at the meadow in front of her. She couldn't see Mia, but it didn't mean she wasn't here. There were so many small and windy walkways looping and criss-crossing through the nature reserve, she could be curled up under a tree reading a book, or listening to music somewhere. Or down by the lake and café.

She'd already searched the castle grounds and the small cafés in the centre of town and she knew Eric had already looked here, but that had been hours ago now, Mia may be here now. There was nothing to say she'd stay in one place all day.

'Mia! Mia!' Standing in the middle of the meadow, Kim twisted around, her voice being absorbed too quickly by the blanket of trees surrounding the small meadow. How was she ever going to find her? This place was huge. Closing her eyes and turning her head up to the sky, she listened; she listened for any noise out of the ordinary. The laughter and delighted cries of children playing at the nearby swing park floated through the air, but nothing to suggest Mia's whereabouts. What was she expecting to hear anyway? The quiet thud of bass from her iPod? The ringtone from her mobile?

Turning right, she marched through the long grass and wild-flowers towards the woods. A tiny droplet of water on her arm made her look up as the clouds opened, pouring rain from the sky in true summer fashion.

Scrambling up one of the steep paths etched into the side of the hill from hundreds of feet strolling and pounding the ground for the past century or two, Kim gripped branch after branch to help her stay upright as the rain lashed down in front of her saturating the mud underfoot. There were so many of these walkways throughout the hilly woods surrounding the meadow, each one either turning back on itself or leading to some small clearing or out of the nature reserve entirely. She could be anywhere. But she could be here. She could. It was the perfect place to hide away for a few hours.

'Mia!' As the ground evened out beneath her, Kim began running, oblivious to the twigs scratching her arms and catching her hair. She had to find her. She had to explain.

A noise, a brushing of foliage, a snapping of twigs and rustle of leaves propelled her forward. 'Mia, is that you? Mia?' She was there, just up ahead. It must be her. She was sure of it. 'Mia?'

Running faster now, Kim pushed herself forward towards the noise ahead. Eventually coming to a clearing, she was in time to see a muntjac deer startle and run back into the safety of the trees. It wasn't her.

Sinking to her knees, Kim covered her face with her hands, heaving sobs escaping her lungs. She was never going to find her, was she? Mia didn't want to be found. She could be anywhere by now. Evening was quickly creeping in, gathering the last of the sun's rays and swallowing them with the murky darkness of a summer's night. She'd been missing for hours now; she could have got on a bus, a train, hitched a ride, to anywhere.

'Kim!'

Jerking her head up, she watched as Danny came pounding into the clearing and knelt down next to her. 'Danny?'

'Diane rang me, told me everything. I came here looking for Mia and saw you heading this way. I've been trying to catch up with you for the last ten minutes or so.'

'Why didn't you call out?'

'I didn't want to get your hopes up.'

'You've not seen her then?' Please, please be here to tell me she's been found.

Looking down, Danny ran his hand through his hair and shook his head. 'I'm sorry. You're soaked.' Shrugging out of his coat, he lay it across her shoulders before pulling her to her feet.

Allowing herself to be enveloped in his strong arms, Kim buried her head in the nape of his neck, the tears soaking his T-shirt quicker than the rain ever could.

'We'll find her. She can't be far.'

'She could be anywhere. She's probably taken a bus or a train somewhere by now. She could literally be anywhere.'

'The police have the stations covered; everyone will be keeping their eyes open. Is there anywhere she may have gone? Back to Hulberry?'

'No, there's nowhere. It's always just been me and her, and Diane and Eric. There's no one else. There's nowhere else she could have gone.'

'Well, she's got to be about somewhere then.'

'But she's not.' Looking up at him, she wiped her face with her hands. 'We've looked everywhere. We've rung all of her friends, she's not been in touch at all.'

Breathing heavily out of his nose, Danny looked away.

'What?'

'Nothing.'

'That wasn't nothing. You blame me, don't you?' Stepping away from him, she let his arms fall by his side.

'No, no, of course not. I was just...'

'Yes, you do. You were huffing. You blame me for Mia having run off. And yes, maybe it is my fault. Not maybe, it is. It is my fault, I've handled the whole stupid mess wrong, but I did what I could, what I thought best at the time. You'd gone, what would have been the point of telling Mia about you when you'd gone? And it was you who wanted me to tell her.' Pointing a shaky finger at him, Kim took another step back. Yes, it was. If he hadn't forced the issue, she would never have found out like she had. They could have told her properly.

'I never asked you to tell her on the day of her party. I would never have asked you to do that.'

'No, but you came to the party. If you hadn't come, she wouldn't have found out. She wouldn't have guessed there was anything wrong.' Why was she shouting at him? She didn't really blame him, it was her fault. All of it, she knew it was. It was her who had driven Mia away, not Danny. Taking a sharp breath, she slipped out of his coat, letting it fall to the wet floor and turned around, pushing her way back into the woods.

'Kim, please? Wait.' Bending down to retrieve his coat, he ran to catch up with her. 'I don't blame you. I don't blame you at all. Not now. Not for Mia running off and not for keeping her from me. I spoke to Eric and Diane last night. They rang me up and invited me out for a drink. They told me about you losing everything and everyone after you fell pregnant. They told me about you trying to find me to tell me. They even told me about you and Eric stalking my parents' old place. I should have let you explain. I should have listened.'

Pausing, Kim slowly turned around.

'I'm sorry. It was just a shock, a massive shock, finding out I had a daughter and that she was a teenager already. The whole situation just seemed so screwed up. I mean, I'd been talking to her, we'd had a laugh together, even planned her party together and then she was suddenly mine.' Danny shook his head. 'I just kept thinking about everything I had missed out on, the sleepless nights, her first day at school, parents' evenings... everything. I wasn't there when she needed me. I wasn't there to help her when she fell over and hurt her knee or even when she was being bullied. I was angry that I had missed it all, but I understand now that it wasn't your fault. You didn't know where I was and you'd tried to contact me.'

Nodding slowly, Kim bit her bottom lip. Did he mean it? Did he really not blame her?

'Plus, I realise now that none of that matters. I have the chance to be in her life now and to share all the firsts that are yet to come.'

'But she's gone.' Holding her arms out, Kim let out a shuddering breath. It was too late. Everything was too late.

'She's not gone. She's just run off. She'll be back once she's had time to think about it.' Looking at the floor, he held the bridge of his nose. 'Have you checked the arcade?'

'No, Eric looked at the beach, but I don't know if he checked the arcade.'

'Okay, that's worth a shot then, isn't it? What teenager doesn't like spending time at the arcade?' Laying his coat back over her shoulders, they carefully picked their way back down to the meadow. 'I've got my car, we can take that. It'll be quicker.'

Nodding, she allowed him to lead her towards the car park.

'We'll find her.' Taking his car keys from his pocket, Danny unlocked the car and held the door open for her.

'My phone!' Scrambling in her pockets, Kim wrapped her fingers around her mobile. Someone had found Mia! They must have. Unless... shaking her head, she tried to push the dark thoughts away. Pulling her phone out of her pockets, she fumbled, her fingers too cold to hold it steady, and watched as it fell towards the ground. Falling to her knees, she grabbed it from the mud. With her mouth dry and her hands shaking, she forced herself to answer it and held it to her ear. 'Hello?'

'Kim, love, it's Eric. She's home.'

Letting her mobile fall to the ground again, she dropped her head into her hands and rocked, forwards and backwards as she knelt, oblivious to the murky puddle underneath her. She was home! Mia was home! She was safe!

'Kim? Is she okay?' Danny's voice, barely above a whisper, penetrated the air.

'She's home. She's home!' Tears streamed down her cheeks as her body shook uncontrollably. She was safe. Mia was safe.

Dropping to his knees next to her, Danny wrapped his arms around her, his hands cupping under her armpits and gently lifted her up. 'Let's go and see our daughter.'

28

Stumbling from the car, Danny right behind her, Kim ran through the front door and into the kitchen. Glancing around, she could see Diane and Eric sat at the table with Mia on a chair between them, their backs turned towards her.

'Mia?' Slowing her pace, she walked towards Mia who turned to face her, her face was pale and her eyes rimmed with red.

'Mum! What happened to you?'

Looking down at herself, she was suddenly aware of her mud entrenched and blood smeared jeans, her dripping wet hair and the sting of the graze across the palm of her hand. 'I... I've been looking for you. Where have you been?'

Pushing her chair back, Mia ran the few feet towards Kim, falling into her arms, her head filling the gap between Kim's shoulder and chin. 'I'm sorry, Mum. I'm so sorry. I wasn't thinking. I didn't mean to worry you. I was just so angry and upset; I just needed to get away fora bit.'

'Where? Where have you been?' Gripping her tightly and sinking her nose into Mia's hair, she took a long, deep breath, the familiar coconut fragrance filling her lungs. She was still her Mia.

'I went to the nature reserve for a bit and then I went to the small museum by the beach, but then Tilly rang for like the hundredth time and I answered it. When she said the police were looking for me, I got scared and came home. I'm sorry, I didn't mean for it to go this far. I just wanted you to feel a little bit like I did, like my whole world had been flipped, but I didn't mean to scare you.'

Coughing, Kim blinked back tears. She didn't know whether to feel angry or happy; her emotions had twisted in her stomach. She didn't even recognise how she felt any more. 'Well, you certainly did that.'

'I love you, Mum.'

'I love you too, Mia. More than you'll ever know. I am so so sorry for not being honest about Danny earlier.'

Mia nodded. 'It's just weird. I never thought I'd have a dad.'

'I know, and if I could have changed things back then, I would have. You know that, don't you? I never wanted it to turn out like this. I always wanted Danny to be a part of your life. It just didn't happen before.'

'I know.'

'There's so much to be said still. So much I want to, need to explain to you. And I will, I promise. And I promise that's the end of all the secrets. From now on I'll be completely honest with you about everything, okay?'

'And you can ask me anything you want to as well.' Slowly approaching them, Danny cautiously placed one hand on Mia's shoulder and one on Kim's.

Lifting her head, Mia looked at Danny. 'Thanks.'

* * *

Coming back into the kitchen, Kim patted her hair dry with the towel draped over her shoulders.

'Are you feeling a bit better, love?' Patting her on the forearm, Diane indicated a chair opposite Eric and Danny before turning back to the oven.

'So the police were defiantly okay about it all? They weren't annoyed that their time had been wasted?'

'Not at all. As that PC Compton said when Mia walked through the door, they'd rather have spent time looking and have a happy outcome than an awful one.' Taking a sip of lager, Eric grinned at her. 'What a day, eh? Mia definitely knows how to keep us on our toes, doesn't she?'

'She certainly does. Thanks for everything today, both of you.' Kim looked from Eric to Diane and back again. She really didn't know where she'd be without all of their support. 'It hasn't put you off moving down here?'

'Not likely. You both keep us young. It'll be the perfect tonic to old age.' Chuckling, Eric slapped the table in front of him.

'Perfect timing, Mia, love. Come and sit next to your mum.'

Turning around, Kim waited until Mia had sat down before leaning across and squeezing her hand. Things could have worked out so differently today. 'Okay?'

Nodding, Mia looked up at Diane as she placed a plate brimming with egg and chips in front of her. 'Thanks, Granny.'

* * *

Quietly backing out of Mia's bedroom, Kim paused on the landing, listening to her breathe. Mia hadn't wanted her to sit on her bed until she fell asleep like that for a long time now. She had been exhausted and had fallen asleep almost as soon as Kim had tucked her in but Kim had promised her that they, Danny too, would sit down tomorrow and talk about things properly.

Going into the small living room, Kim perched on the sofa next to Danny and clasped her hands in front of her. 'I'm sorry about everything. I didn't mean for this all to happen.' Sweeping her arms in front of her, she bit her bottom lip. He'd said all the right things downstairs, that he forgave her, that he wanted to be a part of Mia's life, but that had been in front of Mia, Diane and Eric. What he really truly felt might be completely different.

Leaning forward, towards her, Danny covered her hands with his and looked her in the eye. 'Kim, I meant what I said. I forgive you. The real question is, do you forgive me?'

'What for?'

'For making you think I'd abandoned you all of those years ago, and more importantly for behaving the way I did when I found out Mia was mine.'

Shrugging, she looked at him. 'It's understandable. It must have been a shock.'

'You can say that again! I really am sorry for the way I spoke to you and blamed you. Today has put everything into perspective and I think I was angry at myself more than you. I was angry for not trying harder to find you when I got back from travelling. It kills me when I think of what you went through, pregnant and scared, grieving for Miriam. You must have felt so alone. I should have been there for you.'

'Diane and Eric looked after me. I honestly don't know what I would have done without them. They've helped me so much.'

'I think we need to accept that we can't change what's happened in the past and how we got to this point, but we can change the now and the future.'

Looking down at the rug, she sighed. There was no point

raking over the past, thinking about the what if's and if only's. 'You're right.'

Danny grinned. 'I can't wait to get to know her properly. We'll have to introduce her to my parents! They'll love to see you again; you were always the golden girlfriend. The one that my parents would constantly judge other girlfriends, even my ex-wife, against.'

'Umm, I don't think they'd be too happy with me now though. Not after hearing that you've got a fourteen-year-old daughter you knew nothing about.'

'I've already told them. I went round there yesterday after the party, before I met up with Eric and Diane and told them, and do you know what my mum's reaction was?'

'No.' Picking at her cuticles, she kept her eyes focused on the rug.

'She had a go at me for blaming you. She said that she'd always known you were strong, but you shouldn't have had to bring Mia up by yourself. She doesn't think badly of you at all. In fact, it was me she was in a mood with. She seemed to think I should have known about the pregnancy before you even did and that I shouldn't have gone travelling.'

Looking up, Kim smiled.

'So you see, it's me that's in the doghouse with her, not you. That aside, she can't wait to meet her granddaughter. She says she's got fourteen years of spoiling and baking to make up for.'

'Oh, that's lovely of her.'

'Anyway, shall we start again?'

'I don't think we can. We've got a teenage daughter, you know.' Her laugh turned into a yawn and Kim rubbed her eyes. It was only just gone ten o'clock, but she felt as though she hadn't slept for weeks.

'Here, come here.' Leaning back on the sofa and crossing his legs, Danny held out his arm.

Yawning again, Kim leaned back, resting her head into the crook of his arm as he drew her closer towards him. 'Do you really think we'll be able to sort this sorry mess out?'

'I know we will.' Leaning down, his lips met hers. 'We were always meant to be a family, life just got in the way.'

EPILOGUE

'It's beautiful, isn't it?' Taking a brown cardboard box from the back of the removal van, Kim looked towards the stone cottage ahead.

'It certainly is. Eric and Diane chose well.' Danny grinned and lifted the box he was carrying higher against his chest.

'It will be lovely having them just down the road.' Pushing the wrought-iron gate to the front garden open with her foot, she leaned against it, holding it open for Danny.

'Thank you, beautiful.' Leaning towards her, his lips met hers.

'Urgh, you two are disgusting.' Pushing past hugging a black bin bag full of clothes, Mia pulled a face before calling over her shoulder. 'Stop being so soppy, Dad.'

'Love you too, Mia.' Grinning, Danny turned back to face Kim, his eyes sparkling. 'Did you hear that? She called me Dad!'

Smiling, she watched as Danny's face filled with pride. It had taken a good few months, but it seemed that Mia was finally accepting not only the fact that Danny was her dad but also Kim and Danny's relationship. 'I heard.'

'You know what that means, don't you?'

'No, what?' Keeping pace next to Danny, they weaved their way up the short path towards the front door, being careful not to step on any of the forget-me-nots sprawling across the cracked slabs.

'It means we can think about moving on with our relationship.' Looking across at Kim, Danny smiled.

'You mean you want to move in?' Please say yes, please say yes.

'It would make life easier, you've got to admit.'

'In what way?'

'Well, for starters I would be able to spend more time with Mia and, of course, help out with the B and B more. You've got your first corporate team-building event coming up next week, haven't you?'

'Yes.' Scrunching up her forehead, she paused by the front door, waiting for him to finish.

'See, just imagine if I'm there to help fry eggs in the morning.'

'Okay, so you want to move in so you can help fry eggs?' She shifted the box in her arms. Was he seriously suggesting they move in together to make life easier?

'Absolutely! I don't understand how you've coped without me.'

Kim watched as his lips twitched at the corners and shook her head, trying not to grin. 'I think I have perfected frying the eggs, thank you. So, unless you're going to offer to load the dishwasher after the perfect breakfasts I cook, then I'm afraid your help won't be needed.'

'Oh, not the dishwasher.' Lowering his forehead to the box in his arms, he looked back up at her. 'What if I told you the real reason I want to move in is to be able to spend more time with the two girls I love most in the world and to finally be the family we were meant to be all those years ago?'

'Then I'd say yes.' Grinning, she leaned towards him, puckering her lips before turning away and laughing. 'And thank you for promising to load the dishwasher.'

'What? No, that bit was a joke. Wasn't it?' Raising his eyebrows in mock terror, he followed Kim into the living room and lowered his box onto the floor. Standing back up, he stretched his back. 'What have you got in those boxes, Eric? Rocks?'

'No.' Looking at the label on the side of the box, Eric looked up at him. 'That one there has all of my tools in. Are you okay carrying it through to the shed, please?'

'I thought it was heavy! Yep, will do. We've got something to tell you all first.' Danny looked around at Diane and Eric, who were unpacking photo frames. 'Where's Mia?'

'I'm here.' Carrying a tray through from the kitchen, she handed everyone a glass of water. 'Let me guess, you're moving in?'

'What? How did you know?'

'Mum spoke to me about it, didn't you, Mum?'

'I did indeed.' Kim smiled. She had known Mia would jump at the chance of having them all live under the same roof, but it was only fair she checked with her.

'Oh. So you're saying you were planning on asking me?' Looking across at Kim, Danny slapped his forehead. 'I didn't need to bribe you with my amazing dishwasher loading skills, did I?'

Laughing, Kim rubbed him on the shoulder. 'No, you didn't, but I'm afraid there's no going back on a promise.'

'Umm, I know you too well. You won't let me forget that one, will you?'

'Nope. I might let you have a day off on your birthday though if you're lucky.' Smiling, she looked around; life now was a million miles away from how it used to be. Mia was absolutely thriving at school and was even rehearsing a song to audition for the upcoming school production. Closing her eyes momentarily, she let the warmth from the room and the people she loved wash over her. Moving here had definitely been the right decision.

ACKNOWLEDGEMENTS

Thank you, readers, for taking the time to read *Berry Grove Bed & Breakfast*. I hope you've enjoyed reading about Kim's new start at Berry Grove and finding love with Danny again as much as I enjoyed writing her story.

A huge thank you to my wonderful children, Ciara and Leon, who motivate me to keep writing and working towards 'changing our stars' each and every day. Also to my lovely family for always being there, through the good times and the trickier ones.

And a massive thank you to my amazing editor, Emily Yau, who reached out and believed in me – thank you.

Thank you also to Shirley for copyediting and proofreading *Berry Grove Bed & Breakfast*. And, of course, Clare Stacey for creating the beautiful cover. Thank you to all at Team Boldwood!

ABOUT THE AUTHOR

Sarah Hope is the author of many successful romance novels, including the bestselling Cornish Bakery series. She lives in Central England with her two children and an array of pets, and enjoys escaping to the seaside at any opportunity.

Sign up to Sarah Hope's mailing list for news, competitions and updates on future books.

Follow Sarah on social media here:

- facebook.com/HappinessHopeDreams
- x.com/sarahhope35
- instagram.com/sarah_hope_writes
- bookbub.com/authors/sarah-hope

ALSO BY SARAH HOPE

Escape to...

The Seaside Ice-Cream Parlour

The Little Beach Café

Christmas at Corner Cottage

The Bramble Patch Craft Shop

Berry Grove Bed and Breakfast

The Flower Shop on Serendipity Lane

The Wagging Tails Dogs' Home Series

The Wagging Tails Dogs' Home

Chasing Dreams at the Wagging Tails Dogs' Home

A Fresh Start at the Wagging Tails Dogs' Home

Printed in Great Britain
by Amazon

40356853R00145